Marlene,
I've always summed
this book up as "never quit."
Fans like you keep me
going. — JK

AMERICAN EXODUS

AMERICAN EXODUS

A POST APOCALYPTIC JOURNEY

A Catalyst Series companion novella
by JK Franks

Published by Red Leaf Press
Made in USA

RED LEAF
P R E S S

American Exodus
Copyright © 2017
J.K. Franks

Cover art: José Julián Londoño Calle
Editor: Richard Peevers

ISBN: 978-0-9977289-8-9

v 81020120

To Holly, Cameron, and all those who wander.

Author's Notes

When I was developing the Catalyst series, the idea of a connected novella wasn't part of the plan. That changed when I was asked a relatively simple question. "What would you do to get home if the CME happened, and you were a thousand miles from home?"

From that, this story was born. At its heart, it is a simple "get home" journey, but embedded in it are clues to more of the Catalyst stories. I have written this in-between writing book one, two and now book three, so this book is influenced by all of those but is a stand-alone story. Fans of the series will see threads from the other books, and in some cases, rather similar situations dealt with in a very different manner.

This story takes place essentially during the same timeperiod as the first book—Downward Cycle. Revisiting the aftermath of that disaster I first wrote of several years ago was more fun than I probably should admit. It was also nice to explore the struggle to survive from a different point of view as well as visit scenes we may have only glimpsed in the earlier books. I believe you will enjoy this novella. It certainly fits with the series and includes some very pivotal information to the greater story, but in and of itself, is a solid tale which I hope you will enjoy reading as much as I have writing it.

1

He fumbled with his belt, trying unsuccessfully to find the loop while finishing a cup of coffee. His overnight bag stood by the door, watched intently by his wife's most ardent advocate, Buckles. The cat was the bane of his otherwise idyllic existence. Buckles was the reason his trusted friend Elvis was in a fenced compound on the back corner of the expansive lot. Looking out over the yard still covered in morning fog, Steve saw the silhouette of his eight-year-old mutt standing like a lone sentry by his fence. *I need to check on him before I go*, he thought before mentally going through the punch list of other priorities before he headed out of town later this morning.

The small flat-screen TV on the granite counter was showing the latest headlines of political scandal, celebrity gossip and a teaser of a live chat with a NASA astronaut in the next half hour. Steve checked his watch. "If it's not on this break, I should get a refund," he said quietly to himself. He idly waited as the cell phone, insurance and pharma commercials played. Then he saw his familiar and striking spokesmodel standing in front of his Ford dealership and smiled. This ad was one of three he had airing in currently. Since adding the 24-hour news channel to the mix, his traffic increase had been substantial. While most of his competitor's ads aired during the evening hours, he found the early morning seemed to reach the more serious buyers and resulted in better rates.

He went to kiss his wife, Barbara, goodbye. As expected, she seemed to barely register the peck on her cheek. Quickly he wondered if she would even realize her Stevie was missing for the next few days. He traveled frequently for work, but this one was one of the major business trips he had to take each year. He walked down the hall to his son's room, inhaling deeply before entering. He expected his son would likely be awake. "Trey, you up?" He saw no sign of the boy. He was still a "boy" in mind only. His son was nearly eighteen.

"Don't call me that," came a mumbled response from the closet.

Steven approached the door which was cracked open. "Oh yeah . . . I forgot. S-P-3 it is now . . . right?"

"Yep! I gonna be a rapper."

"Trey, it's 'I am going to be a rapper.'"

"Really?" his son said excitedly. "You gonna be a rapper too?"

His dad laughed, "No, son. I was, well, nevermind. Look . . . "

"I know, I know, you gotta go." Trey stood and walked out of the closet. His broad shoulders and six feet of height dwarfed his father. The look on his face was pure sadness. "I have to stay with BarBuRuh."

Trey had been a challenge, more so than the boy's mother had been able to handle. Steve's ex was long gone from both of their lives. He and his current wife, Trey's stepmother, had been married for almost five years. While she said and did all the right things, the true emotional connection had just never really formed. Barbara had a full life, and giving Trey the level of attention he needed was some-times challenging for her. While his son looked like a man, he was mentally more on the level of a first or second grader. "Trey . . . I mean S-P-3, be nice. She loves you and tries hard. She's never mean to you, is she?" He briefly recalled the time she had let Trey go into an enclosed playground at a fast food restaurant. Even though he could have easily climbed out, he got confused and scared. The other kids were making fun of him. He balled up and rocked back and forth until someone on the staff went in and pulled him out. The episode set them back months in the already slow developmental progress. She did try to do the right things though, that was more than most.

Trey looked at the floor and shrugged. "I dunno. I guess not. It's just more funner when you're here."

"More fun for me too, buddy . . . I have to work though, so we can live here, and you can go to that nice school and summer camp. You like camp, don't you?" He knew his son liked going to the wilderness camp. It was for special-needs children and cost a fortune, but it was worth it. Trey loved the outdoors; something his father was far less enthusiastic about. The camp was in two weeks, and *hopefully*, he and Barbara could spend the private time repairing their somewhat strained relationship.

"Yeah, I like camp—I wanna be a Cherokee this year. How long before I go?"

"Just over a couple of weeks, son. We'll see if you can be a Cherokee—maybe I can put a word in with the chief."

Trey started running around his bedroom doing Native American war whoops. "Shhhh, son . . . that's enough. You will wake your stepmom."

"Sowwy, dad."

"You think you can take care of Elvis while I'm gone? Check his food, and he needs fresh water and to be walked every day."

"Why?" his son asked.

"Why do I want you to do it? Because I think you are a big boy, and you know how to do it."

"No, why does he need to eat and have water every day? Buddles doesn't eat like Elvis, and he is fine."

Trey just couldn't get the cat's name right no matter what. Barbara constantly corrected him to the point that he was pretty sure Trey just did it to spite her now. "Well, son, Buckles is a freak . . . an anomaly. Something that shouldn't exist." He laughed inwardly at his son's confused look. Trey tended to take everything literally. "Sorry, the cat eats . . . just not as much as a dog. He also seems to prefer to eat when no one is looking, so we don't usually see him do it. All animals need food and water to survive."

"I need food . . . and water," his son said softly. "Am I a fweak too? Some of the kids at the old school used to call me dat."

Oh Lord, why did I use that word?

"No, son, you are not a freak." He walked over and hugged the boy. "Definitely more of an anomaly," he said with a smile.

"I'm an ano . . . an omelet? Is that something like a rapper?"

"Let me think on that . . . could be similar, yeah."

He finished his goodbyes, shooing the cat from atop his bag and stuffing his bag of vitamins and pain pills into a side pocket before loading it in the big new truck. Backing out, he glanced out to the fence in his backyard and briefly considered driving away before shifting the truck back to park. *I'll get to Charlotte at some point.* Walking through the dew-covered grass, Elvis's tail was wagging like a propeller before he was halfway there. One more goodbye to make before he hit the road.

2

H e watched in semi-boredom as the colorful cars circled the track, again and again. His seat here in the luxury suite overlooking Charlotte International Raceway would have been a dream prize for most of the hundred thousand crowding the massive grandstands. The luxury suite's windows were open to the sounds and aromas of the famous raceway. Each time the cars whooshed by, a wave of heat and the acrid smell of burnt fuel washed over him. The sound, though, that was what was making him nauseous. "Oh God . . . please no—not a migraine," he whispered to himself. The roar of the engines was unbelievably loud, and it was overloading his senses. *I have to get out of here.*

Steven Porter found it ironic that he, of all people, was here. Of course, it was ironic that he lived the life he did at all. The truth was, he had no real love for cars and a complete disdain for auto racing. On some level he sort of got it, the reason millions of fans were so passionate about the sport, but not him. This was simply business. Something he made himself do. Truthfully, it was just as forced as the grins and handshakes with all the others here in the corporate suite. Giving up, he made his way to the exit in as covert a manner as possible. He could feel himself beginning to shut down.

His head was pounding now. This trip had been a mistake. He'd thought he could manage the three-day conference ending with the NASCAR race and accompanying afterparty. But rubbing his eyes to clear the agonizing haze, he knew he had been wrong. As the owner of one of the largest groups of Ford dealerships in the Southeast, he was expected to be here. He had been expected to deliver the keynote address to the annual dealer meeting two days earlier. Just like he had been expected to keep the Porter dealerships running and profitable after his father finally retired. It was indeed ironic that he lived this life at all.

The blinding August sun was too bright as he exited the building and clumsily walked past the garishly colored race team support trucks and into the parking garage. He couldn't remember where he was parked or even the color of the damn truck he was driving. He pushed the buttons on the key fob in his pocket. Instead of the chirp, he heard those revving engines on the track again and the roar of the crowd as an apparent accident occurred. "Fucking barbarians," he said to no one. He clicked the button again and finally saw the headlights blink on a large pickup in the front row.

With a sigh, he climbed into the specially-outfitted Ford SVT Raptor, which had been custom built by Hennessey Performance and now boasted a 600HP beast of an engine. The already potent truck could probably have run the Baja off-road race as it had come off the assembly line. This one, however, could now tame nearly any terrain. It was showy—bright red, with massive tires, and looked like an animal ready to attack. Inside, the look was more luxury jetliner than truck. Rich leather, wood trim, and every technology that could be crammed into the masterpiece of engineering. The truck was overkill; nobody really needed that much power. Truthfully, it was at best, a mildly interesting vehicle to Steve; he had selected it mainly because it was the one closest to the office door when he left the dealership.

Steve started the engine, enjoying the blast of cool air coming from the vents. He looked quickly through the leather messenger bag for some aspirin. *Shit, nothing.* He must've left the prescription pain relievers in his suitcase. That was still over at the conference center hotel. Putting the truck in drive, he sped toward the hotel, the roar of the powerful beast rivaling that of the cars inside the stadium.

The hotel and adjacent conference center was a half-mile away. It had been chosen deliberately to give its better rooms a clear view of the impressive racing facility. Knowing that the race afterparty was likely to run late, he had kept the deluxe room for another night. Walking in, he was greeted immediately by the concierge.

"Mr. Porter, welcome back! Is everything ok? You don't look well."

"Hey . . . um, oh, Thomas, yes everything is fine. Just a headache. Thought I would lie down on that fabulous bed upstairs for a while until it passes."

"Very good, sir." The concierge rushed ahead to summon the elevator. "I'll make sure you are not disturbed. Would you require anything, perhaps an ice pack or a cold beverage?"

"No thanks, I have what I need. Very kind, though."

The elevator climbed to the fourteenth floor, and he stepped out onto the rich carpeting of the penthouse level. He went to his suite, which was massively oversized for what he alone needed, but he didn't complain. The door shut and the sounds of the nearby race diminished significantly. He retrieved the medicine and pulled the blackout curtains tight. He popped two pills with some water from the wet bar. Still feeling queasy, he decided to take the other medicine to help relieve nausea as well. That was going to make him sleepy, but it was better than the alternative. Kicking off his John Lobb shoes, he cleared some of the numerous pillows before lying back on the bed. The luxurious feel of the mattress helped calm his spinning head. Within moments he was out.

STEVE WASN'T sure what woke him up. The fog of drugged sleep still shrouded his eyes with a gauzy haze. He did know he had to use the restroom and stumbled from the bed in that direction. The distant screeches of rending metal and explosions came from the track side of the hotel. This wreck seemed to be going on for much longer than normal. If the race hadn't finished yet, he knew he'd not been asleep nearly long enough to avoid the headache's effects. More sounds of destruction came from outside as he flipped the light switch, but the tiny room stayed dark. Several more attempts produced the exact same result. He shrugged in frustration as he went to pee.

The whirring of something close sounded directly over the hotel. Since Steve was on the top floor, that was a little unnerving as well. *That must've been what woke me up*, he thought as he lay back down. He really should go see what was going on, but the pain and drugs decided otherwise. The throbbing was returning, but this time it was mostly inside his head. He pulled the pillows around his ears in an attempt to keep the outside sounds away.

THE NEXT TIME STEVE AWOKE, it was dark outside, and the sheets around him were sweat-soaked. Did he have *a fever*? Getting up, he realized it was the room itself that was stifling. The thermostat was a blank screen. *Power must still be off.* He stumbled the few steps to the window to open it. Drawing back the curtains, his mind couldn't interpret the view. When it did, he nearly collapsed.

He was still asleep. He had to be, right? This was just a very vivid nightmare.

One entire side of the racetrack was filled with billowing, dark, thick smoke; high flames could be seen roaring in multiple places. It appeared that an accident must have taken out most of the field of cars.

Altering his view, his eyes widened even further. The accidents were not just limited to the racetrack. Just outside the hotel, up and down Concord Parkway, was a line of stalled cars and smoking wrecks. Stumbling to other windows in his hotel room, he could see similar scenes through each of them. As he watched, a large explosion lit up the skyline of Charlotte, which already seemed to have numerous large fires raging.

It took him several minutes to absorb what he was seeing. One other thing—there were no lights on anywhere. The fires supplied nearly all the light outside. *What in the fuck is going on?*

He picked up the remote, thinking maybe the TV coverage would have the answer, but of course . . . *No power, dummy. What to do? Call the front desk?* No, he needed to call home. If they were watching the race when it happened, they would be worried. Trey always worried if he didn't check in. *Barbara, too*, he thought. He felt his way to the large wood credenza and felt across to find his phone. He clicked the buttons to no avail. *Dead. . . . well, great.* He must have slept longer than he realized, as he was positive it had been nearly fully charged when he had come in. He could dig the charger out of his bag and . . . *And nothing, stupid. Need power to charge the phone.*

He checked the room phone, but of course, it was dead as well. His parched throat gave him the next course of action. The suite came with a nearly full-size, and—thanks to the conference, fully stocked refrigerator. Opening the door of the high-end appliance, a welcome blast of cold air greeted him from the darkened interior. He grabbed a bottled water and a sealed tray of cold-cuts and cheese. The halo effect of the headache and nearly comatose sleep was just beginning to dissipate. The water helped, and getting some food in his system was probably smart, too.

Something slammed down the hall. He seemed to recall there were only six rooms on this floor. All luxury penthouse suites like his own. The Ford dealers' conference had rented a number of them as comps to the main speakers.

Looking out the door, the emergency lighting dimly lit a man going through the steel door that led to the stairs. Steve only had a brief look—the man seemed familiar, but he couldn't put a name to the shadowy face. He decided it was probably best to go down and find out what the situation was. He slipped on his running shoes and t-shirt, grabbed the unfinished bottled water and headed for the stairs. The battery-operated emergency lights were only working on a few of the landings. Much of the descent was in relative darkness. A heavy door slammed shut many floors below. Steve was in good shape for his forty-two years, but the stairs left him winded.

Emerging into a small corridor off of the main lobby, he was immediately less sure it'd been wise of him to come down. The expansive lobby was dark, no sounds, no people, as far as he could tell. The colorful fires from outside cast a flickering light in the space, and as he crossed the lobby, his shoes began crunching and sliding on something. Looking down and then to his left, he realized several of the floor-to-ceiling windows had been smashed. He was walking on broken glass.

"Hello . . . is anyone there?" He foolishly had the thought that making any sound was the wrong move. *You're being paranoid.* Still, he quietly moved back deeper into the shadows. "Have I woken up in a horror movie?" he whispered to himself through clenched teeth. Should he go back to his room? The idea of the climb back up made him loathe that option. *Check the phones at the front desk.* Yes, that made sense. He worked his way over to the empty kiosk of guest services.

He leaned on the counter, but the perpetually smiling face of the guest manager was nowhere to be seen. Slipping around the desk, he fumbled around until he found the large switchboard phone. Picking it up, he heard only silence. None of the buttons produced any signal or sound. Flashing the receiver hook several times had no effect either. He looked at the framed pictures of two young girls on the desk—probably the concierge's daughters. To one side of the photo, a sticky note said, 'Alice and Bree—dentist appointment Thurs. 3PM'.

He leaned again on the wooden desktop, trying to come up with a plan. *Where is everyone?—What has happened?* While he had his flaws, Steve was not stupid. He knew something was seriously wrong. Was this an isolated problem? Just here in his immediate area? . . . No, the fires in Charlotte told him it was wider than that. Fires, traffic accidents, no power . . . the clues added up to nothing he could identify. Another thought occurred to him—he had seen no emergency responders. No flashing lights, no firetrucks, or even police.

It was all too confusing. Probably best to just wait in place for help or for the situation to improve. *Where did the man . . . what was his name? Tom . . . yeah, Tom, where did he go?* he wondered, and where was that guy he had followed from upstairs? He looked again around the darkened lobby. Maybe someone in the restaurant next door could help. The hotel also was home to one of the top steakhouses in the state. He had eaten there once already. Just maybe . . . assuming anyone was there, a decent meal would be a welcome treat. Something simple though—no steak. He headed down the long passageway to the entrance.

The door to the dining area was closed and locked. Frowning, he looked in the adjacent bar, which was also dark, but this door was open.

"Come on in, mate."

The voice was familiar. Slowly his mind began to match the voice with a face in his memory. Names were his specialty. His dad had drummed into him the importance of remembering everyone's first name, at least. Peering into the darkened room, he saw the silhouette of a man sitting on a stool at the bar. The glow of a cigarette visible in the man's hand.

"End of the world . . . least we can do is 'ave a drink, right?"

The Australian accent finally forced full recognition.

"You are . . . Drago?"

"Close, mate, Dragovich. How ya doin? This is some shit, aye?"

Steve now remembered this was the man who had given a well-received talk on personal defense during the conference. His near comedic banter was matched with some solid survival skills and had been offered as an intermission of sorts to the non-stop sales, marketing and car discussions.

He leaned in close and flicked his lighter. "Oh, I knows you. You're the big-wig bloke with all the big dealerships down south. Wait . . . don't tell me. Peters Auto Group."

"Also close . . . it's Porter's Auto. Nice to meet you, officially. I enjoyed your talk the other day. Using everyday items for self-defense. I would never have considered using a ballpoint pen that way."

"Aww, much obliged. You guys were a great audience. Sometimes these conferences are just too uptight to listen to someone like me.

They usually bring me in as filler or to keep the wives entertained while the hubbies talk shop, but glad I got my time in front of you guys. Really sucks to end this way though."

Steve nodded absentmindedly and said, "Yeah . . . looks like hell outside. I guess I missed one hell of a storm. Do you know what happened, Dragovich?"

The man emitted a small laugh and took a final pull on the cigarette before snuffing it out. "Call me Blake. I guess you saw what happened ove there at da race—you were there, right?"

Steve shook his head, "No . . . I wasn't feeling well. I left early and came back here to rest."

"Crikey mate, you missed it all then." He stood and leaned over the counter. "What ya drinking?"

"Ummm, whiskey, Irish or Canadian, if you can even tell."

Bottles clinked. "Here we go. Bring it with you, let's take a walk."

A splashing sound then a tumbler of liquid was pushed into Steve's hand as they walked back in the direction of the lobby. "You're just going to steal a bottle of liquor from them?"

"Trust me, mate. They ain't gonna mind." Blake poured a few fingers for himself before continuing. "I never got this car racing thing, you know. Not until today, that is. It's something you just have to experience to understand. All that raging power . . . the sounds, the wrecks. That shite is awesome."

"So . . . what happened?"

"Oh right, oh right, right. Well, the race was nearing the end. They were all bunched up, and one of the favorites was making a move, when all of a sudden, the power in the luxury box went out. That wasn't the half of it. An older man I was speaking with dropped to the floor dead. I was looking around for help when I heard the crashes begin. Not all the cars died when the power went out, but those that did became a deathtrap to others behind them that were still moving. The explosions and fires began at once, and shite . . . in seconds at least fifty cars were in the pileup.

"It was massive, mate. The next thing was the damn camera choppers. Both of 'em went silent and began to spin out of control. One came down in the infield, exploding over a group of caravanners . . . I mean, umm, motorhomes. The other hit in the grandstands. It had to be awful; the fires were everywhere. People stampeding over each other to escape. What was it? . . . I guess maybe a hundred thousand people trying to get out those tiny little exits at the same time." He shook his head, grimacing. "It was awful, mate. Worse even than what happened on the track."

"Jeezeus . . . that's terrible," Steve said. "I don't understand, though. What was wrong with that man? . . . How long did it take for emergency services to get things under control back on the track?" He pushed the door open to the outside.

"That's the thing, see—there was no response. None of the safety crews could get their trucks or ambulances going. Fire trucks wouldn't work. Even the radios for the security staff were dead. The damage was everywhere, and most rescuers were helpless to do much for anyone. Someone went to do CPR on the poor man, but when he tried, he found the man had a scar and large lump on his chest. Pacemaker, I think they said; it had just stopped working."

From where they stood Steve could see the fires from the raceway. It seemed they were beginning to die down, but the flickering light was somehow brighter, everywhere. "What could cause a power outage and crash cars and helicopters?"

Blake was easier to see now that they were on the side of the parking lot. They sat on the curb as Dragovich poured himself another drink and put the bottle between them. "That," he said flatly as he pointed up.

Steve looked up at the dark, overcast sky, which in places was backlit with spots of color. Where the clouds seemed thinner were glimpses of pinks, reds and lavender that flickered across the sky. "*What the fuck . . . ?*"

3

Steve was mesmerized by the glimpses of color and light breaking through the clouds. "I don't get it, what would cause that? It's weird, but what does it have to do with . . . with all this?"

The Aussie took another sip and looked around. "Several things could cause most of this. A nuclear bomb could produce an EMP blast that could fry all electronics, and I was thinking that was it until those showed up. Now, I'm assuming it is aliens."

Blake lay back on the grass and looked at the gray sky with the tiny burst of occasional color.

"Yep, we're completely fucked."

The Aussie laughed and turned toward Steve. "How far from home are you?"

"I don't know, maybe six hours by car. Just over 400 miles."

Blake nodded. "Which of these little beauties is yours?" He was waving to the parking lot where the brilliant colors of the sky danced over a lot full of shiny cars.

"The pickup over there."

"Oh man . . . she's a beaut. Wow, that is sharp. Lots of power in that I bet. Is that the Velociraptor edition?" Blake nodded approvingly. "Yeah, that is one great ride. I bet she handles the off-road as well as the highway."

Steve said he didn't really know.

"Well, its completely useless to you now," the man said, his tongue getting a bit thick giving him an even more pronounced accent. "Real bummer, but that magnificent beast will never start again." He laughed.

"Sure it will start; it's brand new."

"Nope, I'll bet you . . . " he pulled a wad of bills from his pocket. He started counting, then just slapped them all on the ground between them. "I bet you this that it won't. Go see."

"I don't have too; it has remote start." Steve pulled the key fob from his pocket and clicked the start button. Nothing happened. He clicked the unlock button, then the lock. . . . Nothing. "What the fuck?"

Blake was laughing lightly. "Sorry, mate. I bet that thing is loaded with computers and electronics. Only old cars without all that crap would have survived."

Steve went over and used the actual key to unlock and try the ignition before giving up and coming back. "You win. Shit, I guess calling a tow truck is not going to happen either. Sorry, I don't have any cash. I will have to owe you."

"No prob, mate. The cash is probably worthless as well by now. Same for all those plastic cards in your wallet."

"Why would cash and credit cards be useless?"

"Well, two reasons—the cash simply because inflation will be crazy, prices for anything may skyrocket, but also, your government may no longer be functioning. If the aliens took them out, then nothing real is backing the currency. Same thing in my country. Most of our money is just little blips and dashes on a computer some-where. You can believe all of that shite is fried as well." Blake poured himself another drink and downed it before continuing. "Yep, what-ever you have on you or can get quickly is going to be all you have from this point forward."

The man was already drunk, Steve knew that, but it didn't mean everything he was saying was wrong. Something was certainly going on, something very bad. The man had some survival skills. What else could he learn from him? "So, Blake, what would be the smart thing for me to do, in order to get home?"

The man had lit another cigarette now and exhaled slowly before answering. "Get away from this city, any city. Get you a traveling pack . . . a 'get home bag,' light on clothes, heavy on water and food, and start walking. Find a bike. If you get lucky, steal a working car. Pretty soon you can forget cash, but anything else you have of value may mean life or death. Oh yeah, get a weapon, even if it is just a stick."

"I have a bag upstairs and food and water in the fridge."

"Really . . . up there?"

Steve was getting annoyed. "Yeah."

"Up there, behind the impressively solid door . . . with the electronic lock?" Blake took another long drag.

The man was right. Steve closed his eyes and punched himself in the head. "Fuck, I was so stupid."

"Don't sweat it, mate. My stuff is locked up as well. I couldn't even get into my room once I got out of the madhouse at the racetrack. Probably not much in there you really need anyway. Think about it."

Again, he was right. He had expensive shoes and suits, his phone, and an ultralight laptop both of which were likely dead. He really had nothing much there. He had no reason to go back up fourteen flights of steps. "You're right, man. Other than food and water, not much. And I suppose I could get that elsewhere."

"I wouldn't worry much about food—too heavy to take all you need, and you can actually survive a long time without eating. Won't be pleasant, but you won't likely die of starvation. Water is a different story; a couple of days without it and you're a gonna. Take all the water you can carry. I saw cases of that back behind the bar. You will need to get a bag of some sort, preferably a backpack or rucksack."

"I'm no prepper, Blake. I know nearly nothing about survival."

The Aussie laughed deeply. "Well fuck, man, I am, but it isn't doing me a bit of good. Don't think prepper—that is as much about having the knowledge as having the tools and supplies. Think more . . . hmm, what would you call them here? Hobos, homeless people. You know. Those guys know how to survive. It ain't pretty, but it'll work. You just have to focus on the things you can control; ignore all the other shite."

Steve leaned back, his mind was still cloudy from the headache, the drugs, and now the whiskey. What the hell does this guy know? . . . *Aliens!* Just absurd. The idea of acting homeless seemed unthinkable to him, but all that didn't mean it wasn't a good plan.

As if the man knew what Steve was thinking, he grinned. "You are homeless now friend; so am I."

Steve nodded, dropping his head in reluctant acceptance. "So, what about you, Blake? How will you get . . . home?"

"Oh . . . no chance, mate. This is it for me. The aliens have totally buggered me. I have plenty of booze. At some point tomorrow, I'm going to bust the door down to the steakhouse and eat myself silly. Then I'm just gonna wait for the end."

"So, that's it? All that survival talk was just bullshit?"

"Steven, look, part of surviving, the biggest part, is having the will. Truthfully...I just don't anymore. No one really waiting for me back home. I spend ten months a year going around the world teaching women how not to get raped or mugged. Now it will be every man for themselves. I'm a fighter—I won't make it a week before someone decides I have to go. Ya see mate, right now you will have cats and rats. I'm a cat. I'm just a drunk, lazy cat. You, my friend, you need to go be a rat."

Steve thought about it. That remark should offend him, but for some reason, it didn't. *Think Steve, think!* He could go try and find someone who might know something more official. The police maybe, or even his contact for the conference. He had no idea how to get home but thought he should get started. The headache had faded. Blake was lying back on the soft grass beginning to snore. *Think Steve, think. Water, go get water.*

4

Steven's mind was clearer, but he still was having trouble processing all this. He had been awake for just over an hour, and apparently, the world had fallen apart while he slept. His pragmatic mind couldn't accept an alien theory, but something had happened. Something dreadful. Did it warrant him making an almost certainly suicidal march toward his home in South Georgia? He knew he was no longer a young man. Not someone that people would think of as a survivor, but he was not completely incapable. He had been an athlete in high school, managed to keep the weight off and jogged a little almost every day. That was not the same as making it hundreds of miles on foot. *Shit, there has to be a working car I can buy.* He needed more cash just in case he found something.

He had grabbed his messenger bag from the truck, leaving everything else that was in it. He filled the bag with bottled water. Behind the abandoned guest services desk was a small pantry with snacks and pastries. He took all of the granola and energy bars they had. He left a note for Tom to add it to his room charge. He marched back out of the lobby past the still sleeping Blake. He looked one last time at the truck and then back at the hotel. *Might as well go see what I'm up against.*

He looked again south toward downtown Charlotte. The dark, angry-looking skyline seemed to hold more threats than hope. Fires were now clearly visible from some of the buildings. They were in the general direction he would need to go. First, he decided to go see for himself how the speedway had faired. Smoke was everywhere, but no fires remained visible on the track. He didn't so much have a plan as just a morbid curiosity to see first-hand if the Aussie was being truthful. Also, some of the other dealers might still be around—maybe with working vehicles.

The sky was more overcast now, thankfully blocking out the weird lights above. As he walked down the gentle slope, a light rain began to fall. *A rain jacket would be nice,* he thought. His wants list was growing fast. As a man used to having everything he wanted . . . this was going to be challenging. He had to keep reminding himself to simply focus on what was actually needed. How were Trey and Barbara doing? She would be frightened, he knew that much. Trey would be angry, looking for a solution. Like his grandfather, Trey preferred absolutes. His was a world of black and white; this would not be an easy situation for the boy.

The smell of burnt fuel triggered a twinge in his head . . . just an echo of the migraine. *Shit, my medicine is up in that locked room.* Steve wandered on, toward the track and an increasingly foul odor. Not an odor of death or decay, but worse. He flashed back to a school field trip during his fourth grade year. They had visited an enormous hog farm, one of many in the area around his hometown. The smell of the muddy pigs that day was unforgettable. Like most of the kids on that trip, he didn't want to grow up doing that for a living. That was the smell . . . the same as now. Only...it wasn't pigs.

The surviving fans of the Charlotte Motor Speedway had numbered nearly 118,000, and they had exited the arena of horrors only to discover they were stuck. No way to leave the area other than the handful of classic cars that were still running. Those cars had left loaded to the brink with extra passengers. The fans that were left had rampaged through the concessions, luxury booths, and nearby restaurants to fill their stomachs with food and drink before collapsing in the grass parking area. The piss and shit combined with the mud, sweat, and other bodily odors now filled the night air.

"Oh my God!" Steve said as he topped a hill and saw the mass of people. Small, makeshift campfires dotted the open field ahead. He tore a piece off his sleeve and tied it around his nose and mouth as a makeshift filter. The sounds of people fighting, women screaming, even some babies crying added to the mix. He watched in morbid fascination as a group of men attacked another man who apparently had just managed to get the lights to come on in his car. The scene of chaos continued as far as he could see on all sides of the racetrack. This was not what he was looking for. The tableau of misery was too much for him to focus on.

The darkness covered other routes—he tried to remember what lay in other directions. He turned away and headed due south or as close to that as he could guess. The walking got easier after a few miles, and he crossed onto a loose gravel road heading in the same direction. *How far could a man walk in a day?* He wasn't sure but did some rough calculations and guessed somewhere between fifteen to twenty miles. *Could a person do that day after day? What if it wasn't on a road but maybe a field or forest? Were there mountains between here and Georgia?*

It was crazy, he couldn't just leave for home—nothing could be that bad. Just wait for the sun to come up. In the light of day, he would find help. He was beginning to feel foolish. The Aussie had planted a whopper of a tale, and his paranoia was letting it consume him. The drizzle of rain was coming in fits and starts now. He moved underneath a large tree and thought through what little he knew once more. *The power is out, not just electricity but everything electrical. How widespread would it be? Couldn't be out everywhere, could it? Nah . . .* he felt like it had to be just the city or maybe a few neighboring counties.

What else did he know? Hmmm . . . well, everyone in charge seemed to be gone. Hell, the only place he saw people was at the racetrack. So, emergency services were likely overwhelmed or unable to respond. Did he know anything else? A glimmer of pink light in the sky showed through in the distance . . . *yeah, there's also that.* He was still clueless as to what that meant. An EMP is what Blake had said. An electromagnetic pulse. *Those only happened when a nuke went off though . . . right?*

Those three items added up to . . . nothing. How was he supposed to make a plan when he was totally clueless about the problems? *Damn, I wish I had a radio, or even better, a working phone.* Maybe he could find someone with one. That sounded smart . . . he needed info. That was now his primary focus. A better explanation than aliens.

He had been walking for nearly an hour when the surroundings opened up into a small meadow. There was a reflection coming from something in the middle of the field, and as he listened, whispered voices. The sound of a radio was also heard. The hiss and tinny sounds were unmistakable. It was too dark to make out much detail, but he guessed from the lighter shades that it was a barn with curved tin siding, maybe one of the familiar Quonset huts of years past. He was ready for a short break anyway, and the drizzle had restarted again. The thought of finding a jacket or a tarp had moved from a want to a need. The closer he got, he could identify lettering on the side of the . . . barn? It no longer seemed the right shape, too long and too skinny, and the side of the "barn" was a good fifty feet above the ground. "OODYEA" was all he could make out. Lighter letters on dark background with a lighter gray section above and below. He had seen this yesterday. The blimp sponsored by the tire manufacturer had been circling all day. "Hello . . . anyone there?"

He heard someone say, "Shhh." He walked a few feet farther holding his hands halfway up hoping he didn't look threatening. "It's ok, I'm alone. Just trying to find out what happened. Would either of you have a working phone or . . . radio?"

A voice in the dark said, "Yeah, but be quiet. Are you really alone?"

The question seemed odd, but he decided to be honest. "Yes, it's just me."

A small but powerful flashlight flicked on, and he saw two men. One was untying a rope; the other had the light. The voice came again, "Its ok, we were about to leave. That crowd over there is getting a bit rowdy. We put her down after the fireworks, but our ground crew never showed, and no one is answering our radio calls and, uh . . .well, sorry, both our phones are dead."

Steve placed the man's voice as Upper Midwest. "But the blimp itself is ok? No problems with electronics?" Steve asked.

"Oh yeah, she's fine. Just a big balloon. The motors are simple and operated by old-school mechanicals and hydraulics. The radar, radios, and such are all out, but we fly by terrain and landmarks all the time."

This night kept offering more questions than anything else. Steve knew he couldn't walk 400 miles; he was mainly counting on getting far enough to be in a less affected or unaffected area. Any rescue coming this way would have to deal with the carnage at the race track first anyway. *No matter what had gone wrong here in Charlotte, it couldn't extend more than . . . what, forty miles, maybe a hundred or so. Right?* He knew he was trying to convince himself more than anything. Dragovich's words haunted him though. He didn't want to stay put and wait for the end. He had to get home.

Steve quickly reached a decision. "Where are you heading, and could you use an extra pair of hands getting there?"

AN HOUR later they were ready to launch. The two pilots, McKay and Lambert, had shown him what needed to be done and made room for him in the tiny cabin. They had also ditched some extra ballast to account for his weight. As soon as the small engines started, they began to hear shouts and saw flashlights in the woods. People were coming to investigate—lots of people. "Hang on to something—this is going to be a tail dragging launch."

The tiny gondola was firmly attached to the blimp. As lines were tossed loose, Steve and Lambert rushed to join the pilot as the blimp pitched sharply up at the nose. The rear did indeed come close to hitting the ground, but McKay expertly leveled out just as the group below rushed into the area they had been in. A few of the more daring found tie-down ropes still dragging low and grabbed on thinking they could pull the craft back down. After being dragged roughly for a few dozen yards all let go.

The Goodyear blimp was airborne and heading somewhat toward its home base of Fort Worth, Texas. Steve had asked, and the men had agreed to drop him in Georgia as they passed over. The wind took them toward the city of Charlotte which all could see was now almost fully engulfed in flames. "What would have caused the fires?" Steve was unsure as to the person speaking as the cockpit was completely dark.

McKay, he thought, offered an opinion, "If it was an EMP, then powerlines and even large transformers could have exploded, but best guess on the fires is natural gas. As the control valves and switches are all electronic, a power surge could have wiped them out causing a pressure surge in the lines. Once it began to rupture, it probably happened all over the city. Then a single spark would have set it off. I spent my college years doing co-op jobs in oil and gas down in Houston. The stuff is wonderful . . . until it isn't."

The other man said, "Trim is equalized; you can take us up if you want to get above this mess. Cloud ceiling is about 1,800 feet."

"Roger that," and in a sudden but fluid move the craft angled sharply upward through the clouds like a whale breaching the surface of a silvery sea.

In unison, all three men gave various expletives calling on God in various forms as well as a well-chosen term of incestuous lovemaking. *It was not aliens.*

The sky was alive. The Northern Lights danced through the heavens. The more familiar greens and blues, but also pinks, lavenders and reds. Steve was dumbfounded by what he saw. The aurora flickered, ebbed and flowed. Meanwhile, its shadowy reflection was mirrored along the sea of clouds now slowly moving below them. The dance of colors stretched to the far horizon. As a man who had never seen the Northern Lights, it was mesmerizingly beautiful. The co-pilots had another reaction entirely. Lambert refused to look; his face was buried in his hands. McKay was staring in horror out the small window. "Guys?" Steve said tentatively. "What does this mean?"

"It's not good . . . " McKay said.

"But it means it wasn't a nuclear bomb, right? This is just something natural. That has to be better than a bomb or war." He recalled that the Northern Lights were a normal occurrence up in the Arctic, although he couldn't remember what caused them . . . something to do with the Earth's magnetic field, he thought.

McKay picked up on his question. "I wish that were true, man. This . . . " he waved his hand all around. The reflected light in the small cabin was bright enough to read the labels on the knobs and switches now. "This means it was the sun—a solar flare. To be precise, they call it a CME, a Coronal Mass Ejection. Not technically a solar flare, more like a bit of the sun got pinched off and flung at the Earth. It means things are much, much worse."

Steve felt suddenly cold. "What do you mean . . . worse?"

"This could mean the rest of the planet is just a dark as Charlotte."

Solar flares happened all the time. Steve remembered reading about some of the problems in the past. Nothing overly significant, some blackouts, but more commonly just cell phone outages and planes needing to re-route. "I've never heard of a solar flare or coronal thing doing anything like this."

"That's because there hasn't been one like this. Well...not in a few hundred years or so." Lambert was speaking now. His head still hung low, but he was now also watching the mesmerizing light show. "In one of our flight training courses . . . maybe it was recertification, we got some briefing on it. The odds were not high, but it could happen. Last time was back in the horse and buggy days, and only a few people were injured. Not much of anything electrical to speak of back then. Today . . . well, you saw what happened today. Imagine that going on everywhere at the same time." Steve decided not to mention he hadn't actually seen it happen. He had seen the aftermath.

The scene was mesmerizingly beautiful and otherworldly frightening. He thought about his son and wondered what home would be like. "How long do you think it will take to repair the power?"

Neither of the pilots spoke for a while. Then McKay said, "I don't know, Scott."

"Steve."

"Oh, sorry. Umm...I don't know, Steve. I never did much with electrical, although one of the companies I worked for was a supplier to the Texas power grid. I know they often talked about how expensive the LPTs were and how long it took for one to be built. Those are what are so vulnerable to a CME or EMP. Those huge transformers go out, and...well, they said back then, it could be years to get a replacement."

"That's insane. Why would we leave one of the most vital parts of our power grid that vulnerable, and why would they not keep tons of redundancy?"

"I fly a balloon for a living, man . . . I have no idea."

5

He had faded back to sleep sometime later. The hypnotic ribbons of light lulling him into another world. A world of fantasy and "what ifs." A world where he had the life he really wanted instead of this one. A life of daring and intrigue and not a car salesman. As he awoke from the dreams he did realize that . . . this one had definitely gotten more interesting.

The light show was fading as the morning sky began to lighten. Lambert was at the control yoke now; McKay appeared to be dozing on a small cot on the opposite wall. He pushed his way into McKay's seat with a "Good morning" to the other pilot. This was really the first time any of them had actually seen each other. Lambert was older than he had thought, probably early sixties. The face was pale and deeply etched with age lines. "Thanks for letting me tag along. I have to admit, never thought I would be on a blimp trying to get home. I'll be glad to help out any way I can."

Lambert nodded, eyes returned to the dead instruments, then to the horizon. "Airship."

"How's that?"

"We refer to her as an airship, not a blimp. You are welcome,

Steve. Just help us keep an eye out for problems. We rely on our ground crew and spotters and instruments. None of that no more . . . "

"Where are we now?"

Lambert pointed out the side window. "I'm guessing over northeast Georgia. That's I-85 down there. We will follow it in toward Atlanta. That is probably a few hours away, but I can see a smudge on the horizon; that is probably the city."

Steve briefly looked up at the sky in the distance then back to the highway below. The blimp—*airship*—was lower now. The details of the usually busy road were very clear. It was now an unbelievably long parking lot, interspersed regularly with horrific-looking accidents and people. *My God, the people.* Hundreds, more like thousands, all walking in a joyless march toward what? He was damn glad he hadn't tried to get a car and drive—it would have been a disaster.

"All those poor people stranded. I can only imagine what Atlanta is like."

"Aye, it's scary. Nearly every city we have passed has been in ruins. The roads have been packed like that as long as I have been able to see. Hundreds of miles of stranded motorists. Everyone wanting to get home, and those that do will just find more of the same. The cities will be the worst. I am going to wake Mike up in a bit. I think we need to steer well north or south of Atlanta. Do you have a preference where we drop you? Or . . . have you decided you want to keep flying west with us? Just stay up here above it all?"

He thought about it for a few seconds. "No, thanks, but I need to get home." The obvious direction was south of the city as that was closer to Steve's home, but he was now thinking about the route, and maybe it was smarter to avoid certain areas than simply choosing the quicker routes. "West of the city I think would be best; the south side has some unsavory parts, and it has the airport. I think possibly closer to the state line might be quieter."

The pilot just nodded and kept staring ahead.

≈

THE SENIOR PILOT, McKay, had other ideas. When he woke up, the airship was within thirty miles of Atlanta. Looking over all the gauges he shook his head. "We need to fly straight through. That wind last night took too much fuel, and it is still blowing us south. I don't see any traffic lined up to land at Hartsfield, so let's assume everything there is grounded. He pointed at a laminated map in his hand. Take a line south of the city and just north of the airport. We can try for this little airport here on the west side to let Mr. Porter out."

"Roger that," Lambert replied.

Steve knew he was talking about Hartsfield-Jackson Airport, normally one of the busiest airports in the world. He was still watching the crowd marching and camping along the interstate below. It was a human migration. It reminded him of all the families fleeing the war in the Middle East. Leaving everything behind as they marched into uncertainty.

"Sure you wanna get in the middle of all that?" Lambert asked sarcastically. "You could stick with us to Texas."

McKay gave Lambert a look. He wasn't in the mood to be as accommodating.

Steve ignored whatever was *not* being said between them. "No, this is as close as you will get to my home. I will say I'm not looking forward to what comes next, but I have to try."

The men nodded. "You got any supplies in that bag of yours?"—it was McKay this time.

"I really don't—some water and a few granola bars. I literally have nothing that I am going to need to get home."

The senior pilot nodded. "Wish we could help, but we don't keep anything in this thing. In fact, if you could spare a water or two we would be much obliged."

He hated to give up any of his precious water but couldn't refuse the men for what they had already done. He removed two of the plastic bottles and put them in the drink holders attached to the seats. He left a few more on the cabin floor. "Thanks, guys, I'm not sure I could have made it this far without your help. You easily cut my trip in half."

"Aye . . . no prob . . . man," Lambert offered before—"Holy shit, Mike. Do you see that?" Both men were leaning forward, looking over the instrument cluster at something ahead. From his position behind the two flight chairs, Steve was just beginning to catch sight of the high-rise buildings of downtown. Like Charlotte, it appeared fire had raged through parts of the city. The interstate they were following entered into a massive multi-level interchange off to the right, and the sight of thousands of stalled cars and tens of thousands of people on the overpasses was unnerving.

On the left side of the airship was the solid granite facade of Stone Mountain. *Some things can never change,* he thought. The gray rock looming out of the sea of trees still seemed so out of place as to not be natural. None of those were what McKay and Lambert were focused on.

Just coming into view was part of the enormous airport. In lines stretching off in multiple directions, regularly spaced columns of thick black smoke plumed upward. "Those are airliners, jumbo jets," one of the men said in a somber voice. The lines of smoke were arrow straight, mirroring the take-off and landing approach vectors. "Jesus, Mary and Joseph," Lambert said before crossing himself.

This was the airport Steve used on a regular basis. He knew from the stats that it was one of, if not *the* world's busiest. A flight left or arrived every forty seconds, well over a hundred and twenty flights an hour. With even more traffic at the adjacent international runway, he could only guess at the numbers. Tens of thousands of lives lost from these crashes alone. Again, he saw only a few emergency vehicles at the crash sites.

McKay had deviated to fly closer to the tarmac. The devastation was everywhere. At the end of the runway, a scorch mark ran for hundreds of yards before ending in a blackened lump. Obviously, a take-off that never happened. At the terminal building a large section was collapsed and burning; the silver tip of a wing one of the only recognizable signs of the cause. Just as scary, everywhere they looked were people. Many must have fled the terminals onto the tarmac, and all those sitting on planes about to take off or just landing had eventually hit the emergency doors. The sagging remnants of inflated slides were hanging from every stopped jet like an animal trailing its insides.

Many people stared up at the brightly colored blimp overhead. They must be feeling their pain and despair on display like at a sporting event. "We need to go," said Steve.

The men up front seemed to realize this as well. The airship turned away from the macabre scene and was away from the airport in seconds. That was when they realized someone was shooting at them. A hole appeared in the fiberglass floor just in front of Steve. "Holy shit! What was—" Another cracked the glass windshield.

"Losing pressure in the envelope, Mike. Get us out of here."

The pilots sounded concerned but were not panicking. Steve looked over the side to see neighborhood streets filling with people looking up and pointing. He no longer felt as safe up here as he had. "Can't we go higher, get out of range?"

McKay yelled back, "Some but not much. We mostly fly map-of-the-Earth only about 1,500 feet up. With a full load of gas, we can add 500 more feet, but not today. He shoved the yoke forward and to the right, working the control pedals at the same time. Steve could see more of the city skyline filling the view, the old Olympic Stadium and former home to the Atlanta Braves coming into view. The city was unrecognizable; fires were raging out of control, and nothing was moving down there but waves of people out on the streets.

The city of Atlanta had always been one of his favorites. It was still relatively young and vibrant and not so large that you couldn't get around. Great restaurants, museums and excellent luxury hotels. He and Barbara had spent many nights here over the years. Now, it looked dead—sinister even. It was no longer the city that he loved. He watched as the Westin Hotel, one of the iconic landmarks downtown passed by, a deep gash and black charring taking out most of one side. Something had impacted it hard.

McKay swung the craft back west and let the wind carry them away from downtown. Steve leaned forward. "Captain, what about the airship? Do we need to check for damage, fix something?"

"Not much we can do. The ship is designed with redundancies. The outer envelope will trap most of the escaping gas. I would say only a couple of the internal gas bladders were struck. You see, the airship it is not just one balloon, but many, all surrounded by the outer shell, the envelope, as we call it. We should be fine unless we run into more of that. Come up here and look out to tell me a good place to set you down."

6

Steve watched as the giant craft rose gracefully back into the sky, the landing rope sliding through his hands until he was sure they would clear the hangar. McKay had brought the airship back to Earth at a small abandoned, rural airstrip well outside of Atlanta. Steve had exited the craft, and they were back on their way in minutes. The horrific scenes they had witnessed the previous night, and especially the last few hours, had left them all shaken. Few words were spoken other than wishes of good luck to each for their journey home.

He turned to leave the grassy field as soon as possible. The large, colorful blimp would have been seen. Others would be coming. That, he now knew, could likely be very bad. The few neighborhoods and houses were mostly to the north and east, so he headed south. With few supplies and no real plan, he simply wanted to keep moving. Avoid large roads and big towns. This part of Georgia was unfamiliar to him, but he had selected it for several reasons. It was less developed; it had good roads and a large river flowing south. Truthfully, it was simply the least bad option. He would have loved to have caught another blimp flying south, but you work with what you have.

So much had changed since yesterday, and yet he had no idea

how much. The lack of information was driving him mad. He could be out here risking his life for nothing. In less than twenty-four hours his life was unrecognizable—the world he had seen so far was in shambles. He recalled a friend of his had a Ford dealership in a town about thirty miles away. For no other particular reason, he decided that would be his first destination and began moving in what he hoped was the right direction.

The August heat in Georgia is something you can either deal with or not. He was ok with it but knew the water wouldn't last long with temperatures in the high nineties and the sauna-like humidity. Within thirty minutes, his clothes were soaked through with sweat. Even the waxed-canvas messenger bag strapped across his back was soaked. He needed to focus on something else, and his mind drifted to his family. How were they doing? His current wife, Barbara, had not been the first Mrs. Porter. He had defied his parents and married his first wife for love. Marie was pretty, simple and kind. She had been an art major while he was in business school. They had fallen in love, and she had gotten pregnant. His father had very nearly disowned him. "The woman is a goddamn Democrat, Steve. What were you thinking?" To alleviate further family shame, his mother had given him money to go to Vegas for a quickie wedding. Sadly, Marie lost the baby two months later. The miscarriage devastated her, and she never was the same again. The scar of loss reshaped her from the woman he loved to someone looking for an escape. Her path got darker as the years passed. After bouts with alcohol, then prescription pills, they were finally divorced, his father feeling vindicated by his opinion that "the girl was trash."

With few other options, Steve had reluctantly joined his father's business. While he hated sales—and having no love for cars in partic-ular—he proved to be a valuable addition to the business. What he possessed was a unique ability to observe people and gauge needs. His father had made him work in every department at the company before giving him a management position. He realized quickly that the service side of the business was both the most profitable and the department with the most potential to grow. Over the years, the

Porter family of dealerships grew because they were so service oriented and customer focused. His service department managers were always the highest-paid people in the company. The dealerships were really just fancy garages that leased space up front to the manufacturers to move their product. Money was not made on the frontend—the new car sales—but instead, most was made on the backend, mainly in service and in finance. The sales were simply a good supply pipeline to get more people into Fords, which in turn, fed more work for the service department.

A sound ahead snapped him out of his mental time travel. He was in the woods about fifty yards from a two-lane highway. He crouched as he saw movement on the road. Two men in camo with guns slung lazily across their chests. Could just be hunters, but he had to be sure. *Be a rat.* The Aussie man's words came back to him over and over. He watched and stayed hidden.

"Hey, you! Stop right there," one of the men said. Both men were running now. Steve thought he might have been spotted and ducked even lower. The men kept running as they went by, and then one took a knee and fired his gun. "Shit, man, can't just be shooting at people for fucking wid ya stuff."

The other man stood back up. "I can, and I will. Our stuff may mean life or death right now. Things have changed, Will." They turned and walked back in the direction they had come.

Who in the hell were they shooting at? He had not seen anyone else come by, but he didn't always have a good view of the road. Highways are dangerous, he needed them for navigation but now was wishing he had a GPS or a compass instead. Not that he knew how to use a compass, but he was becoming convinced that he needed to do something different. It was slow going through the woods, and if he caught a root and twisted an ankle or broke a leg he would probably die there. "Shit, shit, shit." The best of the bad options was to stay concealed, closer to the road, but not on it, and watch the road as well as the path ahead. He stopped to think about what he was wearing. *How much would it stand out if someone was looking?* His clothing was dark but not made for roaming through the woods. Twill pants and a dark gray dress shirt. His running shoes were originally bright but well-worn; the day in the forest had them already stained and dirty. He rubbed some soil onto his face and the same on his exposed hands.

He hated working with limited knowledge. He was used to being in charge—being the most informed and usually able to accurately predict outcomes. It made him a good businessman, and in his opinion, a good husband and father. Right now, he wasn't even being a good rat. The men with the guns had not seemed evil but had no problem defending themselves. That told him something: unlike the cities where seemingly random violence, death and probably even looting was already a fact, here it was more like people being opportunistic than outright thieves. Small towns and rural communities had their own way of dealing with problems. He was from a small town. All of his dealerships were in relatively small towns. He understood the mindset of those people and could appreciate it. Protect what is yours, don't trust strangers, be prepared to meet danger head-on.

The afternoon sun was beginning to dip, but he knew this time of year it could stay light until nearly nine. Shelter was a concern, and one he had no idea how to solve. Walking out of sight alongside the rough-paved road, he'd seen no other houses, barns or even shelter of any type. Had no idea how to craft anything, nor if he even needed to build one. The night wouldn't be cold, not that many predators were around, wasn't really bear country or anything. He was considering this as he noticed the roadblock just coming into view ahead. He was deep enough in the woods to not be seen but thought briefly of stepping out and strolling up to see what was up. The idea of being turned around and sent away was more than he could handle, though. He was a rat. Sneak up close enough to listen to the people and see what he could learn. Observe, little rat.

The roadblock consisted of an older truck with a Carroll County Sheriff emblem, an ancient and rusty station wagon and a large, yellow piece of road paving equipment. It would have been effective had anyone been driving, but if you stopped to look, it was something less than official. Steve got close, then lay on the ground and slowly began crawling up to within earshot. Two men and a woman leaned against the truck and wagon chatting. One of the men was in uniform and armed. The other two may have been officers, but he couldn't see any weapons.

The conversation was well under way when he lay back and began focusing on the words, " . . . wire, and he said it was the same all over. The fucking Russians done nuked us, we are at war."

The other man: "You don't know that and don't go spreading rumors. The powers out, that's all."

"Then why won't our cars start? Huh? Why did them jets fall out da sky? You the assistant sheriff, Clay, you sposa know these things."

The woman spoke for the first time, "I heard it was space weather, some freaky solar storm fried everything."

"Solar flares don't do all that. Shit, they happen all the time, Lori. . . . damn. Might lose service on your phone, but wouldn't make the whole world go to shit."

She huffed, "So you are an expert now? How did I forget the time you spent consulting for NASA? You don't know shit. But, Clay . . . what in the hell are we doing out here? Nobody has been down this road all day."

The deputy said, "Keeping people from coming into town. The mayor and council said to expect people to start flooding off the inter-state and out of Atlanta and the bigger cities. Turn them away as whatever resources we have are ours to use. Even if they have family here, we are to send them away. If they are walking, it is probably too soon for them to be showing up, but later tonight, definitely tomorrow, we are going to start seeing 'em. One of the guys at the meeting is a ham operator, and he said lots of other towns are already having problems."

"Did he say how widespread the blackout was?"

"He didn't know. Said everyone he had reached so far was reporting the same thing. He hadn't been able to reach his pops up north, but gathered from the others that all of the U.S. was affected, probably much more."

"So, how long before its fixed?" the woman asked.

"No idea Lori, no idea. . . . It's bad. Real bad."

The conversation kept on for a while. Steve just lay there in the cool carpet of dead leaves and pine needles listening to his empty stomach rumbling and the idle chatter from the roadblock. One was sitting in the station wagon flipping channels on the old radio trying to find a working broadcast. They stopped on what sounded like a weak AM station. A preacher, by the sound of it, condemning everyone, saying that God's judgment had been cast. *The only way forward was to battle the non-believers and spread the Lord's message.* Steve cringed—why would that guy be the one broadcast that was still getting out? As the shadows grew longer, sleep overcame him. He had found shelter, and it was going to be right here beside the roadblock.

7

I t was late the next morning before he saw the first real signs of civilization. They came in the form of numerous stalled vehicles. He stayed inside the tree line and avoided the cars. As he neared the small town ahead, he realized it was nothing more than a rural community. A church, small store, repair shop, several other squat buildings and a few homes clustered near an intersection. He had awoken before dawn to the sound of cars and equipment being moved. The woods were dark, and he had bug bites all over, but the sleep had been needed. The trek so far had been uneventful. This, he doubted, would continue.

The crew manning the roadblock had gone north. He assumed they were extending the blockade farther out. As he neared the cluster of homes and buildings, he was forced to walk on the paved road. The forest had turned into fenced pastures; the last thing he wanted to do was be caught trespassing in a farmer's field. Having grown up in the even more rural, southern part of the state, he knew about farmers and ranchers. He consciously took his hands out of his pockets and kept them slightly raised as he walked toward the store. He could feel the eyes on him. He fully expected a local to step out with a gun and block his way forward at any moment. It didn't happen.

He heard the unmistakable sound of a small engine behind the store and realized a neon "Open" sign was lit. *They have a generator.* He eyed cautiously up and down each of the roads but knew he needed supplies. If they were selling, he needed to be buying. The door was an old screen door with a spring to keep it closed. He pushed on it, noticing the rusted image of the Merita Bread company logo on it. The store was dimly lit. A single lantern stood on a counter, but the two small windows provided a bit more light. While most of the shelves were nearly empty, the store was neat and tidy. He again felt eyes on him immediately. Two men were talking to an older woman behind the counter. As a businessman himself, he tried to think the way she might be thinking. *Was this man someone she knew? No. Was he a threat? Did he have money?* Quickly working out the basics of a plan in his mind, he walked forward to the counter.

"Morning, just curious if you guys might have any information on what happened?" He gently removed the strap on his backpack and lowered it to the ground, again showing his empty hands. "Name is Steven Porter, not from around here . . . obviously, but trying to get back home." They all eyed him with interest, but none seem overly concerned.

The younger of the two men, wearing jeans, boots and a t-shirt, asked, "How did you get past the roadblocks? Deputy sheriff said they started turning people away yesterday."

He quickly decided not to play games with these people. They may be rural, but unlike stereotypes, that didn't mean stupid. They were also likely untrusting of all outsiders. "I'm embarrassed to admit, but I was in the woods when I saw them. It was nearly dark, and I fell asleep waiting for them to leave. I'm from South Georgia, and I have a long way to go. The thought of heading back toward . . . well, up there, was more than I could stand."

The woman gave a brief chuckle. "Can't blame you there. Bet those people in Atlanta are going nuts by now."

"It's a mess alright," he said. "So . . . I won't bother you, just wanted any news you might share and if you have any supplies. I have a little cash." He had lied to the Australian; he always carried a few hundred dollars, two in his wallet and several more folded up under the insoles of his shoes.

"They have mostly cleaned me out already, hon." The woman said. "Feel free to look around, not sure when we will get another order. I do have a pot of stew on. Had to start cooking off some of the things in the coolers and from home. Cup of that will run you four bucks. Everything else is whatever price is marked."

"Thanks, just some water and dry food . . . things that I can easily carry I guess."

The younger man nudged his pack on the floor with a toe of the boot. "Don't pay for water man, get one of those empty plastic jugs over there and fill up at the tap. We are all on well water here. It's free."

"Much obliged, mister."

"South Georgia, huh? Well, you're about as out of the way as possible to get there. Where the heck you coming from?"

Steve picked out several bags of rice and pasta from a nearly empty shelf. "I don't know that you would believe me if I said. I was in Charlotte watching the race."

"Damn, man, that looked like some mess before the TV cut off. I hope Jr. made it out ok. He looked to be about to take the lead. Wow . . . that's something. So, you made it all the way from there already? Your car must have been a lot better than all ours."

"Nah, my car was dead too. I managed to hitch a ride with some folks heading this way. Charlotte was in pretty bad shape; Atlanta was worse. I-85 is a parking lot with thousands of people walking. The scene at Hartsfield was . . . "—the scene erupted again in his mind—". . . it was a nightmare, crashed jets stretching back for miles."

The woman said, "Yeah, we heard a couple crashed over near Carrollton. This is crazy, man. So, it's this bad all over?"

He put the few items on the counter before answering her. "I think so . . . we have to assume it is. A pilot told me that it must have been a solar flare—something called a CME. The Northern Lights and all. That means the effect could be over most of the country."

"We pretty much figured the same thing. Douglas here has a ham radio and was passing along a few things he heard last night."

The younger man seemed like the type that rarely got bothered by anything; the older one was his complete opposite. Douglas put down the Pepsi he had been drinking and slowly responded. "Word is, there is a lot of people dead. Big cities must have just been death traps. Smaller towns are doing a bit better, but most of them are starting to block themselves off just like we are. All of that is just to help in the short term 'cause no one knows how long it will be before things get better. My wife is a diabetic, and we were supposed to get her more insulin this week. No way to get it now; no way to keep it cold once we do. We can keep refrigerators running off generators until the fuel runs out, but then what?"

Steve just nodded as his attention was captured by the aroma of the stew simmering nearby.

Douglas continued, "One of the guys said it was an EMP or maybe that geomagnetic storm that Newt Gingrich had been warning us about for years."

Steve knew Gingrich was the former Speaker of the House and was also a native of Georgia. While unaware that he had been prophesizing the possibility of such an event, Steve had a lot of respect for the man's opinions. The smell of the pot of stew was becoming overwhelming. "Could I get a bowl of that as well?" he said pointing to the crockpot plugged into the extension cord. The owner nodded and went to get him a bowl. "So, have you heard anything more?"

The older man, Douglas, answered slowly, "Lots of panicking, people with wild theories. The general perception is that it is going to get worse, a lot worse. Best prepare for the long term. The quicker you react and prepare . . . the better. Within a week, may not be anything left to get. Emergency services are nearly gone, hospitals will be closed once medicine and generator fuel are gone. Anything using microprocessors is probably useless now. Most communications—internet, TV and radio. Power generation and distribution, fuel refineries and, of course, trucks and food distributions system. All toast at this point."

The younger man looked at him. "Mister, you will still be on the road in a week if you last that long. What will you find once you get there? It'll be too late to start preparing then. You might just want to find you an abandoned fishing cabin somewhere and hunker down there. Unless whatever you have back home is mighty special . . it isn't worth the risk."

Steve nodded glumly. He liked the practicality of people like this. "Believe me, my friend, I have thought the same thing. I have family there, a son, in particular, who needs me. My wife as well, but she . . . well, she is probably doing ok on her own. Like most people out here, I have no idea what I am doing. I have a little water and a couple of granola bars to get me several hundred miles. That's as close to a plan as I have."

The young man offered him a plastic spoon from a nearby cup full of them as the woman put the cup of stew in front of him. "Mr. Porter," the young man asked, "how many of the stalled cars on the road did you try and break into on the way here?"

"None. I'm no thief."

He nodded. "How many homes or barns did you take shelter in?"

Steve was more focused on the smell of the food at this point. The stew, which looked more like soup, was hot. It seemed to be a mix of a few vegetables, chicken, shrimp and sausage. He decided it must be a gumbo. With his mouth now full, he gestured to the bowl. "Ummm," after swallowing, "this is the best food I have ever had." He looked at the young farmer. "None, I told you I slept in the woods."

"Mr. Porter, you look like an honorable man. Probably successful —expensive watch, decent clothes and shoes . . . or at least they were before you became a hobo. Right now, you assume the same rules apply as a few days ago. Let me tell you, friend—if you want to survive . . . to get home, you are going to have to make some changes."

"Like what?" Steve asked before taking another spoonful of the gumbo.

"Every car you passed may have had supplies in the trunk. A

knife, roadmap, tools, possibly even food and water. It will have some fuel which could operate a motorcycle or an older car maybe. If nothing else, you could use it to easily start your fires. You should be checking before someone else does. Just because they aren't good for transportation doesn't mean they are worthless."

"But they aren't mine, they belong to someone. Someone who will want them back when this is over."

"Your car is where . . . in Charlotte? Do you care what is happening to it right now?"

Steven shook his head finally understanding. "No, not at all."

"Exactly," said the man. "Cars are easy. Large trucks are even better as they may have food and lots of supplies, but you'll need to be cautious . . . make sure they are empty. Houses the same way. You seem like a cautious type—watch to make sure no one is around, knock on the door, walk away and watch some more . . . then break in if you have to. It may not seem right, but this will keep you alive."

Steve finished off the soup but was hanging on the words of the stranger. "That makes a lot of sense. Thank you. By the way, what is your name?"

"I'm Will, this here's my mom, she runs the place." The two men shook hands.

"How are you guys going to weather this? You don't seem too concerned."

The woman laughed. "Trust in the Lord, Mr. Porter. We didn't have much before and probably won't have much after. We're pretty simple people. Some things will be tougher, but our hogs don't care if the lights are on. Chickens rarely get upset if the internet goes down."

"This really just affects us . . . people will have it the worst."

Doug added, "People will also be the biggest threat, Steve. You can't trust anyone out there. In a few days, people will kill you for what little bit is in that bag. You are going to need to move fast and avoid people."

"Already been doing that," he said with a laugh.

Will picked up the messenger bag and looked in it. "Wow, you don't have anything. You ok if I add a couple of things to your purchase?"

"Be my guest."

He grabbed an empty box and wandered into the dark recesses of the store, C,oming back minutes later with several new items including a tarp, cheap multitool, lighter, candles, headlamp and fishhook and line.

"Thanks, man, I didn't even think of anything but food and water."

"You can only haul so much, but this stuff won't add much weight and could save your life. You really need to find some better clothes, too. T-shirt and jeans in this weather and probably going to want some extra socks in a few days. I would check clotheslines as you walk. Most people won't miss a single change of clothes. Don't worry if they are too big, I added a few nylon Ty-Raps you can use to cinch 'em up."

"Wow, I'm overwhelmed. After seeing the craziness in the cities, I was scared to even come in here, but thank you so much. You have undoubtedly saved my life."

He paid for the items and headed for the door. His bag now full, he carried the rest in the box. If he had a shopping cart to push he would indeed look like a homeless person. The more he thought about it, a cart would be handy. Something else for his wish list.

8

The advice from Will had been spot-on, and he took it to heart. With a good meal in him and a sense of direction again, he was making good time. He stuck to the roads and checked every car he came across. The multitool had a prong to use for easily breaking a car window. By now, he'd already used it several times. On one, he got lucky and found an old bookbag in the trunk. Storing his supplies in that allowed him to discard the small laptop bag and the box. Before he tossed the box, he took note of the label. The food distribution company was a name he recognized and was in the same town as his friend's dealership. That was still twenty miles ahead, but he was making better time now.

Early afternoon, he scored a change of clothes. Not from a clothesline but from a charity collection box in front of an abandoned store. He had used the multitool to jigger the lock, but once the door was open he had his choice. He only took what he could use and changed right there, putting his expensive slacks and shirt back in the box. Now he wore khaki cargo pants, t-shirt, and he also found a musty windbreaker that went into his pack. Unfortunately, no socks, but he was doing better.

Steven kept walking until well after dark. He was getting accustomed to being outside and felt better moving. It was very late when he stopped to rest. He moved well off the road, keeping a small hill between him and the highway. Spreading out the tarp, he lit one of the candles and started a small campfire. Quickly he realized it gave off too much light. Taking stones, he mounded up a wall on all the sides of the fire to block it from outside view. He had found an old can in the ditch and now cleaned it out to be a cooking pot. Adding water, he set the can over the heat on a couple of stones. The water came to a boil quickly. He added some of the rice and stirred in a cube of chicken bouillon for flavor. No protein and few calories, but he hoped it would fill him up.

The cool ground felt good after two days of walking. He waited on his dinner thinking about how different things were. He was no survivor, but he wasn't a quitter either. Steve knew that he was a man of action. Sitting around waiting for someone else to do something was just not his style. While it would be nice to find the government was sending FEMA in to rescue stranded travelers, he didn't think that likely. Unfolding the map that he had gotten at the store, he ignored the risks for a minute and used the small headlamp to plot a course.

He lived in an exclusive community in Arlington which was near Albany, Georgia. He estimated it was 240 miles at least from where he sat. Will was right, that would take weeks. He made note of the roads and shut off the light. *Man,* what he wouldn't give for a working car or motorcycle. In his truck, he could have been home in a few hours. Walking, it would be a couple of weeks. *What shape will my son be in by then?* He felt awful knowing his son would assume he had abandoned him. Barbara was not Trey's mom, she was Steve's third wife. Trey was the result of an incredibly brief whirlwind relationship and marriage soon after his first had fallen apart. Steven Porter was not a man who was lucky in love. She had left and taken the boy when he was still an infant. As Trey's special needs became more recognizable, his ex-wife had suggested joint custody and eventually gave up all her parental rights. His autism, although not severe, had been more of a burden than she could handle.

He used the multitool's pliers to retrieve the hot can from the fire. He had also saved his plastic spoon from lunch. The meal went down better than he expected. It was hot and somewhat nourishing, but that was as much praise as it deserved. Thankfully, he had never been much of a foodie. Eating was more maintenance than anything. When Barbara would drag him to some new swanky gastropub, he would enjoy it, but he was also just as happy picking up a few burgers at the drive-through. They had taken trips to Paris and Italy in the past few years, spending exorbitant amounts for tiny pastries, cured meats and dishes that he could never pronounce. Barbara had been delighted with every mouthful; he had enjoyed watching the joy it brought her. To him, it was just a meal. That was just one of the differences between them . . . somehow indicative of the deeper issues they were having these days.

He doused the campfire with dirt and lay back on the tarp, using the bookbag for a pillow. The trip to Europe was fresh in his mind, so easy it had been to get around the continent. He idly wondered if those countries were having the same kinds of problems. *How could things be this bad already?* He was not used to looking back, but kept wondering what he should have done, what the country should have done to be ready for a crisis like this. People were dying; many were already gone. While no spring chicken, he knew he was luckier than many. What if he had a small child with him? What if he was old or had a medical condition? In the grand scheme of things, he was relatively close to home; the weather was manageable. Despite his situation seeming dire, he was a lucky one. He had survived the first twenty-four hours. Now his goal was to simply survive the next week.

9

The morning started off innocent and calm, belying the dangers ahead. He had gone to sleep watching the flickering lights dance again in the night sky. The sight left him mentally off-balance. His world, which was normally so orderly and logical, had suddenly shifted out from under him. A light morning fog obscured the road and offered him a rare chance to use the pavement with little fear of being seen. *The rat scurrying down another turn in the maze*, he thought with morbid amusement.

He heard dogs barking off in the distance. Dogs usually meant people, so his rat senses went on alert. He crept low in the grass near the trees to see if anyone was approaching. He realized he had not seen a working car in two days. He wondered if all the cars on his lots were dead. Rough calculations on the current inventory held at the dealerships he owned outright or was partnered in would be about 2,500 vehicles. The staggering dollar amount that equaled would be financial ruin. His insurer would cover only a small portion. The sudden bark of a dog off to his left caused him to jump. He had to focus better than this—his mind just kept wandering.

He saw the lone dog, a mutt by the looks of it, running off into a pasture on the scent of something else. If he kept hiding at every little noise he heard, he would die of old age before he made it home. *I need a weapon*, he thought idly. Didn't need to be a gun, or even a knife, but something for protection. He remembered reading a book as a teenager about a boy who survived a small plane crash mainly by using a hatchet. He had one when he was a boy scout; he remembered the little leather pouch it fit in. *That would be really handy right now,* he mused. Seeing nothing else for several minutes more, he began moving again.

Later in the afternoon, he noticed a pickup on the side of the road, more in the ditch than the road. His thoughts had been centered on protection all day. He sat and watched the truck for some time, debating on whether it was abandoned or not. Once he felt confident it was unoccupied, he walked by giving it considerable room. He continued to walk for several hundred feet just to make sure no one was nearby or using the truck as bait. Satisfied, he circled back and began to scout for useable items. The doors were locked, but he was thrilled to find a solid-looking walking stick in the bed along with some old tools. Most of the tools would be nearly useless and too heavy to carry. He peered in the windows—a part of him still hated damaging someone else's vehicles. There, on the floorboard, though, were some items he could really use: a laundry basket with old clothes and a small bottle of bleach.

He used one of the tools to break a side window, unlocked the door and inspected the find. The clothes all appeared to be kids' clothes. A girl's and a boy's he guessed. The bleach would be good, he thought he remembered it could purify drinking water, so he took that. Looking through the storage compartment, he found a few other items including matches. Behind the seat was where he found his real treasure—a large machete. The blade was dull and the handles well-worn, but it was awesome. He couldn't believe how happy he was to have this one simple thing. He stowed the large blade in his pack and went back to the bed to look at the tools again. There . . . there it was: he picked up the somewhat rusty flat metal file and added that to his haul and quickly walked off, putting distance between him and the truck.

As darkness settled in, he boiled up some of the chicken-flavored rice and began sharpening the knife. It took him a while to get the right angle, but he was taking it slow. He didn't want to ruin the edge by being too aggressive. By the time he had eaten and cleaned his cooking can, he was too tired to work on it further. He spread the plastic tarp and went to sleep.

MAN, a cup of coffee would be great right now. Instead, he took a swallow of lukewarm water from the plastic jug. As he neared the next destination, his anxiety increased. This town was the largest in the area. It sprawled from the homey downtown with the old courthouse square to the interstate almost eight miles to the east. Steve was content moving around the less-developed western edge. An area of mostly industrial parks and support businesses with fewer residences and retail stores. He would need to walk down Highway 59 several miles to the start of automotive row. He wasn't sure why it was important for him to see his friend's dealership, but it was. He wanted . . . *hoped* . . . for something normal to hang onto.

This town would be dangerous; in his "rat" mode he knew he should just avoid it. To bypass it though, he estimated a full day just to get around it. This was a dilemma—he needed more food, protein of some kind, and water. He felt he should be able to find more food and water, possibly even a working car, at one of the dealerships if he was lucky. But since the interstate was so close, he assumed the town would already be overrun by stranded travelers. He decided to try his best to look like a local. That meant his backpack was a problem—it screamed traveler, stranger, newcomer. But it was too important to leave behind. He would see what other people were using and decide then.

His feet were dragging by the time he passed the city limits sign. The farms had given way to more homes and now subdivisions and shops. All closed and dark, but faces peered out warily from windows and doors. Steve tried to look innocent, which he was. Just a routine trip into town—nothing to see. His legs were wobbly though.

Around every curve, he expected to see a police roadblock, but none materialized. As he made it closer to town, he began seeing others on the roads. Some coming toward him, and a few walking or riding bicycles in the same direction. Most of those he crossed paths with looked even worse than him—few raised their eyes to meet his. A few simply nodded as they passed. The shared misery was evident for all. He had just turned onto Highway 59 when he met what appeared to be a family coming toward him. He could see a young mother and father and what appeared to be three small children. The father just looked down, but the mother smiled and walked directly into Steve's path. "Excuse me. . . . Excuse me, sir . . . mister."

He knew she was talking to him but didn't want to respond. He moved to go around her. "Sir," she persisted, "would you have any water or food you could share?" Steve shook his head and kept walking. "Please, mister, not for me—just . . . just for the kids. Anything?" He made the mistake of looking at the kids, their sad eyes and stumbling footsteps broke his heart to see.

"Sorry, ma'am, I have nothing—trying to find supplies myself."

The man looked over at him for the first time. "Bullshit—you got a pack. You got stuff. You want to let my kids die out here? "

Steve knew discussing this further would not end well. He was not going to point out that the children were not his responsibility, nor would anything he offered make a real difference to them. Thankfully, the woman saw someone else down the road and began calling out to them. He walked on past the little group quickly, the haunting eyes of the smallest child watching him as he passed. *Shit.* He had been expecting something like that, lots of it in fact, but it still unnerved him. He thought he was mentally prepared for seeing others like himself, but the kids . . . that was too much. In another day —maybe two—those people would probably just attack him and take his stuff instead of asking. Was he willing to fight to save the meager contents of his pack? He didn't know.

10

Steve moved off the highway and into the parking lots that lined most of the road ahead. The foot traffic was increasing, and he saw his backpack was not out of place. Nearly everyone was carrying a bag of some kind; some were even pulling wheeled luggage down the road. He also noticed how many were now carrying rifles or had pistols in holsters. He still hadn't seen any police presence, which disturbed him greatly.

He was passing through the parking lot of a relatively new motel when he saw the first real signs of trouble. People spilled out of every door, some trying to get in and others seemingly trying to get away. He made himself small and crept past, hidden by the parked cars. He could hear the yelling. "Just let us in, give us a room, place to sleep, some water." The shouts mostly seemed to be similar in nature. Others were almost running to get clear of the place.

Suddenly, a man who looked like he came from India, or maybe Pakistan, ran into the crowd with a baseball bat. "Jou mos leave now —private popertee. We have no rooms, no water. You pigs have been sheeting in my halls. Go away now."

A large man in a baseball cap said, "Look, Patel, I paid good money for my room. I ain't going nowhere til my truck gets fixed. You can just get yo short, hairy ass back up behind that counter." The irate owner took a sudden swing with the bat that connected to the trucker's head with a sickening sound. Both seemed equally surprised. The driver dropped to his knees, then slowly pulled a small handgun from his pocket and pointed it up at the owner. "That was a mistake, friend." The hotel owner began backing away, then dropped the bat and began to run, but the crowd laughed and pushed him back toward the downed man.

Steve lost sight of the melee as he moved on past, but minutes later he heard a series of small pops coming from that direction. He hustled farther down the road. He noticed that every store had broken doors and windows. Most seemed to have been emptied out. Not just the places that would have had food or drinks either, but everything. The looting had been indiscriminate—from restaurants to banks and auto parts stores. Trails of discarded boxes and bags littered the space in front of every store. Broken items were also becoming a common sight, from computers to flat-screen TVs—most with cracked screens or mangled in other ways nearly beyond recognition. He was increasingly more pessimistic about finding anything at the car dealerships coming up.

THE DAY'S march had taken its toll. Steve's stomach ached for food. He was getting low on supplies already and had nothing he could quickly eat. His plan, if you could call it that, was to get into his friend's dealership and hunker down for the night. He felt more confident about making a fire and cooking his ration of rice inside, away from curious eyes. He was already losing track of how long he had been on this journey. *The power went out three, four . . . was it five days ago?* he wondered uncertainly.

The first car dealer was an import line. He saw immediately that most of the cars had windshields broken out. The large windows on the showrooms had also been smashed in. The next two were similar, but he could also see people inside of these ransacking for whatever they might find. Nearly at the end of the row of dealerships, he could just make out the familiar blue and white sign. His friend's place was also a Ford-branded lot, and it was the largest dealership in the area.

As he feared, it was in no better shape than the rest. The hundreds of shiny new Fords were all damaged beyond belief. While he could understand someone trying to get a car started that they could "borrow," what good did tossing a hunk of concrete through a windshield do? Most of the damage just looked random and pointless. He mentally calculated the amount of money his friend had tied up here. Most of these would have been on the floor-plan—a short-term loan that most dealers used to keep a large inventory on hand but with as little cash tied up as possible. If you could move cars quickly, it worked great, but most only went for about four months before you had to pay it off. His friend would be on the hook for probably ten million that his insurance wouldn't cover.

A part of him knew this mental exercise was pointless . . . none of this mattered anymore. Besides, he felt sure all of his dealerships were probably in the same shape. Still, the waste of it all was shocking. He crouched down and watched the building for twenty minutes, but neither saw nor heard anyone inside. He cautiously made his way to a showroom door that was hanging open. All the glass had been broken out.

He had been in this place many times over the years. In fact, he was in the picture hanging high on the wall of the ribbon cutting for the new showroom six years earlier. He sat in one of the sales chairs and looked and listened. The hunger and the sadness were overwhelming, but he needed to know he was alone before he went exploring. His feet ached, and his stomach rumbled, but he forced himself to focus on his surroundings.

Finally satisfied no one else was in the building, he went to the supply closet. The small room was nearly hidden near the parts counter. Every dealer keeps cases of bottled water for customers, and he knew his friend kept a supply here and more in the break room. The door was open, and even in the dark space, he could tell no water remained. The breakroom was just as bare. Even the snack machines had been pulled down and ripped apart.

Frustrated, he took a new direction. Heading back into the service area he looked for the shop break area. The technicians and service writers usually had a place to eat that was separate from the customer areas. He couldn't recall if this one did, but it was worth a shot. He located it on the back side of the parts department. Lockers lined one wall, a refrigerator, sink, coffee maker and microwave on the other. Two picnic tables with cheap plastic tablecloths ran down the middle. He pulled open the refrigerator and quickly shut it. The smell of rotting food was already overwhelming. He knew he needed to give it a good inspection but decided it could wait.

Turning, he faced the lockers—no sign that anyone had been through them yet. Most were locked, and the ones that weren't had little of value—some clothes and a pair of sneakers in his size. He sat those on the table. He needed to get into the other lockers. He needed a tool to pry open the doors or cut through the locks. Looking back out at the shop he realized the obvious: while most of the mechanic's toolboxes were locked, plenty of spare hand tools remained scattered about. These were not his focus, though. Most dealers have a supply of heavier, more expensive tools that everyone shares. Using a prybar, he found the storage room and managed to locate the pneumatic cutter. The electricity was out, but the compressors usually keep a shop's air tanks full. He walked back to the nearest air connection to the breakroom, connected the airline to the cutter and keyed the trigger. The strong whirring sound spun the abrasive wheel up to the max.

Fifteen minutes later, he was cutting the lock off the final locker. As it fell away, he released the trigger on the compact little tool. It took a few seconds for his hearing to return, and it occurred to him that the sound had been too loud. People from far away may have heard it and would come to investigate. People . . . who he needed to avoid. He made quick time going through the rest of the lockers, finding an assortment of mostly useless items like cell phones, pictures, car keys and empty plastic food containers—the food having been previously consumed. It was not a total bust, though. A few of the lockers were veritable treasure troves. Ok, that might be an overstatement, but by the new standards . . . it wasn't far off. Several high-quality knives, lighters, a lightweight jacket, gloves, bottles of water, packs of crackers and most importantly, a nearly full case of granola bars. He tore into one of the nut and oat bars and saw a plastic container with a photo of a body-builder—a high-protein energy drink mix. Reading the label, he was surprised to see how high the calorie count was. He set it in the "keep" pile. Finally, he wrapped a rag around his nose and took another try at the refrigerator.

His backpack was nearly overflowing. He had even removed a few items, mostly clothes, which he had replaced with better now. The few items he had salvaged from the fridge went on top: partial jars of peanut butter and jelly; a bit of cheese that he had cleaned the mold from; a half jar of olives and some spicy mustard that seemed ok. He walked out the backside of the shop and eased himself to the ground. He had to get away from the stink inside and just breathe fresh air for a few minutes. He was looking at the fenced-off storage area of the dealership where employees parked and service customer cars were stored. Much calmer back here than up front. He popped an olive into his mouth and nibbled a cracker.

As he looked at the cars back here, an idea began to take shape. Actually, it was more of a question than an idea, but still was worth investigating. *Would any of these cars have survived the CME? Since they weren't running at the time, would that make a difference? What if they had the battery or alternator out?* He knew at shops there were always cars waiting for parts to complete repairs. He wasn't a mechanic. Maybe he could change a battery out, but beyond that, he'd be pretty lost.

Maybe one of the employee's cars would be something older, something that might still be working. That didn't make much sense either as they would have undoubtedly taken them if they were running. The question kept nagging him. He shouldered the backpack and began to walk the several lines of cars. What had the Aussie said about older cars? Something about no computers would be better. Steve knew computers had been in cars for many years now and electronic ignition went back decades. He needed a classic, not just a beater trade-in. He saw the group of cars that were probably being held for wholesale. Trade-ins with too many miles or too rough looking to put on the used car lot. They were likely slated for one of the weekly dealer auctions to get whatever they could out of them.

Only one of the cars back here was old, and it was not what he would call a classic. It was a 1980 International Scout, a type of early SUV. They were big, heavy, utilitarian vehicles, and few remained around in any condition at all. He couldn't recall if they were four-wheel drive as well, but he thought, *probably so*. Looking in the windows, he saw tools and parts on the floor.

11

"Shit, shit, shit!" Steve looked down at the empty space where the engine *should* have been. "Man, can't I get a break?" Slamming the heavy hood, he glanced up at the sky. He had been in church most of his life. Had given more money than anyone else to the largest church in town. He was a deacon and took a turn teaching Sunday school several times each year. "I've done my part for you, Lord. I was . . . I am—a good man."

He wanted to blame someone for all this. It was just so damn frustrating. Here he was, afraid for his life, struggling to find enough food to get by. Wearing borrowed clothes . . . *okay, stolen*. Drinking water from old dirty milk jugs. The pity party continued for several more minutes as he aimlessly walked back toward the building. He stopped suddenly when he heard a shout. The slamming car hood had been too loud—the rat had been discovered.

"Hey! There he is. Hey, man, you have a car?" The four men were running in his direction now. *Time to go.* But his supplies were at the back of the building. As meager as they were, he knew it was the difference between life and death. He ran, ducking low behind cars, first toward the back of the lot, then cautiously back toward the shop door. Looking through the dirty windows of cars, he could see the

men spreading out and looking under cars. "C'mon dude." They
yelled. "We just want to talk. We need help."

The tone of voice was not one of weakness. Everyone needed
help; these boys wanted to help themselves. To get to the rear of the
shop he would be exposed in the open for at least thirty yards. *Not
good, not good.* The men were nearly to the old Scout he had stupidly
slammed the hood on. That would be as far away as they would likely
go before turning back. He weaved his way through the labyrinthine
maze of parked autos until he was as close to the building as he could
get. He glanced back in the direction of the four, waiting until they all
seemed to be facing away and made his break. The sound of his feet
running on the gravel crunched underfoot, and he had taken only a
couple of long strides when he heard one of them shout something
unintelligible. He disappeared around the corner, quickly scooped up
his bag and fled back into the shop, carefully closing and locking the
door behind.

With luck, the men would keep going around the building
assuming he would be smart enough not to try and hide. But hide
was exactly his plan. His heart was thundering, adrenaline pumping,
and his breathing was already labored. The fear more than the exer-
tion was causing his body to implode. His legs went weak as he heard
the door he had locked rattle from someone pulling on it.

He had to find a place to hole-up. Somewhere concealed, small,
dark. Thinking quickly, Steve thought of his own dealerships. Many
were very similar to this, old core building clad in new corrugated
sides. They were often remodeled and added on to countless times,
which sometimes created orphaned spaces that could no longer be
used. He heard the voices outside going around to the front. They
would be inside the building in a few minutes. He quickly opened the
parts room door and froze. It was pitch black inside the crowded
space. The smell of parts, fluids and grease permeated his senses.

He pulled a flashlight from the bag and clicked it on once to get
the layout, then made a move for a set of stairs on the far wall. This
would lead up to a mezzanine where larger parts, body panels and

such were stored. The sound of the men was inside the shop now, catcalling for him to "come out and play." Reaching down, he quietly removed his shoes and slid his feet across the plywood floor in the direction of an outside wall. He heard one of the pursuer's kick open the parts door below. He was focusing on the deeper shadow against the wall. As he got near, just as he guessed, the floor dropped away. His toes extended over empty space where the mezzanine floor met the beams for the outer wall. It would be tight, but he managed to stuff his pack in one spot and then his body sideways in the narrow opening. It dropped about four feet until the next crossbeam. It wasn't great concealment, nor was it comfortable, but perhaps it was enough.

Why are they after me? he wondered. *I look like a bum. I have nothing they couldn't find elsewhere easily.* He heard footsteps and laughing below. Slowly the answer bubbled to the surface. *Because they can.*

He lay there sideways on the ledge, a crossbar bearing down on his shin and a ragged edge of the plywood floor abrading his neck with each breath he took. Through the cracks and pegboard lining of the lower floor, he saw flashlights sweeping back and forth.

"The bastard has to be here. Mac would have seen him if he escaped around the front."

"No shit, genius. Now just tell me where," another voice responded.

The sounds of feet on the metal stairs rang out through the space. They would surely find him; he felt sure he had only minutes. *Why am I this scared?* He hadn't even seen any weapons.

Fifteen feet away. He could no longer feel anything; his feet were going numb.

Ten feet . . . five. He heard the footsteps pause.

Loudly, one of them said, "Over there!" Steve was about to jump up and make a break when he realized the footsteps were heading away. He cowered lower.

"Well, fuck."

"Just that chickenshit Ford driver," the other said laughing.

"Yeah . . . has that dude won anything in years? Come on, its hot as hell up here."

The sounds and the lights receded, and silence returned. Cautiously, Steve pulled himself from the coffin-like space and sat on the edge of the wood floor. His breathing wouldn't slow. He was sure he was having a panic attack. He was not going to leave anytime soon —he waited in the hot space for hours. No sounds had been heard for a long time when he finally eased over to the steps. His foot brushed against something near the stairs, and he reached for it. He could just make out the cardboard silhouette of a NASCAR driver in a blue-and-white racing suit. He had one just like it in a corner of his show-room—part of a promotional press kit Ford Racing had sent out. Funny thing was, he had actually met this driver at the dealer convention just a few days ago. *I wonder if he survived the race? You may have just saved my life buddy . . . thanks!*

12

———

T he night spent in the dark dealership was one of the most difficult of Steve's journey. Odd, he thought, with all the other places he had slept the past week, that this one scared him the most. His body ached, and he still found himself jumping at nearly every sound. He was sure the boys were long gone but figured he would run into more just like them. Dawn was breaking—he wanted to be well underway getting out of this town before people started moving about. Would he have to avoid people and towns altogether? Surely not everyone was this bad, this desperate. How were his wife and son dealing with it?

His wife . . . thinking about her as her son's only caregiver during all this sent chills through him. Barbara Hyde-Porter was young and beautiful and no doubt with him mainly for his money. It was an awkward basis for a marriage, but both accepted the falseness and the benefits—so it mostly worked. So much of his world had been an illusion. He knew that now. The appearance of success and happiness instead of the real thing. How had it taken the end of the world to show him what an empty shell of a man he really was?

Steve drank a bottle of water with some of the protein powder mixed in and downed a dry granola bar. *Time to go.* Slipping out the back door, he darted for the sparse cover of trees and shrubs behind the building. He was intending on heading under the interstate about a mile to the east but changed his mind once he saw what was there: thousands of people, many gathered around smoldering campfires. Everyone who had been on the road when the CME killed their car must have walked to the closest exit. Here, forty miles south of Atlanta, the road had been even more crowded than those he had flown over in the airship. From his hiding spot a quarter mile away, he could see more than enough. People were up; most looked to be exhausted. Many wandered around aimlessly. One large man was literally dragging a young woman over to a blue tarp spread over several cars. Sounds of fighting were evident as was the smell of decay and human excrement.

The misery of the mass was evident everywhere. Countless Americans were now on an exodus from one point of misery to another. A flash of a dark wing drew his eye to a far corner of the macabre tableau. A crow and several vultures perched atop a massive mound of . . . of—dead bodies. *Oh, God.*

Ok, he would not be going through that. He backtracked a few hundred yards, then picked his way across the abandoned vehicles on the road and headed south. This would take him through the older section of the town. The original downtown. Once he got his bearing, he would go east again. He found himself having to walk more in the street as manicured lawns with wrought iron fences lined each house. Being this exposed was unwise, but he had to weigh risk with rewards. More established middle-classed neighborhoods like this felt safer, but that, too, was probably an illusion.

As the morning sky brightened, he began to recognize more of the area. His friend had brought him down these streets several times. A small, upscale shopping center was ahead with a really nice restaurant, a gastropub. He thought again about happier times here. His friend had been a gregarious man, so full of life. Somehow, he knew or felt deep down his friend was gone—just another life gone. *How much of America is disappearing right now?*

Turning the corner, his heart sank as the shattered glass and garbage strewn from the front of the gastropub came into view. Looters had already descended into this area as well. He paused, realizing those looters were probably people from the surrounding neighborhoods. Wealthy, privileged, and unprepared . . . just like him. The term "looter" was not a class distinction anymore, the "haves" had joined the "have-nots." While he had only wanted to get home, his descent back to Earth had been a harsh wake-up call. He and his friends had wealth, but no longer had value.

Dejectedly, he wandered past the shops, doubting he'd find anything still intact anywhere in this world. The sounds of someone yelling, possibly a fight from behind, made him pick up his pace and move again into the shadows. He crossed cul-de-sacs and gated drives with caution, scouting ahead. A thought occurred to him. On another trip to this area, he had stopped to buy cheese and bread from a small cottage down a side street. He stopped and listened, but the angry sounds had faded. Several blocks ahead and he turned left and found the shop tucked beside a florist shop in what was a mostly residential area. The front window had the name in small thin print, as if advertising or anything overt would have been too common for the establishment. The shop was intact, but the solid door was locked tight.

Steve circled the building. The store had a solid steel back door that was also locked and a dark keypad beside it. No windows that he could see, and no way to go up to the roof to look for access. He could just break the glass and go in that way, but he hesitated. Yes, he was now a looter as well, but breaking glass would likely bring others. More than food, he wanted to stay hidden. Looking through the window he saw bottles of expensive olive oil, copper pots and pans, and hanging in the back were several long tubes. Something registered with him, *the charcuterie.* The shop always had a selection of gourmet dried meats to go with the cheese and bread. Those would probably last a long time and be easy to carry—he had to get inside. That had to be what he was seeing.

On a hunch, he tried the florist shop. The doors were also locked, but the rear door looked more like a normal residential door. He took a paver stone from a nearby walk, and as quietly as possible, broke one of the glass panes. Reaching through to unlock, he was inside in a few seconds. The cloying smell of flowers and greenery was present, also a strong odor of decay. The source of the latter was obvious as he saw the leg jutting out from behind a counter. The man had been dead for many days, probably since the CME. His withered hands were reaching toward a pronounced bulge on his chest. *Another pacemaker*, Steve thought. *Damn. Guess the electronics on those things were vulnerable to the blast as well.*

He searched around the small counter and cash register but didn't find what he was looking for. As a businessman, he knew it was not unheard of to leave a spare key with a neighbor just in case of an emergency. It was a longshot, he knew, but figured these two lone shop owners were probably friends, certainly acquaintances. Having scoured all the normal spots, he reluctantly went to the corpse. The smell was overwhelming, the body having swollen and ruptured judging by the dark stains on the floor and clothes.

His hands shook. He really did not want to do this. *Fuck, fuck, fuck,* he thought as he pulled one pocket out and dipped a finger into the gooey mess saturating the trousers. *Just do it, Steve. . . .* Nothing. Not a key, no phone, not even a coin on the man's body. He looked at the vile mess on his hands and hurried to find a bathroom or some water to get rid of the fetid ichor. The bathroom was little more than a closet with a sink and a toilet. The dark space was suffocatingly hot already. While the taps were dry, lifting the lid on the toilet, Steve saw it still had a reservoir full of water. It was a waste to use it for washing, but he had plenty to drink for the moment. Dipping his hands in, he began to scrub. Looking down, he noticed the crack of light on the floor.

Drying his hands on some paper towels, he knelt down to examine it closer. The wall here was different. He began to tap each of the walls in the bathroom. The familiar hollow thud of drywall board echoed on every wall but the one that faced the gourmet shop next door. This one felt more solid . . . it was plywood. A sheet of plywood painted to match the rest of the space. He could now see the seams in the corners where the board had been cut to fit. Originally, the two shops must have been one building. This room probably was a rear hall or a closet they closed off and turned into a restroom.

Steve went through his bag, finding the multitool and a screwdriver and went to work removing the sheet of wood. Thankfully, it was less substantial than it looked. The wood swung out of the way after prying a single corner loose. Behind the false wall was a door with a simple deadbolt. Sliding the lock clear, he walked into the back room of the other shop, grinning broadly as he took in the bounty of food.

13

The morning was clear, achingly beautiful. The kind of morning the boy would have lived for just a week ago. He rose from his hiding spot where he had slept. He knew he had to decide if today was a travel day or a scavenge for food day. He ate yesterday, so today he needed to be on the move. He still had no idea where to go or even which direction to take. As had become his new routine, he began walking toward the big road in the distance.

He had no idea what had happened to everything. He had been staying with his grandmother for the summer. A woman he barely knew. When his phone died, and the lights went out, he had found her. She was laying on her bed, not moving. At twelve years old, he knew what death was, had just never seen it that close. People died every day, and he knew she was not in good shape. She had an oxygen tank and something that refilled it. He guessed maybe that had stopped working, too. He had tried calling his mom and then 911, but none of Nana's phones worked, so he'd begun walking. He knew he could find a policeman or fireman. They were usually everywhere.

That had been days ago. He hadn't found anyone anywhere who was willing to help. Several times he had gone back to his Nana's house but just couldn't go back in, not with her dead body inside.

Then he got hungry and went to find food. He got lost in the strange town and hadn't been able to find his grandmother's house again after that. That was also the day that people started getting crazy. Not zombie apocalypse crazy, just a mean kind ofcrazy.

The road was hot; cars were stopped everywhere. Lots of people were walking in both directions. Sometimes he followed a group for a while, but no one said much or paid him any attention. He thought it was weird that no one wondered what a small boy was doing all alone on the road. He had asked one kind-looking woman if this road went to Jacksonville. That was where his home was. She nodded and said, "Eventually," so he had stayed on it. He ran out of water during the hottest part of the day, but he kept walking until well after dark. His feet were just shuffling along the pavement. Several times he thought he had been sleeping while he did it. With no lights on anywhere, judging distances was impossible. Finally, he gave up and found an unlocked car to crawl into and sleep.

The following morning, he awoke to rain pelting the roof of the old car. His mouth was dry and his head hurt. His stomach growled so loudly it scared him. He had never been a big eater—always too busy, his mom had said. He watched as the rain etched rivers down the window. Each drop connecting with other drops until they flowed into the chasm at the bottom. Mom and her new boyfriend were doing something called a "European river cruise" this summer. He had no idea what it was, but they were a long way off. That was the reason he had been with Nana. He wondered if his *mom* would *even be home once* he got *there?* He began to cry, his meager tears crawling down his face toward his parched dry mouth.

The noise erupted from his stomach again. It sounded bad and this time was accompanied by a pain. He knew he had to go to the bathroom, and so he quickly fled the car for the ditch.

It was a long time before he was able to somewhat clean himself with wet grass and climb back up to the highway. Now his head and his stomach were hurting, but he was no longer sure about his hunger. He glanced at the car where he had slept, then walked past it.

He was already wet, may as well get moving toward home. *How far is "eventually?"* he wondered.

There were fewer people on the road today, probably because of the rain. He eventually figured out if he held his mouth open while he walked he could get a little water. Then he started raking his hands along stalled cars, then sucking the water off his fingers. It wasn't much, but it helped. He walked and rested until he realized he was doing way more resting than walking. *If I just had a bike,* he thought. Not that he felt like riding. Hunger, thirst and a pounding headache were constant now. Finally, the rain began to taper off.

He forced himself to start moving again, then realized he was walking back the way he had come. Turning around, he started south once again. As the day got hotter he thought he heard the sound of a big truck several times. He didn't see anything, and soon it was silent again. How odd that something as ordinary as a car engine would be so unusual now. *What had happened to everything?* The silence slowly built until it seemed very loud, a snowy white noise that he began to focus on. It was the sound of air, his heartbeat. Ultimately, he decided it was the sound a life makes when it leaves the body. His feet kept walking.

An hour later he topped a small rise in the road and swore that he could smell food cooking. Not just food but hamburgers— hamburgers being cooked on a grill. *My favorite! I have to find it. . . . Surely whoever's cooking them will give me one.*

He passed another of the big green signs with the arrow and spotted smoke and an old bus at the top of the exit. There were a lot of people gathered around, but hunger drove his fear aside. He had never been this hungry or thirsty. He tried to run up the short distance, but his feet just continued shuffling.

A young man in a military uniform sat at a small plastic table writing something. Looking up, he smiled and stood up like he had been doing this many times. "Everyone just come on up, I am with the government and we are here to help. If you just came in on the bus, then you have heard this already: America was attacked." A collective gasp went up from the crowd, and everyone started talking and yelling questions. The soldier smiled and put up his hands in a calming gesture. "Look, all of that in time. For now, let's just get you registered and ready for transport to one of our aid camps. There is water in the barrels over by the tent. Please help yourself while we get your info."

The boy kept looking for the burgers. He still smelled them, but couldn't see anyone cooking. The smoke seemed to have cleared as well. He found a plastic cup and joined the line waiting to get water. An old man eyed him from nearby. "I ain't going to no goddamn FEMA camp. That's where they take people to die." The man scared him, so he got the cup of water and headed in the opposite direction. He went looking for the food. The soldier was speaking loudly again.

"Sorry, folks, I can't answer your questions, mainly because I don't know myself. We are working with the State Patrol and Department of Transportation to get people rescued off the roads. Eventually, they will get you back home. We don't have much food here, but we can offer a little. There will be more food at the aid camp. The bus heading there will be along shortly."

"We smelled cooking," someone shouted, followed by, "Yeah," "Me, too," and "Come on, man."

The soldier shook his head and sat down. He passed a form to the next person in line. The boy got another cup of water. It was warm and tasted like metal, but he didn't care anymore. He needed it and wanted food. He joined the line in front of the soldier. He now noticed there were a lot of soldiers, many in a different color uniform, most carried guns, too. *Why would they need guns?* Weren't they here to help people?

The man in front of him in line spoke to the soldier. "Look, son, my wife needs help. She is diabetic and lost a leg. She couldn't walk with me, and she needs her medicine. Can you send somebody back to her?" The soldier nodded and said, "Absolutely, sir." He nodded over to one of the men in the gray colored uniform who came and led the man away.

It was the boy's turn. He stepped up. The white plastic table shook as the man continued to write something. "Name?" the man said in an oddly pleasant voice.

"Johnathan, although my friends usually call me JD."

"Oh. Sorry, kid," the soldier said looking up. "Where are your parents?"

"Umm . . . don't know. Europe, I think. I haven't heard from them . . . from her I mean. My dad is gone."

"Well, JD, you were with someone. Who is taking care of you?"

"Mister, can I just get some food? I am really hungry."

"Absolutely, just need some information first. Who are you with, and what is your last name?"

Why do they need all this? he wondered. He just wanted a burger. "I was spending the summer with my grandmother, but she wouldn't wake up. I am pretty sure she was dead. I tried to find help, but then I got lost."

He gave the man the information who wrote it all down, then stamped his wrist with something like you might get at an amusement park. "Be ready when the white bus pulls up. You want to take that one. Someone at the camp will help you and get you checked out. Go over to the tent back there and ask for a plate. Show them the stamp."

"Is that a Femar camp?" JD asked, remembering the old man. The soldier just smiled and waved the next person in line to come up.

14

He wolfed down the burger. It was dry, cold and tasteless, but he was so hungry. The sounds coming from the group on the exit ramp were increasing. An air of nervousness descended as the sounds of a vehicle approaching could now be heard. JD began gathering his few things and stood. He couldn't see through the crowd of adults but assumed it was one of the white buses coming to take them to the camp. He heard sounds that reminded him of the squeaks and hisses of his school bus back home. An occasional glimpse of white ahead was all he could see.

People jostled him, and he nearly fell several times. Then a hand rested lightly on his shoulder. He moved to get away from the grip, but it stayed. He had little room to walk, much less escape. His heart began to race.

A quiet voice said, "Kid, you don't want to get on that bus."

Looking up, he saw the man who was speaking. He was tall, gray-haired and one hand was attempting to steer him to the side of the group. "Why not?"

"Please just trust me for now. . . . I am not going to hurt you," he whispered.

Now JD was really scared. What should he do? He had been

taught to listen to policeman and avoid strangers. He struggled to make the man release him. The man pushed him roughly through more of the crowd. No one seemed to notice . . . or care. He started to scream, and the man's other hand clamped over his mouth. "Gimme five minutes kid, you will understand." Leaning in closer, he said, "What is your name?"

The hand moved away from his mouth. "Um . . . JD."

They broke free of the group just as someone began speaking near the bus. He was telling everyone to line up and show the stamp on their hand before boarding. The tall man directed him behind some stalled trucks before releasing his grip.

"JD, you are alone here, right? No family?"

He nodded, still too scared to speak.

"Ok, listen . . . " the man went down to one knee.

JD could smell the guy's breath as he leaned in. His heart was pounding. *The man was too close.*

"My name is Gerald. I want to help you. Those people there—they aren't here to help."

JD could see the man was old and wearing a dress shirt that was stained and torn. His beige pants ended with what appeared to be a pair of new athletic shoes. While the man's appearance seemed like an office worker, his tan face and the way he talked didn't quite fit.

"Look, mister, I don't know who you are, but I just need to get home. My Nana died, and those people do want to help." His eyes were watering, and he felt his legs begin to shake with fear.

Gerald took his shoulder and turned him to face the bus. Very quietly he stated, "Watch what they do when the people go to get on."

JD dried his eyes and focused in on the front of the line waiting to board. One soldier was checking the stamp marking each person as processed. The next was doing a quick search. It reminded him of what the airport security had done to some of the passengers when he flew up a few weeks back. They seemed even more thorough, if that was possible. Everything was removed from pockets and back-packs. Whatever they were carrying was taken and piled near the bus. Angry shouts could be heard coming from the crowd, but the soldiers kept at it. Reluctantly every person in line gave up everything they had and stumbled up the steps to take a seat. "Why are they doing that?"

The man pulled him back out of sight. "My guess is they are mainly checking to make sure no one is taking a weapon into the camp, which I could sort of agree with. But taking the food, water, spare clothes . . . everything. That can really be only one of two things —they want everyone in the camp to be completely dependent on them for everything, or . . . they won't be needing any of it again."

JD's young mind tried to make sense of it but failed. These people were in authority—you had to do what they said. It was the right thing to do. No way they would be out to hurt anyone. They were nice, they fed him, although the burger hadn't tasted right and it was cold.

Gerald saw uncertainty on the young boy's face. He sat all the way down on the ground and looked up at JD. He wasn't sure why he felt the need to look out for this innocent, but something about him had struck a familial chord deep inside. To survive, JD was going to have to grow up very quickly. "Did you ever see any of the old black and white news from World War II?" Without waiting for a response, he continued, "Ever see the Nazis loading Jews on the trains? Beside those trains would be piles . . . hell, mountains of suitcases, bags, coats. They loaded them onto cattle cars and shipped them off to die. There were so many they tattooed numbers on 'em to keep track."

JD looked down at the inky stamp on his hand. His eyes drifted up to the growing pile of belongings in the weeds. The tears came again; this time he could not stop them. "Those people are going to be killed?" he managed to say.

The man shrugged. "Killed, die, stay locked up until they starve . . . I don't know. I am just certain it won't be good. Whoever is ordering the round-up wants these people off the highway and out of sight. No way FEMA or DHS or whoever it is has the food supplies staged to handle everyone stranded out here. They are simply cleaning house."

Gerald stood back up, stooping low to stay hidden. The bus was nearly full now, and they were pushing people away to wait for the next one. "Kid, you have to make up your own mind. I can't stop you. However...if you want to survive all this, you should come with me."

JD wasn't sure. He was still hungry, and he could smell cooking food again, but what the man said had seemed genuine. His mom would be mad if he went with the man. He was so scared and confused but picked up his meager pack and headed off into the tall grass behind the man.

15

Steve looked at the remnants of his meal. It was not all that different than other meals he had enjoyed regularly: crackers, imported olives, some hard cheese and various sliced charcuterie including a dry coppa, which was his favorite. He had laid it all out on a gingham napkin and opened a bottle of wine he'd found behind the counter. If he concentrated hard, he could almost ignore the rank of his own body and the stench coming from the other body lying in the shop next door.

He wanted to keep eating, but his stomach had obviously shrunk over the previous week's neglect. The shop had a lot of very expensive cookware, knives and kitchen gadgets of which a few would be useful. His main desire had been the small, nearly hidden section of gourmet foods. Besides the cured meats and cheeses, there were exotic coffees with exorbitant price tags. Spices, preserves, nuts and olive oils. While he had never hurt for money, even he would have resisted indulgences of this level on most days. Most . . . *normal* days. This was anything but normal.

He wiped his mouth with another of the linens and looked around thinking about what he should take. He wanted to carry it all . . . or just stay, but neither was an option. Trey and Barbara would likely be running low on food by now. Hopefully, the water supply would hold out, but he had to get home. He had room in his pack for some supplies, but much of what he saw would add a lot of weight. He looked through his stash and decided to upgrade several items. He tossed a couple of the knives he had acquired and replaced them with two top quality Wüsthof carbon steel knives from the shelf. A small pot and pan were also added.

He scoured the shelves and found several handmade soaps which went into a side pocket. *Who knew that soap and toilet paper would be such a valued commodity now?* Several tins of canned anchovies, nuts and wax covered cheeses went in as well. Then as many of the cured meats as he could carry. A few baguettes with only slight discoloration from mold. Several candies, sea salt and finally, a couple of the rather heavy but tasty-looking jars of preserves. He hoisted the bulging backpack on and thankfully realized it was not as heavy as he had feared. Eyeing a canvas shopping bag by the counter, he filled it with more of the store's inventory before sighing and heading for the rear door. He felt guilty at what he was doing but admitted he would gladly have paid if an owner had been around . . . and willing to sell. He mentally tallied the total cost and winced. "I'll stop by one day when all this is over and settle-up," he said to no one. He may be a rat now, but the businessman still lurked inside him.

STEVE HAD BEEN on the streets for about an hour before he heard sounds of a vehicle. He panicked and rushed to find a hiding spot. Nestled up behind a boxwood in front of a small cottage-style home, he watched as a large passenger bus passed by. The nondescript white bus had a small logo and official-looking type on the door. *"Did that say DHS?"* The darkened windows prevented him from seeing any of the passengers, but the sight gave him both hope and dread. He briefly thought about rushing out and trying to flag it down, but that seemed risky. After seeing the sheriff's patrols days earlier blocking roads, he was less confident in any officials being truly interested in his welfare. He was curious about where they were going to and . . . coming from. It had approached from the south. That was where he was heading, so he decided to see what was there.

16

Steve's mind drifted back again to happier days. Like his dad, his business had become his pride and joy. Also like him, success at home had been harder to attain. His son, Trey, could be very challenging, and he found few people to have the patience the boy required. His wife, Barbara, was a caregiver by training, so she seemed to take an interest from the very beginning. In the years since, even her measured enthusiasm had faded. He was under no illusion as to why she was really with him, but the arrangement worked. They did have happy times, but they were rarities these days; he had to work on that when he got back.

While his son was not overly fond of his wife, he rarely complained about the way she treated him. Still, Steve tended to worry about the boy more when he traveled for business, which was too often. He knew that Trey could get agitated and even violent over the smallest things. The doctors had explained where his son was on the development disorder spectrum, but none of it had ever made sense. Steve loved him and knew there was a bright, happy person locked inside if he could just somehow find a way to reach him. He marveled at his every achievement. Things that most people took for granted could be an impossible hurdle for the boy. *Hang in there, Son.*

The houses in the area were becoming more isolated as he finally neared the southern edge of the town. He had seen no other buses and only a few people out since leaving the ritzy neighborhood far behind. The backpack and bag were heavy and made noises with every step as the contents jostled and settled. With his stomach still painfully full, he decided not to camp but to keep walking as long as he could.

The familiar sights and sounds of a summer night began to unfold. The chirping of crickets faded into the windup of a cicada as distant frogs croaked. Soon, the darkness was punctuated by dozens of fireflies signaling across the horizon. The sight reminded him of his childhood and camping out. Despite all the tragedy, there was a beauty now; something he would have avoided or ignored a week ago. With no cars, no house or street lights, nature was once again center-stage putting on a show for everyone to see.

Steve shuffled his feet along the road, careful not to catch an unseen rock or another obstacle. Hour after hour he kept at it. The partial moon offered some light, but he wandered off into the weeds each time the straight road curved. If he focused really hard, he could just see the cut in the tree line where the road was. The silhouettes of the tall pines were just slightly darker than the night sky. Several times he thought he heard someone . . . or something in the darkness. Like a roach caught out in the open when the light comes on, he froze in place each time, waiting for confirmation that he wasn't alone. *What had it been? A scuff of a shoe on pebbles? An intake of breath? Someone snoring up in the woods?* Each time the sound failed to recur, and he would hurry quietly away.

The sense of time was hard to gauge. He had tried to use the movement of the stars and moon as a reference but had no idea how long it took them to navigate the heavens. Eventually, it was his weary feet that caused him to take a break. He maneuvered as far into the woods as he dared in the dark and stowed his pack on a limb. Sitting at the base of a large tree, he removed his shoes and socks and drank a bottle of water from the canvas bag. He wasn't making very good time—not nearly enough miles. That had to change, or he would be months, not weeks, getting home. *Where is everyone?* he wondered. The roads, which had been busy just days ago, now seemed abandoned. No faces peered out of the houses as he passed. People had to be getting more desperate—more dangerous—but was something else going on? He nodded off wondering once more about the bus.

THE KICK KNOCKED all of the wind out of him. "Wake up you fuck," growled a voice from above.

The attack had come with no warning. Steve struggled to catch his breath, then bile caught in his throat and a torrent of vomit rushed out. His blurred vision vaguely registered a weathered pair of leather boots dance backward out of the spray of his discharge.

"Watch it, fella. . . . Damn. That's nasty. What the fuck did you eat?"

Through watery eyes, Steve could see the man holding the shopping bag he had been using.

"You got some good shit in here, man." He held up a meat stick with obvious delight. He ran the delicacy under his nose like a fine cigar, then took a huge bite off of one end. The expensive salami began to disappear into the man's open maw. "Damn, that's tasty. What else you got in here?"

A racking cough followed by a long stream of sputum dropping from the corners of Steve's mouth. His ribs hurt, but he could focus on the man now. His attacker was skinny, white, mid-forties and was alone. Apparently, his nighttime hiding spot was not sufficient as he could clearly see the road in the gray morning light just as the man had apparently seen him sleeping soundly.

"I thought you uz dead lying up 'ere." The man said kneeling down, still gnawing on the meat. "You was lucky I found you before some of those mean ones did. I just want your food. I know you gots more, whar is it?"

Steve had stashed his backpack out of reach in a tree when he bedded down. He forced himself not to think about it now. He would hate to lose the nearly full shopping bag now firmly in the man's grasp but knew that would be minor compared to losing the pack. "Look, you can't take my food, I'll die. I need that." He reached a hand out and the wiry man just laughed. He felt beside him for the walking stick.

"We all gonna die, friend. Just a matter of how. This here bag is mine. If you want food, just head over to one of dem government camps."

"What government camps?"

"I dunno, State Patrol and National Guard or sumpin started rounding up people out on I-85 and busing 'em off somewhar. One of 'em said it was a refugee camp for stranded travelers. Thing is, I saw 'em also taking some people out of their own houses."

Steve was attempting to stand now, and the man backed up a few more steps. Realizing he was a good head taller than the man, he held the wooden stick and approached him with more confidence. "Why did you attack me?"

"I . . . I wuz hungry." An edge of fear creeping into his attacker's voice. He continued taking bites of the meat as he slowly continued to step backward. Steve took a swing and the stick connected with the man's knee.

"Owww, you fuck!" The man rubbed his knee but kept eating and grinning as he stepped back farther.

"Why don't you go to the camp if you want food? Maybe get that leg looked at."

"Been locked up before, bunch of times. Don't want that again. I'll find my own food." He tipped the ragged end of the salami as if to prove his point. "That bus . . . the way they loaded dem folks up looked like prisoner transport to me. I knows what that trip is like. Gonna have to catch me first to put me back in the pen."

Steve was confused but wanted his stuff back. He charged the man who quickly drew a nasty looking knife and waved it. "No, no . . . now you don't want to do nuttin foolish, mister. You lost this round, just leave it at that." With that, the man turned and trotted awkwardly away with his stolen bag.

He started to run after the robber, but with his newly bruised ribs, he barely made it a dozen yards before stopping in agony. He heard the guy laughing as he disappeared up the road. Stumbling back to his unsuccessful hiding spot, he began searching for the tree that held his backpack. He spotted it several minutes later with great relief and pulled it on in a quick motion, wincing from the sharp pain in his side. Cautiously, he began moving south avoiding the road again. Being found so easily had unnerved him, as did losing his bag of supplies. He wanted to put as much distance as possible between him and the attacker. The man may have friends around.

STEVE HAD BEEN WALKING about an hour when he topped a small rise and saw the familiar lines of the interstate a short distance ahead. While abandoned cars still littered the roadway, the lines of people walking was not happening here. Instead, he saw a small cluster of people around an olive-colored tent and several older State Patrol cars and military green Humvees. The smell of cooking meat reached him, triggering fond memories of summer barbecues. He had eaten well the last two days, though, so hunger was not his driving force at the moment. The warning from his attacker earlier still rang in his head. Something about what he was seeing just felt wrong.

Working his way through the dense undergrowth in the wooded hillside, he struggled to get a closer look. Soon he noticed the sound of an approaching vehicle. Steve watched as a familiar-looking white bus lumbered up the opposite ramp, and brakes squealed as it rolled to a stop by the tent. The bus had a small insignia, which he couldn't make out from this distance, but guessed it was the same as he had seen earlier.

People began to queue up as the uniformed men instructed. He noticed that they were searching each person, often removing an object from pockets or even full backpacks and bags. *Guess they don't want any weapons being aboard.* Some of the passengers resisted the search. Those were roughly removed from the line, searched more thoroughly by multiple troops, then marched onto the bus. *What the hell is this?* he wondered. *Are they taking them to safety? A refugee camp maybe?* If so, why did it also remind him of a prison transport? Maybe his mugger did know what he was talking about.

Part of him still wanted to run down and line up. This was the first *somewhat* hopeful official response he had seen so far. At the very least, he should be able to get information, but he stayed put. The sight troubled him, and it just wasn't the earlier warning from the mugger. *Be the rat*—he would hide and watch.

Once it filled, the bus pulled away. Most of the line had made it on, but a few at the end were turned away. Those individuals stood awkwardly for a few seconds before wandering away to find some shade to sit and wait. It took Steve a few minutes to register that the pile of belongings was still there. He had assumed those would be loaded into the luggage compartments, but no. The soldiers began tossing the pile of bags into a large pile of trash off in the weeds. He had noticed the trash pile earlier, but thought nothing of it; now he was shocked to see what it consisted of.

He suddenly felt the weight of the pack on his own back. Not just the physical weight, but the mental and emotional value. It held all he had—his life was in these tools and supplies. He had been willing to fight and possibly die protecting it. His aching ribs reminded him of the value it held. The people getting on that bus no doubt felt similarly, yet all of it was removed from them and discarded like trash. A simmering rage was building deep within. Indeed, something was very wrong with what was going on.

17

J D watched as the man who called himself Gerald silently moved through the trees at a low crouch. They were still close to the interstate and the soldiers, but he had decided to trust the man. . . for now. The truth was, the uniformed men scared him more than the man did. He wasn't sure why, just the almost mechanical way they were treating the other stranded travelers, maybe. No talking, very little interaction. They knew they were in control, and that was something that just bugged him. Some of his teachers did that, and he never liked it. The ones that showed him kindness or treated him like a person were the ones he would listen to and learn from. The ones like these guys, he just wanted to ignore or piss off more than anything.

Gerald waved to him to get his attention, then motioned for him to come his way quietly. He put a finger to his lips and used his palms to signal. *Slow and quiet,* JD thought. He still was not sure why they were hanging around but figured the man had a plan. Sounds from the encampment began to change. It seemed the troops might be getting ready to leave. Glancing through the tangle of vines and small trees, he could see them loading crates back into trucks. *Man, I would have liked to get another of those burgers before we left.* As he joined Gerald, the man smiled and nodded.

"Looks like they are moving on," he said softly. "Guess they cleared the section of road."

JD nodded. "So, what are we doing?"

"Waiting."

THE SOLDIERS and cops were loaded and gone in less than an hour. Virtually no sign they had even been there remained. Gerald and JD stayed concealed but began moving toward the far side of where the troops had been. The large pile of trash loomed in front. *Not trash,* JD remembered. The stuff the soldiers had taken off the people getting on the bus. Lots of garbage bags, but also backpacks, suitcases, grocery store sacks. It looked like trash, but even at his young age, he knew there could be valuable supplies inside. Gerald put a restraining hand in front of his chest. Looking up at the man, he saw him shaking his head.

"We're not alone," he mouthed silently.

Following Gerald's gaze, JD saw a man emerge from the woods on the far side and cautiously make his way to the pile. He was moving oddly, kind of like he was injured or something. The man's eyes darted around furtively. Gerald's hands pushed against his chest, guiding him back a little deeper into the shadows of the trees.

"Stay here, JD. If anything happens, get away from here."

He nodded and watched as Gerald silently moved out into the open on the opposite side of the pile from the man. JD's knees were shaking, but he didn't know why.

The man stopped his digging through the piles when he heard Gerald approach. "Hey, friend, don't be alarmed. I think we both had the same idea." Gerald was holding his hands up slightly in a non-threatening manner.

The other man didn't speak but went for something in his bag. "Whoa, whoa now," Gerald said with a laugh. "Don't get excited, plenty here to share." They were only about ten feet apart. Gerald was still very casual and speaking in an almost jovial manner. The other man now held a large knife and kept looking off to each side as if expecting attackers other than just Gerald. "Tell you what friend, why don't you search this side, and I'll stay on the other? How does that sound?"

JD watched as the other man seemed unsure, then made a lunging move toward Gerald who just calmly stepped aside. He never even lowered his upraised hands. "Mister, I gotta say you don't seem to be too trusting. Are we really going to have to fight over a pile of trash?"

"It's mine," the other man snarled. "Get the fuck away."

"So, you're taking all of this?" Gerald waved one of his raised palms to gesture at the pile. "Where is your truck, do you have a trailer? I'm a little confused."

"It's mine," was the only response.

JD watched from his place of concealment as the drama unfolded. He couldn't understand why the other man wanted to fight so badly, or even more odd, why was Gerald apparently so unconcerned.

The man made another attack on Gerald who simply faked a block with his hands then kicked out at the side of the man's knee. A snapping sound was followed by the man's howls of pain. Gerald still had both hands raised in contrition.

"Sorry, man, I didn't mean to hurt you, you just surprised me."

"You ruined my fucking knee man!" he yelled. "Oh my God, it hurts. Shit!"

"Yeah, pretty sure you broke it. Listen, can I put my hands down now?"

The man, who was now lying in the grass writhing in agony, just looked up with at him in rage.

Gerald lowered his hands as he kicked the large butcher's knife away from the man. "I would have shared," he said quietly. "Come on out, JD. This man is not going to be a problem."

JD had been amazed at how smoothly his new friend had moved, how easily he had taken down the armed attacker, but now he was focused on something else . . . *someone* else. A dirty bearded face peered out of the trees thirty feet away.

18

J D moved out of the shadows up near Gerald who was binding the fallen man's hands and inserting a gag to stop the screams. "We're still not alone," JD whispered as he picked up a bag and began going through it.

"I know . . . the man in the trees. Saw him earlier, don't think he is with this clown." He touched a foot to the man at his feet. Looking up, Gerald raised his voice, "You can come on out. We mean you no harm and are willing to share whatever we find. Unlike this piece of shit." He nudged the man's ruined knee with his shoe. A muffled yelp was the immediate response. "Come on out now—you're making us nervous."

Slowly the undergrowth began to shake as a man stumbled out of the shadows. He was holding his side and dragging a walking stick and old backpack behind him. His other arm was upraised as to show he was unarmed. Gerald looked the man over. "Name's Gerald. My friend here is JD. I'm not too sure this guy has a name, but we can call him . . . retard."

The stranger flinched, and his nervous eyes darted between the bound man on the ground and Gerald. "I'm. . . I'm St..Steve," he said with a nervous stutter.

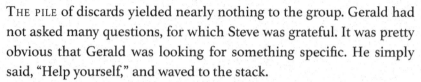

THE PILE of discards yielded nearly nothing to the group. Gerald had not asked many questions, for which Steve was grateful. It was pretty obvious that Gerald was looking for something specific. He simply said, "Help yourself," and waved to the stack.

"Not much of anything good," the boy said.

Gerald leaned up and wiped sweat from his brow. "Most people didn't pack for the end of the world, kid. Even those of us who probably knew better didn't normally carry around much in the way of survival gear."

JD grimaced but nodded. "Yeah, I guess that makes sense, but why would they carry all this stuff for miles? Laptops, tools, radios and all these clothes."

"People have a hard time separating the essential from the valued. What was important to them yesterday can't be worthless trash today. They just can't wrap their heads around that—their attachment to stuff just won't stop. What did you say about radios? Show me what you found."

Steve watched as Gerald seemed excited about what the boy was holding. Something made Steve think this man had a plan or knew more than he let on. "Hey, Gerald, what's so important about a radio?"

The man just smiled as he opened the battery compartment on the small handheld. "You have any idea what happened? To the electricity, the cars?"

Steve's nodded. "Yeah, I think I know. I don't understand it but some kind of solar flare. A crazy huge solar storm or something. I really don't know why that caused the blackout, much less the cars and electronics to stop working."

Gerald nodded. "That's pretty much it, best I can tell. An EMP or CME was what I was guessing. Both of those should be relatively limited in scope, but it appears whatever happened . . . this event is everywhere. At least ...everywhere that concerns us," he said with a sigh. Gerald held up the radio smiling. "With this, maybe we can find who is still broadcasting. These radios are great, not like a big rig, but they can reach pretty far. Hopefully, we can get some decent information and find out how far this shit goes."

"Hmmm, well, I can tell you it goes pretty far." Steve watched as Gerald stopped what he was doing and looked up questioningly.

"How's that?"

"Just, I was in Charlotte when all this started. It was at least that far. I also heard a radio broadcast that next night from out west, Texas maybe, said the same kind of stuff happened there."

"Wait . . . you made it from Charlotte to here in—what's it been? —ten days?"

Steve nodded. "Yeah, sounds right. I made it halfway the first night. Since then I have barely made it forty miles."

"Still man, that's a solid effort. Headed home I guess? Where's that?"

"Ugh, south another two hundred miles. Near Albany." Steve wasn't sure why he was sharing this much with the man, but Gerald had seemed to be nothing but helpful so far.

"South? Seems like all of us are heading down a similar route. JD is wanting to get to Jax and see if his family is ok. I got some property down in Crisp County. Think it will be a good place to hunker down. Steve, JD and I haven't really discussed it, but might be a good idea for us to travel together. I mean, everyone is on their own, but strength in numbers and all. Just throwing it out there if you want. Feel free to check us out for a day or two first—wouldn't blame ya for that."

The offer caught Steve by surprise. While a few other strangers had shown him kindness, it was getting to be unexpected in this new world. His aching ribs reminded him to stay wary, but also being with others could be safer. "Um, thanks, Gerald . . . and JD. I'd like a bit of time to decide but wouldn't mind hanging with you tonight at least."

Gerald nodded as JD let out a whoop. JD's hand emerged from a massive purse with a box of cookies. He set that aside and also pulled out a nickel-plated revolver. "Careful there, JD. You know how to handle a pistol?"

"My friend's dad showed me how to shoot, but not one like this. His was more square with a thing that slides back."

"Ok, well, set it aside and I'll go over it with you later. Just the basics and how to handle it safely. Check to see if she had any extra rounds for it."

"Rounds?" JD said questioningly.

"Ammo . . . extra bullets."

Steve whispered to get Gerald's attention. "You think that's a good idea? He's just a kid."

"What do you want me to do? Go take it away from him? Personally, I think we should all be armed. I am hoping we find several more of those in this pile. That 'kid' has as much a right to defend himself as any of us. More, really—he can't compete physically with a grown man. He needs a weapon. Even if this scrawny shit snuck up on him, JD would need help."

Steve nodded in growing comprehension. Gerald was in good shape, not just for his age, either. Steve had seen what he had done to the other man. He had no doubts the older man could also take him should he want. It then dawned on him that the 'scrawny shit' sitting bound below Gerald looked a lot like the same asshole that robbed him earlier. He was pretty sad looking. Now he felt more embarrassed he had let the man rob him. His stolen shopping bag would have to be out in the woods nearby. He made a mental note to find it before dark.

Gerald interrupted his thoughts, "So, why didn't you come down and get on the bus, Steve?"

It took a minute for him to shape his thoughts into words. "I'm not entirely sure. It just felt wrong . . . just wrong in every way possible. The buses were also heading north; I need to go south."

"Oh, you'll see some going south, too. I haven't figured out how far apart the camps are, but it seems like we must be one of the last collection points for this one. The buses came from the south but only had a few people on them when they stopped here."

"Who are they, what agency, and why are they moving people into camps?" Steve asked.

Gerald was shaking his head. "Not sure the agency even matters —probably all fall under Homeland Security now. Could be DHS, FEMA, TSA or something completely different. Never seen troops in those gray uniforms, but the point obviously isn't to help the people —more likely just to clear the roads."

"You state that as fact more than feeling. Do you know something about all this?"

"I am retired from public service, gave my country thirty years. I heard stories, contingency plans and such. It was enough to scare me into finding a little place off the grid and stock it full of supplies . . . just in case. I also passed one of those camps, up near the city. Damn lights lit up the sky for miles. Lights, mind you, when everything else is black. The thing was massive, and they had huge trucks spooling rolls of heavy duty fencing out across huge fields. No buildings, no tents even. That's where the white buses stop. It reminded me of descriptions I've read of North Korean political prison camps. You know the ones where they don't just put the prisoner, but his entire family, even grandparents and babies? I don't know what they are going to do with them, but I do know they don't have the logistical ability to feed or care for them for more than a few days. It will be a death camp."

19

The two men sat in the darkness, their individual memories of the past days flowing and ebbing like giant rivers. JD had sacked out earlier, and his soft snores could be heard above the insects' sounds in the night. Steve again thought back to "normal"—the mundane issues he had dealt with every day and how silly it all seemed now. The piles of discarded bags like so many cast off souls. The final remnants of a being's existence. If what Gerald had said was true, there was no returning from those bus rides. What had become of his country, his home?

As if reading his mind, Gerald set down a small notebook he had been writing in and asked, "Steve, what are you going home to? I mean, I get why you are going home. Just wondering if it is the right move for you."

It was a question Steve had asked himself over and over for days, but he was not ready to express those doubts to anyone else. "What do you mean? It's home. My family is there."

Gerald's voice came back slowly, "Do you have any proof they are there? Are you going to be any real use to them when you arrive? Not like you are pulling in with a truckload of supplies. You will just be another mouth to feed. At the rate you are going, it will be a few more weeks before you even get there. Do you think the stores will have anything left? Your neighbors? Your church? Anyone down there friendly enough to take food out of their family's mouthes to feed you?"

Steve was getting angry. "What the fuck, man? I can't leave them there on their own. I'm not totally useless, I've been a good provider —I'll . . . I'll find a way."

He saw the silhouette of Gerald's hands raised in the air. "Sorry, friend, just asking the tough questions. I'm sure you've thought of it already. Point is—the window is closing. That's all I am saying. Right now, you can still find supplies to scavenge. Honestly, plenty of food around if you look hard. Might be best to find an empty house far enough out to not be an easy target and load up everything you can find. Might could even start a late garden. Get a place on a lake or river so you could fish and have clean water. Hell, a few well-fed chickens can keep a man alive for a long time. I'm just saying—your family has been on their own for a while now. Don't you think they may have gone somewhere else for help? If not already, how will they hold out for the next few weeks waiting for you?"

Silent tears of desperation snaked down Steve's face as he, too, had been thinking that. Thinking that his wife and son might already be in one of those camps, or even worse. "I have to try," he said weakly.

The conversation abated while both men reflected on their plight. Steve spoke quietly so only Gerald could hear. "Something I've been wanting to ask you. Why the kid? I know you said he wasn't family. Why would you have taken an interest in JD? Seems he would just be a burden to you. Just another mouth for you to feed."

"That is one way to look at it, but when I saw him standing there about to make a bad choice, I, well . . . "

His voice trailed off, and Steve assumed that was the only answer he would get. Long minutes later a now very emotional Gerald continued: "Several nights ago, I was working my way down parallel to the interstate. I found myself outside a little town. You know, one of those little pop-up developments with no name, just sort of places that spring up. A convenient stopping point . . . probably the result of interstate exits, fast food restaurants and stuff." He paused, and Steve could see him looking off to the dark western horizon.

Gerald's voice cracked a bit when he picked the story back up. "Most of this area down here is really just a bedroom community for Atlanta. People live out here because it's cheaper and safer, but many work back up in the city. These little pop-up cities exist to serve them, so they can get gas, get a haircut, pick-up some food on their way home.

"Anyway, I was out of water and needed to fill up, so I made my way over to a building off by itself. It was one of the few structures that didn't look looted. I had already snuck in the back door before I realized it was a daycare center." Gerald paused again to wipe his eyes. "Anyway, this woman is standing there. Right in front of me, scared the shit out of me. She doesn't say anything, but then I hear the sounds of kids and the smell. *Oh God, the smell.* Finally, she said, 'They never came.' I knew who she meant. The parents never came back from work that day to pick up the kids. I should have turned and left then, but I didn't—I looked in the rooms. Most of the kids were in bad shape. She had given up changing diapers. Maybe she was out completely, I dunno. It seemed that all of the little ones..." He paused as if reliving the nightmare, "The babies. . .they were all dead." The man let out a small sound as the memory was too fresh and painful to relive.

"The older ones, the toddlers and preschoolers, were in only slightly better shape. The woman was in some kind of shock. Suffering and exhausted. I asked her if she was there alone. She pointed to a nearby bathroom. Opening the door to it, I found another woman hanging from a beam over the toilet.

"'I would have done that too,' the daycare worker said, 'but I didn't want them to be alone. No one should die alone.'

"I tried to comfort her, but she was too far gone by that point. It was pitiful, Steve."

"She told me, 'We have no water or food, everything ran out the first few days. I was too scared to go out there until it was too late.'

"I don't know how many kids were in that building—sixty, maybe more. One large room had been set aside for the dead ones." He grasped his head and leaned over as if he were going to be sick. "I knew I couldn't do anything to help any of them. I have never felt so helpless in all my life."

"Oh, damn." Steve turned to look at Gerald. "I hadn't even thought about that. Geeze, that's horrific, what did you do?"

The man shook slightly and seemed to be staring at the ground. "I left."

Steve had no response to that. It wasn't right; it wasn't wrong.

Gerald leaned up and sighed. "I simply turned around and left. The woman didn't even seem surprised or try and stop me. She just stood there, just as dead as the other woman hanging from the ceiling. It messed me up. Next thing that really registered with me was today. Here at the checkpoint getting some water and a burger and seeing this boy wandering around lost and confused. He was about to put his trust in people that I knew would not take care of him, and ... well,—I had to do something. Maybe I could save one, at least."

"Are you going to get him to his family in Florida?"

Gerald made a sound. "Don't know, we both know they are likely not there. No big city is going to survive this. Gangs and looters will get you if starvation and lack of water don't. I think the chances of him seeing them again are small, but I'll try if he wants. Right now ... right now, I am just hoping to keep him safe for another day."

"I guess I get that. Not sure I would want the added responsibility, not in the middle of this crap especially. He seems like a good kid. Lucky he bumped into you." Steve paused for a minute. "I think I would also like to take you up on your offer. To... to travel with you at least for a few days. I mean, if that's ok."

"Sure, man, glad to have the company."

20

T he trio had been on the road since before sun-up. Gerald wanted them to put as many miles as possible between them and the checkpoint. The shopping bag Steve had recovered was once again dangling from his arm only slightly lighter than it had been. "Did you ever untie that creep before we left?"

Gerald gave a slight smile, "I did, but he started cussing me soon as I removed his gag. So, I knocked him out with your walking stick. Dumb bastard is dead and just doesn't know it yet. Ruined knee and a concussion probably, on top of just being plain dumb. Stupid is now a fatal illness—it will get you killed as quick as anything else."

Steve chuckled. *Serves him right*, he thought.

They had not found as much as he would have expected in all the discarded bags. Hardly any food, some medicine. The one radio and three handguns. Gerald had explained that was probably why the checkpoint guards didn't even bother looking through them. "We're all hobos now. Got nothing of any real value," he'd said.

JD had stayed quiet all morning. Steve wasn't sure if this was normal for him or not. Gerald never pressed the boy to talk but acted like he was just one of the guys. As a father, Steve felt unnatural to exclude him or conversely—treat him like an adult. "JD, do you play any sports?" Nothing. "What about a girlfriend, got any cuties waiting for you back home?" Slight head shake was all. "I don't think he likes me."

Gerald never looked back. "None of us like you. You talk too much and ask too many questions."

Steve took offense with that until he saw the slight crease of a smile line on the other man's face. "I have a serious question. "Why are we walking?"

Gerald stopped in the middle of the road and looked at him. "As opposed to . . . ?"

"Anything. My feet are killing me. I have been walking for more than a week, and I'm exhausted. I know cars don't work, but what about finding horses to ride or something?"

"Hey, I'm all for it, but have you seen any horses? Do you even know how to ride? Also, stealing horses might be a hanging crime again. You do have a point though—should be other ways to get where we are going. We know some vehicles still work, but not sure how far we would get before running into another checkpoint. Most of the highways are jammed with dead cars, too."

Around midday, they took a break in the shade under a bridge. It still had to be nearly a hundred degrees even in the shade, but it felt better, and the trickle of muddy water in the stream helped buoy the spirit at least. Steve broke out one of the sausage sticks from his bag and a bit of hard cheese. He sliced thin slices of each and laid it out in a line on a cloth napkin.

"Wow, look at you, Martha Stewart, nice."

"Help yourself, guys. I am tired of hauling this bag. We need to eat this stuff."

JD smelled the slices of expensive salami and wrinkled his nose but took a bite anyway, then another and another. "This is really good, thanks."

"He speaks!" Steve laughed and pulled out some of the other gourmet items from the bag.

"Don't eat too much, we have a lot more walking to do," Gerald said. "Wait, is that preserves? Oh my God, can I have a bite?" Steve passed the unopened jar and a spoon to the man.

Between bites, Gerald said, "I am really glad you joined us, man. Even if you do talk too much." Bits of sticky, sweet strawberry dribbled down his chin beneath his enormous smile. "Tell me, Steve, where were you when it all went to shit?"

Steve answered with obvious embarrassment, "Umm...asleep. I missed the whole thing."

Gerald laughed. "You're shitting me."

"I shit you not. I get bad headaches. Took some medicine, lay down, and the world came to an end while I was passed out."

"Wow, best story I've heard yet."

After the lunch, the group rested. Steve stared at the stream, trying to ignore the throbbing in his feet. As he watched, an idea began to form. "Boats!"

Gerald was leaning back, ball cap covering his eyes. "Planes!"

Steve laughed. "Not a word game—we could get boats or canoes and use the rivers. The Chattahoochee is not that far. It's a huge river. Flows all the way to the Gulf of Mexico. Even a kayak would work. It would be a lot easier than this."

Gerald tipped the bill of his cap up. "Might have a point."

JD chimed in that he knew how to kayak. His family had some they used all the time. Where would they find any though?

"Houses near the rivers or lakes would have them. Probably some outfitter shops in some of the towns," Steve answered excitedly.

Gerald thought for a moment. "The Hooch is a good twenty miles to the west. The Flint River is the only other major one flowing somewhat south, and it's probably thirty, forty miles to the east. I'm not sure either of those would be worth the detour. From what I recall, neither is very developed, other than a few small towns. Doubt many of them are into recreational sports."

One of the items JD had saved from the luggage was a plastic laminated road map of the Southeast. He had it out, looking now. "I-85 crosses the Chattahoochee little ways down, right at the Alabama line. Looks like a big lake up above that. West Point Lake, it says. Think we could get a boat there?"

Steve and Gerald both leaned in to look at the map. "Damn, the kid is right. If we just stay near this interstate it will take us right to it. I am figuring we are about here. Steve put his finger near a place called Moreland. "That would be what . . . maybe forty miles. We could do that by late tomorrow if we hoofed it."

"I like it. That river is the border between the two states, goes a bit west of where we want, but certainly could cut a lot of miles and days off our travel," Gerald said. "We have a plan. Good work, guys."

21

It was late afternoon when Gerald lightly touched Steve on the arm. "You hear that?"

Steve craned his ears trying to pick out what the older man indicated. Only the faintest of sounds could be heard. "Damn, you have good ears, I am just barely making out something. Maybe heavy equipment or tractor."

Gerald nodded. "Yeah, maybe."

"Should we get off the road?" JD asked. Both men looked at the boy realizing that was a damn good idea. All three hustled into the copse of trees to the side. They continued to walk toward the sounds but also worked to stay hidden. The sound continued to increase and eventually became more distinct. Definitely something heavy, probably multiple sources with an occasional backup alarm sounding.

"It reminds me of the sounds of a highway construction crew," Steve said.

"Don't think anyone would be patching potholes anymore, but yeah, kinda does. Sounds like it is just around that bend up ahead. Let's get a bit deeper into these woods and head toward it; maybe we can see what's up."

Steve followed Gerald with a nod. JD was the first to glimpse what was going on.

"Damn," Gerald said, kneeling down to get a better view. They watched as a unit of heavy equipment moved down the southbound lane pushing abandoned cars and hauling heavier trucks off the travel lanes. "That's an Army rotator, heavy lift tow truck." They could all see what he meant as several of the massive crane-arms were hooking to stalled big rig trucks and jerking them to the side. Other large vehicles had dozer blades on the front and pushed smaller cars into ditches like a snow plow. All the moving vehicles were painted olive drab or desert sand.

"Military?" whispered Steve.

"Yeah, and armed escorts." They watched as numerous Humvees slowly paced the convoy, each with a soldier manning the mounted guns.

As the activity neared, the sounds of wrenching metal and rubber scrubbing against pavement became constant. Within fifteen minutes they were past them to the north and nearly out of sight.

Steve sat back on the ground. "That was damned efficient."

"Yep, the civil engineers have had a lot of practice overseas clearing roads. Remember the 'Highway of Death' in Kuwait?"

Steve did remember the scenes of mile after mile of burned out cars and trucks all manned by burned Iraqi corpses as they tried to retreat up the road to Basra during the first Gulf War. "So, they cleared off all the people using the highway and now are clearing the lanes themselves. Isn't that a good sign? Like things might be getting back to normal? Now they can get emergency supplies around the state."

"I don't know, Steve, but my feeling is no. Our interstate system is part of our domestic military preparedness plan. They may be preparing for a possible invasion or could just be a way to help establish command and control. Control transportation routes, and you go a long way toward controlling a region. What I think they are doing is clearing supply routes. I think it is even more important we get off the roads and on the water as soon as possible."

JD threw a stick into a pine tree. "So, those people wouldn't help us either? They are soldiers right . . . our soldiers?"

Neither of the men had a good answer. In fact, they were wondering much the same thing. Gerald turned to face him and gave a shrug. "I don't think they would offer any help. No civilians were with them, and I would bet plenty have asked. My guess is more white buses will be somewhere nearby, picking up anyone who approached that convoy."

"Well, that just sucks," the frustrated boy muttered.

"Yeah, I'm with him," Steve agreed.

THE THREE CAMPED deep in the woods as night fell. They had indeed seen several of the white buses since the afternoon's road clearing. It was a cold camp; they didn't want a fire betraying their presence. Each man ate some of what they carried and gave a share to JD. "Gerald, I don't get it. The camps, the roadblocks, now the Army clearing the interstate. None of this seems aimed at helping the people. Our country is us—the people—as much as it is the land."

Gerald was playing with the small multi-band radio. He had changed out the batteries and was now scanning the dials listening mainly to static. "Steve, something I learned a long time ago, people in power want to stay in power. No matter what. Now, I'm not sure who is pulling the strings anymore, but I do know, deep-down it's all about power. They will protect their own, but for the rest of us . . . we are a waste of resources to them."

"How can you know that for sure?"

"Logistics, man. Look at it this way. No agency, no government could stockpile enough supplies to take care of a major city in a real disaster like this. How do you think they can feed a nation? Acceptable losses, just like in war. If they can't get the power back on quickly, then they need to depopulate the country."

JD looked up. "What does depopulate mean?"

Gerald took a breath before continuing. "It's a fancy way of saying let us all die." The radio gave a warbling sound, and then a voice talking could be heard. It was a presidential address.

22

A s the radio's signal faded in and out, Gerald stood holding it out to help. "Let's see what our esteemed leader has to say." The president began his address with an expected level of grief, sadness and optimism, all carefully balanced by a crafty speechwriter, no doubt. JD lost interest quickly and retreated to his sleeping mat. Steve found little of anything meaningful in the man's words but was reassured that a functioning government still apparently existed. Once he was done, the president introduced the current director of FEMA and then the secretary of transportation.

The FEMA director admitted being overwhelmed but said supplies were being delivered to relief centers daily. Anyone not sheltering in place should make their way to the closest center. The president has asked each state to activate National Guard units to assist in the crises and where contact could not be made with any officials. The U.S. military was also authorized to act to keep the peace and help restore order. Gerald made several rude noises at this part of the broadcast but didn't comment.

The woman who began speaking next had a name that Steve couldn't ever recall even hearing. She was over transportation and stated that distribution and transportation routes were being cleared as quickly as possible. She had mobilized and expanded the roles of the TSA to assist with the aid of evacuees nationwide. "During this international state of emergency, we will grant additional authority to all members of our security forces to help keep the peace. This may in rare instances include the collection and use of civilian equipment including working vehicles and even weapons. Interfering with or failure to comply with this presidential directive is a federal crime and will be enforced by standards listed in the emergency code, and exclusionary rules are also in effect."

Steve had pretty much stopped listening after the FEMA guy, but Gerald was holding the little radio close to his ear as the woman spoke. Once the broadcasts were over, he sat down heavily and sighed. "Well, shit," was all he said.

"Care to elaborate more?" Steve asked.

"Not really, not yet. I need to think about this for a bit. It . . . it changes things." He took out his small, brown leather notebook and began jotting down something.

Although they had not been traveling together long, this was the first time Steve had seen the man flustered. Something about the broadcast had registered badly with Gerald. He had no idea what, though. The speech sounded like just more politico gobbledygook to him. He did wonder again if he should head to one of the relief centers. That was probably what his wife and son would be doing by now. Maybe Gerald was wrong, and they were actually there to supply aid. He gave up thinking about it and drifted off to sleep.

"WAKE UP, STEVE," came the urgent whisper.

"Huh . . . what?" He leaned up until a sharp pain from his bruised ribs caused him to wince. It was still dark, but he saw the deeper shadow of Gerald kneeling and heard rustling sounds from where JD had slept.

Gerald leaned in, "Get your ass up, we have got to move."

"It's the middle of the night. Is someone out there? Are we in danger?"

"Just shut-up, grab your gear and follow me. JD, you ready? Here's your pack, tie off your bedroll and let's move."

Steve now could see flashlight beams in the distance and heard voices. *What in the fuck was going on?* He quickly gathered his few supplies and crammed them into his pack.

Gerald grabbed his arm. "Keep that pistol in your belt. We may need it."

He felt more than saw the other two as they left the campsite and moved deeper into the woods away from the searching men, whoever they were. "Who is that, Gerald? Who are they looking for?" He got no response. Twice he caught a toe on an exposed root and nearly went down. Gerald and the boy were easily outpacing him through the dark woods. He didn't like bringing up the rear. Then a shot rang out. Then another.

Gerald didn't pause or duck but kept moving forward. "They aren't shooting at us, but let's not give them the opportunity," he said over his shoulder in a low whisper. Steve's pace had sped up noticeably, closing the distance to the other two. Up ahead, he heard JD run into something with a thud, then the boy whimpered in pain.

"Fence," Gerald said. "Barbed wire." "JD, are you ok?"

"Yes sir, I think." He could almost make out the figure untangling himself from the metal hooks on the thin strands of the fence. In the darkness, they had been invisible, and JD had hit them at full speed. They would leave wounds, but that was a problem for later. Gerald helped get the boy unhooked and then parted the two lower strands of wire to let Steve, then JD and himself slide through. More shots rang out, seemingly closer this time. Whomever or whatever the guys were after was coming nearer.

Ten minutes later they broke from the treeline into a cleared pasture. "Run," Gerald said as he took the lead. Steve's chest was on fire, his ribs throbbing, but he ran trying to silence the noise being made by the items in his pack. JD was falling back, unable to keep up with Gerald who seemed like a man possessed. *Damn, the old dude is in good shape.* They made it into the far tree line just as the rays of light began stabbing through the woods they had just left.

Each of them was winded and breathing heavily. Gerald motioned for them to stop behind some thick bushes. The search party emerged on the far side of the clearing. At least a dozen spread out with lights sweeping in long deliberate arcs over the tall grass. "Guess they aren't hunting deer," Steve whispered.

Gerald leaned against his ear. "Don't whisper, it carries much farther than you realize. If they have NCGs, we're fucked. But since they seem to be relying on flashlights, we may have a chance. Just don't make a sound."

Steve nodded, trying to process it. The fog of sleep was fully dissipated now, but none of this made any sense to him. A twinge of pain at the back of his neck sent panic through his body. Tension was an enemy of his as it could trigger headaches. *Focus on the task at hand.* He held an arm around JD and noticed numerous dark spots across his light-colored shirt. That fence had gotten him good, but he hadn't complained. This kid was a trooper, that was obvious. He felt Gerald pulling on the back of his shirt, wanting him to follow. He pulled JD, too, and all three began moving slowly away from the searching men.

It was nearly an hour before they stopped. The first blush of daylight was sweeping across the sky as they came into a clearing with row after row of tall, round hay bales. Gerald climbed on top of the bales and helped the other two up. They moved to the center of the mass and lay down, grateful for the rest.

The hay smelled fresh like it had been cut in just the last few weeks. Steve lay back on the rounded hump enjoying the relatively cool, soft bed. "Think we are safe yet?"

"No idea, but we had to take a break. I haven't heard any shots in a while."

JD asked the obvious questions: "Who were those guys? What did they want?"

"Soldiers of some sort is my guess." Gerald shrugged out of his pack and wedged it into a low spot between bales. "Something woke me up. Guess I wasn't sleeping too well after that radio address. I thought I heard somebody yell, then saw lights coming our way. Figured we needed to not be there anymore."

"Why do you think they were soldiers? Couldn't it have just been hunters or something?"

Gerald shook his head. "They were well trained, moved very precisely and deployed in a way to offer multiple firing lanes. I'm not sure who they were after, but it seemed serious. After the radio broadcasts, I just know we better not take any chances."

Steve was puzzled and rubbed his temples. "Why is that? I noticed you seemed very concerned with what you heard. It didn't sound too bad to me. Made me wonder if we shouldn't all go to one of those relief camps."

Gerald leaned back on his pack and gave a slight smile. "If I had to guess, that was where that person was trying to get away from—the one the soldiers were chasing. I don't think they want anyone spreading the truth about the camps."

"Gerald, why do I again get the feeling you know what is going on?"

23

J ust over 700 miles to the north, a Marine helicopter gently touched down on the well-manicured lawn. The massive wooden door to the stately mansion opened as Madelyn Chambers, the secretary of transportation, was ushered into one of the estate's large wood-paneled parlors. She felt, as always, the opposing emotions of dread and excitement at being summoned here.

"Madelyn," came the clear, feminine voice from behind an enormous writing desk, positioned at the far end of a small conference table. "So very good of you to stop by this morning. Caught your speech last night. Quite a performance, I must say."

"Thank you, Ms. Levy. I appreciate that."

"Let me get right to it. I know you have a busy schedule, and I am heading out shortly. Have you mobilized all of your people?"

"Yes, ma'am, we have just under 70,000 armed TSA agents being deployed as instructed."

That was quite a bit more than any public record would ever indicate, but with an annual budget of almost eighty billion dollars, a lot of things in the Transportation Department could go unnoticed.

"Has David over at Homeland given you access to the CBP forces as well?"

"Yes, he has. Forty thousand agents being temporarily reassigned to work under my department's direction. Some issue in getting the word out to everyone, but we anticipate no problems."

"You should." Ms. Levy paused to take a pill that was sitting on her desk with a drink of water. She held the glass up to catch the morning light streaming in from the high windows. "Amazing, isn't it?" She set the glass back down on the ornate desk. "Madelyn, problems will be part of this, make no mistake. Lives are at stake. Many more will be lost. Dangerous people smell opportunity. Now that Catalyst Protocols are in effect, we all have our jobs to do. I need to know we can count on you to do what is expected. Your combined militia will work with our guard assets who are already in place. You must ensure they secure all vital infrastructure, get the designated individuals to reserve centers, maintain strategic agriculture production and please make damn sure the bio labs are secure."

The secretary paused before answering. "I can do what is expected. I struggle with the suffering I see, but I know we have to do what is best for the country."

"The country. Yes, of course. These are tragic times; the CME was devastating. Who knew a solar flare could do so much damage. It was one of our most dreaded scenarios, but the crises offer us a rare opportunity. We now have the chance for a full reset. Eliminate the parasitic vermin who live on the backs of hard-working Americans. Get rid of our broken political and monetary system that has long struggled to keep pace. Sadly, this, reduction of the *burden* is the only way to achieve this—and we can save the most important among us. The rest will have to . . . "—she faded off—"fend for themselves. Tell me, dear, what is your boss doing about his Navy going rogue?"

Madelyn had heard that numerous fleet commanders and even several in naval command were no longer responding to presidential directives. "He has sent an envoy down to the Gulf and also blocked the fleet from leaving out of port in Virginia."

"The idiot, he never had any real control. Guess that is why we put him there, but you would think he could do something. Madelyn, you know you can be the next one to occupy the White House . . . or whatever we choose to be our next capital. Unlike most of the rest, you would actually know who gave you this position. For that to happen, you do what is needed—you cannot be weak. Do you understand me?"

"Of course, ma'am, of course. We have prepared our contingencies for years: secure the food, the water, the transportation and cut-off the regular military. Full command and control will be ours within the week."

Ms. Levy brushed her hair back and approached her. "Honey, we have always had control and command. We just no longer need to pretend or work through idiots like our president. He . . . he, sadly, will likely not survive the week. I'd suggest delaying any other meetings with him for now. We can't save everybody you know."

"I rarely meet with him in person, anyway," she said. "The broadcast was a rare exception."

"Yes, of course . . . the protocols."

A man in a dark suit opened the door. "Ma'am, your ride is ready."

"Sorry, Madelyn, but I do have to run. Work to do and have to check in on my lovely family. Do be careful on your way back to the capital and meet me at Mount Weather next weekend. We will have much to discuss." She handed the secretary a large sealed envelope before heading out the door. "You are going to need this. Please review it today."

Madelyn stood there absorbing it all. The power contained in this room was enormous. She had just been all but promised the presidency of the United States, and yet, she had never even been offered a seat in this room. Even if she were president, she would not have a seat at this table. She had no idea the true identity of the woman, but her power and influence were astonishing. Once again, she had been dismissed as just another lowly servant while the master left to attend more important matters. She tucked the envelope under her arm and proceeded back out the estate's rear door to catch her own ride still idling on the lawn.

24

The men watched as JD moved across the hay bales and under the shade of a large tree. He tugged on a long, leafy-green vine and began pulling something off and putting them in his mouth. He grinned—"muscadines" the sweet, wild grapes that grew all over the South. All three were soon downing the sweet, pulpy fruit and spitting seeds over the edge of their perch. "Man, these are good," Gerald said.

Steve nodded agreement. "Yep, good find, JD. This takes me back to my childhood. Every summer it was such a treat to go out and find wild plums, blackberries and muscadines. I never see them growing anymore."

Steve looked at Gerald. "You haven't answered my question."

"Never heard a question—you made a statement."

Steve smiled and looked down shaking his head. "You know something, don't you? Or have a pretty good theory at least of what is going on."

"I have . . . an opinion. Not sure I am ready to share as you would probably think I am just another conspiracy nut."

"Whatever you have is more than me. It obviously affects us all, so give us your thoughts."

Gerald nodded. "Okay, but believe me, I hope I'm wrong. Remember, I worked in government for years. I was basically an analyst, forensic accountant by trade."

JD asked the same question Steve wanted to, "What is a forensic accountant?"

"I was the guy they called to 'uncook' the books. I found where money was hiding, misdirected or stolen, mostly by looking at the paper trail. I did stints at Treasury, IRS, GSA, but most of my years with the GAO. The Government Accounting Office. One thing about the government: no one spends a dime that accounting somewhere doesn't know about. Now, it helps that I am paranoid, skeptical and have a bit of a devious mindset myself, but I was damn good at tracking down misappropriations. That made me very good at my job, and over the years, provided me with a catalog of unusual knowledge. When it comes to politics, following the money is always the key."

"Sounds boring," JD said as he went back to picking the fat grapes.

"Kinda agree," said Steve.

"Most of it was, but I like solving puzzles, and at some point, I realized I had a lot of pieces that didn't seem to fit anywhere. Like places that had way more money to spend than they should have, which to an accountant is even worse than having a shortfall. It took a lot of years, but eventually, I came to the startling realization that the people that must actually run our country were not our government. Believe it or not, government agencies are also always conspiracy hotbeds. Some lifers are the most distrustful of big government. I found that I listened to these theories and some—*a very few*—dovetailed into what I had uncovered in my various accounting work assignments.

"As a side project, I began to come up with some scenarios that might fit the clues. In some of the history checking, I researched the founding of the American banking system and the families behind it. You know, after the Revolutionary War, the government was flat broke, couldn't even pay the army. Since then we have become the richest nation on Earth. What most people don't know is that there was just a handful of men, six to be exact, who were responsible for that. They called themselves the Jekyll Island Group 'cause that is where they met. You know Jekyll Island, just across the state from here. Anyway, from those meetings emerged the Federal Reserve Bank."

Steve nodded but was not sure where all this was going.

"I know, I know . . . it's a bit complicated. Bear with me. Think about this, though. A small group of individuals meeting in secret creates something so instrumental, so vital to our country. Something that is pseudo-official, government-ordained, yet none of these people had any real legal authority to do so."

"So what, Gerald? I imagine it just seemed like a good idea at the time. Its time had come. Nothing all that sinister to me."

"But Steve, the Fed is still privately owned, yet they can print money and regulate its value. They set the interest rates. You must see this is inherently wrong. *Problematic* at best and truly evil at its worst. I won't bother getting wound up in a discussion about the Fed as that is not the real culprit. Just understand for this small group, money was never an issue. They owned the banks. What mattered to them was what it could buy. In Washington money buys power and loyalty."

Steve interrupted, "But this Jekyll Group are long dead. Surely whatever machinations they put in place are long gone."

"Well, Steve, that's where it gets muddy. You have no doubt heard of the secret cabals that run our government: the Trilateral Commission, Bilderberg Group, Bohemian Grove and such. People seem obsessed with shadow governments. The truth I uncovered is that it isn't the government that has been commandeered; it is instead, a small group that runs our financial system. Six men or six families maybe, each representing the top layer of what may be truly ancient financial empires. As far as I know, they have no name, but I maintain they are the evolution of that original Jekyll Island Group. I suppose they may even precede that meeting—that one just happened to get some unwanted attention.

"What's so troubling is once I made the initial connections, I could see their hands in everything. Nothing that was ever outwardly illegal, nothing I would ever go to my bosses with, but I swear these people were the ones in charge. I heard rumor of lots of crazy ideas while I was in DC. Plans to collapse the dollar, ruin the housing market, get rid of the social welfare system, neutralize global warming, but the worst ever was how to depopulate the country. That one always had a bit too much of the ring of truth. Supposedly somebody got hold of some documents that told people what to do in various natural disasters to help the effects of the disaster spread across the country and to use it as an excuse to get rid of the undesirables. The masses of humanity that are simply a drain on the economy."

"Whoa . . . whoa, whoa! . . . Uh, uh. So, you believe the government is using the blackout as a cover to what? . . . Depopulate the country?"

"Don't give our government that much credit. It is a massively oversized, slow-to-react behemoth, but in this case, it's probably just another tool being used by this group. But to answer your question, essentially, yes. You see, besides being huge, our government, particularly the politicians, are notoriously bad leaders. A person whose main job is being popular enough to get re-elected may not be the best person to control the world's largest military and largest economy. Yet, knowing that, I realized most of our choices throughout history have been pretty good ones. I am not totally sure this group is evil; it seemed much of what they have done has benefited us as a nation. I do think you would have to be blind not to see our nation's problems. Massive social welfare programs, broken healthcare system, crooked politicians, banking ineptitude, packed court and prison systems, add to that immigration and a long-simmering racial divide. Someone high-up has declared a 'do-over.' That is what I think."

Steve pinched the bridge of his nose, another twinge of sharp pain behind his left eye. *No, no, no . . . not now.* "This is a lot to take in, as someone who has normally followed the rules and assumed our government had our best interest at heart. It seems impossible, but I do accept that something more is going on."

Gerald studied him for a moment. "You feeling okay, Steve? You are grimacing a bit."

"Yeah, just a headache, I hope. Probably from lack of sleep. I occasionally get migraines. I hope this isn't one coming on. Now that you have scared the shit out of me, not sure I will ever sleep well again."

Gerald patted his leg. "Sorry, buddy."

Steve struggled to focus but wanted one more answer: "I gathered something in that speech last night convinced you that this plan was now in place. What was that?"

"Several small clues, one is the emergency orders that were issued. Not martial law, mind you. Through those emergency orders, and especially the exclusionary rules, our constitutional rights have been put on hold. They can imprison us without due process, presume us guilty, even execute us on sight if they wanted. Second, FEMA and the Transportation Department being out front and working together. Those two agencies have a lot of money and people at their disposal. FEMA especially can set-up these . . . these,"—he struggled for the right word—"I don't know . . . 'relocation or resettlement' camps, and Transportation can clear roads and man them with its own agents. Just seems the plans all came together very quickly, yet no sign of aid coming into any areas that I have seen. So, who are they benefiting? "

It really was too much. Steve lay back on the hay using his pack for a pillow. He massaged the bridge of his nose hoping to keep the pain at bay. Gerald noticed, but continued laying out more of the conclusions that he had come to.

"Think of it like this. When the ship is going down, are you going to try and fix the ship, or are you going to gather your friends and find a life raft?"

"Find a raft," Steve said through slitted eyes.

"Exactly. I think they have got their cronies holed-up somewhere safe to ride this storm out. Then they can come out and start over."

Steve struggled to stay awake and focused, but something the man said didn't fit. "There is a problem with that plan, Gerald. It assumes no other country would be in a position to do anything as well. We have allies who would try to render aid as well as enemies who would love to come conquer us while we were knocked down. This blackout maybe is worldwide, I don't know, but I feel sure it didn't decimate every country as badly as us."

"Yeah, friend, that's the rub. Haven't figured out the rest of it yet. Somehow, they would have needed to keep the Russians and Chinese and ISIS, among others, all out of the mix. As it is right now, Iceland could probably come conquer us."

Steve didn't hear the rest. He was out. His tortured head now also dwelling on the possibility that his country had abandoned its people in its greatest time of need. Gerald picked up his leather notebook and began writing again, some new thought occurring to him.

25

Steve awoke to dark clouds and a light rain falling. The mental fog he always felt from a migraine was overpowering. Some sufferers called it a halo effect. He had always dreaded it as much as the actual headache; it was debilitating, like having the flu while suffering the worst hangover of your life. He had no immediate idea of where he was or who he was with. This inability to put rational thoughts together always reminded him that this could be what Trey went through all the time.

He reached a hand out searching for something familiar. Rough, scratchy. Was he lying on the ground? He was definitely outside—the rain told him that much. After what seemed an eternity, he managed to sit up and waited for his eyes to begin focusing. The remnants of the migraine were still there lurking in the shadows. He could feel them ready to unleash a dark tide that would take him back under again. The cool rain felt good, and he opened his mouth to let the drops quench his overpowering thirst.

Finally, after several minutes, he was able to see his surroundings and recall where he was. He realized he was alone. Gerald and JD were nowhere to be seen, nor was any of their gear. The clouds in his mind refused to clear entirely. *Had they said they were leaving? Am I ,on my own again?*

He couldn't recall any of that. Just like his last one back in Charlotte, it left him oblivious to the real world. At least there he had his meds which helped a little. He crawled to the edge of the bales but saw no one. He couldn't blame them for leaving him—he was weak, he would just slow them down.

He retreated back across the wet hay and retrieved his pack, then gingerly dropped off the bales and back onto solid ground. Staring across the field, he could see nothing clearly due to the misting rain. He should probably head south, but with his head still throbbing, he knew he wouldn't get far. Heading to the backside of the bales he would be sheltered somewhat by the trees. As soon as he moved in that direction, he heard JD's voice calling out to him. He then saw both of his traveling companions tucked up under an overhanging bale of hay in a relatively dry spot.

"Sorry man, we couldn't move you, and I figured you needed the sleep anyway. One of your migraines I'm guessing."

Steve nodded, "Yeah—since I was a teenager, tension and stress trigger it occasionally."

"That's rough man. My wife, God rest her, she had 'em sometimes. Every now and again I'd find her curled up in a dark closet when I got home. No idea how long she had been there."

"They are . . . unpleasant. Thank you, guys, you know, for waiting around for me. You didn't have to."

"Nonsense, Steve, you're one of us now. Well, assuming you want to be that is. 'Sides, you got the lovely meat sticks and cheese we've grown so fond of."

JD nodded enthusiastically at that. Steve handed his pack over to them. "Help yourselves. I am going to sit this one out."

They ate while Steve sipped on a bottle of warm water. "Any idea what time it is? Are we going to head out or go back toward the interstate?"

"Guessing it's four or five—my damn watch didn't survive the blackout. You still don't look too good. My vote is we camp here again and get an early start tomorrow. We should be able to parallel I-85 without getting too close. If I am right, the main danger will be south of here about a half day's walk."

"Sounds good to me, just wake me when you are ready. I'm going back to sleep to try and rid myself of the rest of this."

GERALD WOKE up both of his fellow travelers again before daybreak. The extended rest for all of them had been welcome, but he was worried about what the day would bring. After a meager breakfast, they left the relative safety and began the day's trek. Steve was feeling much refreshed but still feeling the after-effects of the headache and the mugger's attack. He had slept hard. The warnings of Gerald's theories kept popping into his sleep in awful, vivid dreams. Something he had refused to think about until now. As he walked beside the older man he brought it up. "Hey, man, I think I know the answer, but what about our money? The money I have in banks and investments. My companies' accounts."

"Gone."

The simple answer was both what he expected and what he feared. "It's just money, right? And if what you said yesterday is true . . . then it never had the real value I thought anyway."

Gerald made a little sound of disgust. "We gave it value. Our trust in the system made it work. All they could do was put ink on paper and say it was valuable. We, the American people, had to buy into that belief. Just look at the success of Bitcoin and the other cryptocurrencies. Nothing backing them but faith, and yet they are working currencies. Personally, I believe the world economy, particularly something outside their control like Bitcoin, which was well out of their reach, scares the fuck out of this group." They walked a bit farther in silence before he continued. "Steve, I haven't asked what you did, but I am guessing you were pretty successful at it. Would that be accurate?"

"Yeah, I was pretty good at making money, I guess. Not that it matters much anymore."

"The money doesn't matter," Gerald said, "but the effort you put into it still does. The merchant class was every bit as important to this country's success as the farmers. Nothing works without trade. You need to think about any other assets you have that aren't digital or in a bank somewhere. Those are gone. But property, jewelry, working vehicles. Hopefully, you have something you can put your hands on. Liquid assets we used to call it. Only now a lot of things we wouldn't have thought of as an asset will be."

Steve understood, but could only think of a few items that might qualify as such. "I just measured my success by dollars, didn't really diversify much. What about you? You don't seem too surprised by all this—where did you put your money?"

The older man took a long time to respond, seemingly unsure of how much to tell. "Well, I was a government employee, and my wife was a teacher, so we never had very much to play with, but I was pretty smart with my money. Like I said, when I started seeing the clues in my work of a deeper hand at play, I started paying more attention to other conspiracy theories, and I started reading a lot of prepper fiction. Much of it was good storytelling but complete rubbish from a practical standpoint. Too dependent on stuff—stored foods, gadgets, weapons. Some of it, though, was very well thought out. Good bushcraft, living off the land, getting back to nature.

"I had just retired when my wife, Nancy, passed away. We were living down here in Atlanta then. I had already sold our townhouse up in DC and took our savings and later the life insurance proceeds, and put nearly all of it into this property down south at the lake. We never had kids, no family at all really, so we always planned to retire early, maybe do some traveling, but to finally live somewhere simple and peaceful." He sighed.

"My friends said I had gone green as I spent a lot of time learning more about gardening, fishing, canning. Things that city life never prepared me for. Anyway, while not much use to me now, most of my money is tied up in that place. It is off the grid and has nearly everything I should need for a long time."

"Wow . . . sounds very smart, Gerald. Way better off than me or anyone I know of in fact. How do you know it's still there?"

"Oh, I am pretty sure no one has stumbled across it yet, and if they did, well, it wouldn't much matter."

Steve wasn't sure what that meant, but before he had a chance to think about it, JD turned around to face them with a look of fear.

"Get down!" the boy said in a loud whisper.

26

The three of them ducked low, although Steve had no idea what or *who* was out there. JD crawled back the fifteen or so feet to them. "Looks like another group of men like yesterday. They are crossing ahead of us."

"How many did you see?" Gerald asked.

"Hard to say. . . just mostly shadows, a few flashlights. I would guess maybe ten or twelve."

Steve was again impressed with the boy's composure. He was adapting to this new reality faster than anyone. They moved diagonally into deeper woods away from the direction JD had indicated. The sounds of the group became evident then faded as they passed farther away. "Gerald, we are in the middle of nowhere, why are we running into patrols out here?"

"I think we are going to find out soon. Just stay alert everyone."

They hiked for several more hours. The going was difficult. They stayed mainly in the deep woods. As the sun crossed the midday mark, they started hearing sounds in the distance. They slowed their pace and were even more cautious the closer they got. Twice more they had seen groups of uniformed men in the woods. The patrols were armed and looked ready for business. "Maybe we should head in a different direction," Steve said upon seeing the last patrol.

Gerald had the map out again. "I don't think we can avoid whatever is ahead. According to the map, we should be coming up to a junction of two interstates. Whatever this is, most likely is positioned right there. I am guessing it is another of those relocation camps."

They smelled it before they saw it. The sheer size took their breath away, which didn't help defuse the odor. From a small overlook, they saw the freshly cleared land laid out on the edge of an interstate going south to Columbus, Georgia. To their west, the camp was bordered by I-85, the road they had been roughly traveling down. A nearby abandoned weigh station appeared to now be functioning as a command center. Gerald had been right about what it was and the location.

The earthy aroma of freshly cut trees and excavated dirt was punctuated by smelly campfires and a foulness that could only be human waste and rot. Line after line of tents, tarps and even cardboard shelters for as far as they could see. "Geeze," said JD.

"Yeah, kid . . . exactly. Damn, there must be thousands of people in there."

Gerald had been surveying the scene with a pair of binoculars he had retrieved from the discard pile days before. "Tens of thousands at the very least. They must have been clearing both of these interstates down here into this one massive camp."

"I came through this way two weeks ago on my way to Charlotte," Steve recalled. "Hell, I stopped and ate lunch in a beautiful little town just a few miles south of here. I can't believe this. Who did this? It really is a prison camp?" He could see people, masses of people, hanging on the fences looking out in all directions.

They spent several hours watching the camp, trying to get a sense of the purpose and how to get around it. Heavy equipment was being used to clear more forest for miles. They were going to have a long detour to be able to keep going southward. "Wonder if they're clearing off land to expand the camp?" Gerald asked.

"I don't think so," Steve answered now using the binocular to survey the scene. "See those trucks lined up on I-185?"

"Yeah, I see them but can't tell what's on them," Gerald answered.

Steve was very familiar with the distinctive green and yellow objects. "Crop tractors. Look like John Deere 7R, maybe 8R. We see plenty of them down around Albany. They are designed for large tract farming. They are clearing fields for planting some type of crops. They must have had them stored in a protected structure for them to still be operational." He handed Gerald back the binoculars.

"Damn, just like in North Korean prison camps," he said, looking in the same direction as Steve. "They are going to make these people feed the survivors."

"Well, that's a good thing, right? I mean they will at least have food to eat." Steve said optimistically.

Gerald turned to face him shaking his head. "I don't know, Steve, but . . . I just don't think so. Not food for these survivors. If I'm right, camps like these will be the new food supply for the country's elite. The ones who are probably holed up somewhere safe right now. If the people down there get more than a few scraps of it, I would be surprised. They have a built-in workforce and can always clear the towns in the area if they need more hands. No wonder security around here has been so tight."

Steve felt a buzzing in his head. "Wait, you are saying this is some kind of forced labor camp that will be used to what . . . feed what's left of our government?"

Gerald nodded. "What does it look like to you, Steve? All I know is what I am seeing, and it doesn't look like any fucking humanitarian relief effort. This corridor between Atlanta to the north and Fort Benning to the south has now been cleared and appears that armed patrols are in charge. I don't know if this is part of my paranoia coming true or something else. I just think it's best not to stick around. We need to be south of the camp as soon as possible."

JD tugged on Gerald's sleeve. "I smell food. Can we eat?"

"Food, really? That is what you are smelling?" Gerald looked at Steve with a bewildered look.

"He's a kid, Mr. Leighton. He gets hungry, I think he's done remarkably well, considering."

"You're right, sorry, sorry. Sure, JD, we can eat. How are we doing for food anyway?"

"Not good, enough water for maybe two days, I have enough food for possibly three," Steve said.

Gerald went through his pack. "Yeah, about the same, and I know JD only has a day's rations in his pack to keep it light. Gentlemen, I think we are going to need to do a bit of foraging as soon as we get away from all this."

"What is foraging?" JD asked as he bit into a hard granola bar.

"Grocery shopping," Gerald answered.

IT TOOK a full day to skirt the camp's eastern edge and then turn south. The three were hot, tired, hungry and thirsty as they had been hiding from patrols all day. The tension was causing Steve's head to throb. He couldn't afford another migraine now. As they traversed the perimeter of the camp, the scale of it was even more staggering. The camp and attached fields were miles across. Whoever did this must have started almost immediately after the CME. Gerald had briefly entertained the idea of raiding one of the trucks for supplies but changed his mind at the sight of a man being shot darting out of the woods attempting the same thing.

They waited until nightfall to cross the four-lane highway that had become a virtual parking lot for military and farm equipment. Steve looked southward down I-185 as he crossed. If he could have just taken one of these trucks, he could be in Columbus in less than an hour and home in just over two. It was so tempting, but everywhere they saw armed and serious-looking troops guarding everything. Even when they were at least two miles from the borders of the encampment, the troop presence was still significant.

They ducked for cover in the darkened median. "Why in the hell are these roads so wide?" Steve whispered. He had never noticed it driving, but now he knew it must be over a hundred yards with fencing on both sides. The first half hadn't been too bad, but they still had the last fifty. A loose rock or scuff of a shoe could give them all away. Steve wasn't sure what misery getting caught might be, and he didn't want to find out. They made it into the woods on the opposite side and over the fence before a bright light turned on and they heard the sharp command to halt. "Oh shit!" Gerald whispered.

27

I t took a moment for Steve to realize the light was not pointing at him or Gerald. In the dash across the road, JD had pulled ahead and away from them by a good fifty yards. He now stood with his hands up in the beam of the light. A soldier had a rifle pointed at the boy's head. The scene immediately enraged Steve who stood to approach, but a restraining hand from Gerald kept him still and silent.

"It's just a boy . . . just a kid, man. Hey, lil dude, what are you doing out here? Have you been in the camp?" They could see a dark-skinned soldier holding the flashlight and talking to JD. Another stood just outside the cone of light holding the rifle. "Lower the gun, dude, he's just a kid. What are you eleven, twelve?"

"I'm uh, I'm uh, twelve sir," JD said in a shaky voice. He glanced briefly in the direction of the man with the gun before looking away.

"Twelve? Kinda young to be in the woods alone. Who you got wid cha?"

Steve just knew the kid was about to lose it. Gerald had belly-crawled closer to the two soldiers. He held his breath waiting for JD's response.

The quake in the boy's voice was even more pronounced. "I got lost, I was on my way home and got turned around in the woods."

"Wait, so you live around here?" the other soldier said.

"Back near town, yes, sir."

Steve was stunned hearing how quickly JD came up with an answer. The boy was sharp. No wonder Gerald liked him.

"What town, LaGrange? You stays in LaGrange?"

"Uh huh, yes."

"Shit, boy, you six . . . hell, maybe seven miles from there." The two soldiers spoke more quietly to one another. It seemed they were trying to decide what to do with JD. "We ain't sposed be detaining town folk yet. Specially not kids . . . that ain't right."

"You take him, I ain't walking that far just to be told to turn him loose."

The other soldier responded, "They don't turn nobody loose, just put 'em to work."

"Look, lil man, you think you can find yo way from here? Yo wayz home?"

"I, I guess so. I think I know where it is," JD answered optimistically.

"Aight, we gonna let you go head, but listen up—you run into any other patrols don't mentions we did this. I got a lil' brother who's twelve, 'bout yo size too. I hope somebody might look after him in all dis mess."

JD seemed almost giddy, "Yes sir, thank you, sir."

Steve let out a nervous sigh of relief. *Start walking kid, get the hell away.*

The one with the rifle turned on his light and pointed the beam behind him and said, "It's pretty much that way. Just walk straight and try to avoid guys that look like us."

JD thanked them and started walking, then stopped and turned. "You guys have anything I could eat? I'm hungry and thirsty. That's what I was out looking for today."

Gerald looked back at Steve smiling and shaking his head. Steve knew exactly what Gerald was thinking: the boy had his respect too.

While the soldiers retrieved some MREs and bottled water for JD, the men quietly worked their way behind them. Several minutes later they were all back together, JD's pack sagging low with the supplies.

ONCE WELL BELOW THE CAMP, they angled back closer to I-85. They could see this section of road had not been cleared. As they approached the first exit to the nearby town of LaGrange, they felt comfortable enough to finally walk along the edge of the roadway. None of them had spoken since the encounter other than to point out hazards in the way. It seemed that the troop presence and patrols were all behind them now, but no one wanted to take any chances.

As the morning sky began to lighten, the traveler's confidence improved. "Kid, I gotta tell you, that was some impressive storytelling back there," said Gerald smiling. "I thought we were all done for when that light came on. You did good, man . . . really good. Can't believe you went back and asked for food after they let you go. Ballsy!"

JD just grinned and nodded. "They seemed pretty nice. I was a little scared at first, but I don't think they wanted to hurt me. How far is it to the river?"

"Judging by the mile markers looks like sixteen miles to the state line. That should be the river," Steve answered. He grinned as he saw one of his dealerships' name badges on the back of a stalled car. The nearly new Ford SUV had been on one of his lots in just the last few months. The thought of it made him smile; just a touch of something familiar gave him hope he might see home again.

"Hey Gerald, I just remembered something. Before I ran into you guys, I was checking every abandoned car for supplies. Since we are running low, we might need to do that again."

"Yeah, I was doing the same, but I have a better idea. Most of these freight trucks sitting around will be full of stuff. Most food stores have to get deliveries every day, so good bet some of them have food—maybe even lots of food."

JD went up to the closest one and jiggled the padlock on the doors. "So how do we get into them?"

"Ah yes, there is that little detail. We need to find a master key. I can pick some locks—just a hobby I got—but I don't want to spend time picking them all. Instead, look for a stalled contractor pickup. You know the kind that a construction or plumbing company might use."

Steve was puzzled at Gerald's request but kept an eye out and pointed out several. Each time, Gerald shook his head. Finally, JD spotted one on the far side that he liked. The white truck had a large job box style toolbox on the bed. Gerald jumped up in the back and tried the lid of the box to no avail. He then reached into his pack and retrieved a small black pouch. He slid out several uniquely shaped tools that looked more like dental instruments. He inserted them into the lock and moving one hand while twisting with the other, sprang the lock in minutes.

"Yes!" Gerald held up a large tool with long handles and a pretty serious set of cutting jaws at the other end. "Master key."

"Those are bolt cutters," Steve said.

"Yeah, same thing."

For the next several miles Gerald would cut the lock off any truck they came across and quickly check the contents. He told them that food deliveries would likely be on trucks by themselves, so they skipped on past any that didn't quickly look like consumables. They encountered trucks full of auto parts, bags of chemicals, machine pieces that no one could identify, clothes of all sorts and trailer loads of lawn mowers, furniture and TVs. The valuable items of yesterday now nearly useless.

They had opened up over a dozen trucks when they came to the first one worth digging through. This one was smaller, and the cargo box had an assortment of items. Most of what they saw when they opened it up were pallets of toys and cleaning supplies. Far in the back, though, they saw cases of cereal and canned goods. "Jackpot!" Steve said.

JD's eyes lit up as he grabbed a basketball from a box and a snack cake from another. "Don't overdo it, only get things we can easily carry," cautioned Gerald, trying not to hurt the boy's feelings. "We may have to repeat this a few times before we get home. I feel sure others will be doing the same thing soon. So...these will be a resource for only so long."

The canned goods were tempting, but were just too heavy to take very many. They decided to make a fire and have a large meal before continuing. Their packs were now bulging with dry goods, beef jerky, drink mix and even some candy and vitamins. Gerald had also grabbed several boxes of large commercial trash bags. "That truck was perfect," JD said.

Gerald agreed. "Probably some local delivery truck from a supply warehouse. Those tend to hit the smaller stores around. The ones that can't handle full pallets of a single item."

Steve nodded; that would make sense. "We will need to keep an eye out for more of those."

"Or just find the supply warehouses," JD said before taking another big mouthful of soup.

Gerald and Steve shook their heads. "This kid's a genius. How does he keep thinking this stuff up before we do?" Steve asked. JD just smiled.

"We are out of date, last year's models," Gerald replied with a grin. "This was a good idea and a good find. We have a lot to carry, and this damn lock cutter is heavy, but I don't dare leave it behind."

It was dusk before they reached the state line. The Chatta-hoochee River ran thirty feet below where they stood on the bridge. They didn't see anything that looked likely for finding a boat or kayak. "I think we should camp for the night and start looking again at sunrise," Gerald said.

They crossed to the Alabama side and began setting up camp under the bridge. Settling in, they built a small fire, and Steve broke out a gourmet meal of canned tuna and crackers. "This turned into a pretty good day despite the way it began."

"Absolutely!" the others agreed. JD was busy eating a mostly melted candy bar and grinning ear to ear, chocolate stains across both cheeks.

Wish they all could be this good, Steve thought, knowing that was a very unlikely wish.

"Careful, Steve, the life of a hobo and a thief is starting to appeal to you," Gerald said.

"Not likely, but I do now know I am willing to do a lot to survive. More than I realized." He felt the outline of the pistol still in his pack. *How far would I be willing to go?*

28

Perhaps it was the exhaustion from the previous day or the relaxing sounds of the river, but none of the group awoke until well after sunrise. Steve came awake with a start as JD was saying something quietly and pointing up toward the highway above.

"What is it?" he whispered.

"Group of guys on bikes," came the boy's response.

"Motorcycles?" asked Gerald who was now also awake.

"Nope, bicycles. The racing kind, you know. They had guns and looked like bad news. They kept going, though."

Bicycles . . . damn, that would have been smart. Why hadn't they thought to get a few of those? They could have made really good time. Steve let the thought linger. *Most likely would have run right into one of those sweeper patrols, too. No way to avoid the roads on a bike.*

"Probably a hunting party from one of the nearby towns," Gerald said. "No matter what, we should eat something and get moving down this river as soon as we can."

The river was wide and looked foreboding. The murky brown water was flowing faster than Steve had expected. It had not looked deep from the bridge above, but today, down here close to it, he was not as sure. "Where are we going to find boats or kayaks or something?

Gerald was eating canned pasta and scanning the banks of the river in every direction. Nodding he said, "I don't know, I'm sure some of the houses nearby would likely have some, but that may not be safe. Do you know of any outfitters or recreational areas nearby?"

Steve thought about it but shook his head. "I don't recall much, only been through here a few times. Light industrial, older homes, just a quiet southern town, West Point I believe it's called. Think there's a dam and reservoir back up the river ten or fifteen miles. Just not sure about anything near here."

"Yeah, I don't want to go north that far. We could just use some logs, drop them in the water and use any that float to hang onto. That way we could scan the shore for houses and boats."

Steve warily eyed the water again. "That seems pretty risky, especially with these heavy bags." He sat looking at the river trying to come up with something. "When I was a kid we would tie old inner tubes together and put boards over the top to make a raft. Most car tires these days are tubeless though."

Gerald snapped his fingers and held one up as an idea formed. "That's a good idea."

"What, tubes? We won't find any, man."

"No, but the same concept. We need to do a bit of scavenging. You guys follow me."

Gerald led them back to the interstate and pointed at a truck on the far side. "You guys remember what that one had?"

JD began to nod, then Steve smiled as realization took root: empty metal drums, a truck full of various sizes.

They tossed about ten of the smaller drums down to the river's edge. Then they found some wooden pallets and wire in another truck to use as a makeshift platform. By mid-morning, they had the drums secured to the pallet raft and had lowered it into the water.

"It floats," JD said triumphantly.

Gerald was scratching his head. "Not going to be too stable, sits too high in the water. Two can ride, but one of us will need to hang on to the side and help steer."

They packed their gear in another empty drum and lashed it to the side with more wire. Steve and JD took the first turn riding as Gerald leaned to push the raft out into the current and jumped in after. "Damn, that water is deep!" he said as he came up sputtering but smiling.

They had broken off boards from more pallets to use as paddles, but the current was strong enough—they mainly used them to help steer. The river depth seemed to be very irregular. One minute it would be too deep for Gerald to touch bottom, the next they would be maneuvering it off an outcropping of exposed rocks. The first ten minutes was a learning experience. The three of them getting used to the water current that kept spinning the makeshift raft in lazy circles. All attempts to actually guide the craft seem to have a negligible effect on direction. After a while, they just gave up and went with the flow.

Gerald climbed mostly out of the water and onto one of the exposed drums. They were passing through lightly developed residential areas on both sides. The tall pine trees regularly giving way to manicured lawns sweeping down to the water's edge. "Keep an eye out for kayaks or canoes we could take."

Steve had completely forgotten about that. Like JD, he was simply enjoying the ride. The three of them began to search the banks in earnest, although the houses and development were sparser here. "What's that?"

The men looked to where JD was pointing down the river a few hundred yards.

"Not sure," said Gerald. A line of something seemed to span the entire river. "Maybe it's the marker for the state line or something. Could be fishing nets even."

As they got closer and passed the objects, they could see it was just a line of white buoys. The river here had to be nearly a quarter mile across. On one side they could see a large brick building, maybe an old mill of some type. "You guys hear that?"

Steve turned his head in the direction Gerald was looking and heard something. The sound was unmistakable. It was a waterfall. "Paddle, JD, paddle!"

The boy looked panicked. "Which way?" he yelled back.

Steve understood now, the waterfall spanned the entire river. It was massive. Gerald was back in the water kicking and pulling the raft backward away from the falls. As they neared the precipice, it looked down at a thirty-foot drop to the rocky riverbed below. The current here was not swift, but trying to guide or even slow the heavy raft was proving impossible. They watched in horror as the raft continued its march toward the precipice. JD and Steve were paddling furiously as Gerald fought the current trying to swim backward with the raft in tow.

The front edge of the raft nosed over the edge as Steve roughly grabbed for JD and pulled him toward the back. He no longer saw or heard Gerald, but the raft slowly ground to a halt on what appeared to be a rock ledge just beneath the water.

"Get off the raft, try and swim to the shore."

It was Gerald's voice, but Steve still didn't see the man. Looking down through the palettes he could just make out his upper body and head between the barrels under the raft. He was using his legs wedged against the top of the old dam to hold the raft from going over.

JD and Steve hurried off the platform and were able to stand on the edge of the dam. The current wasn't strong enough to push them over, but it was still unnerving. The river just disappeared over the ledge inches away. The jagged boulders jutting from the water below would have been the end of the short journey for the trio. He reached back to try and help Gerald steady the raft just as the rear tipped up and began sliding over the top. He watched as the raft sailed over the edge with Gerald still holding on underneath.

29

Her hand trembled slightly as she lay the envelope down and stared out the window. The message was clear, but she still shuddered in disbelief. She was ambitious, craved power in fact, but this . . . this was nearly too much. The CME event had decimated the U.S. government, and many of the top people in the administration were missing or dead. As the sitting secretary of transportation, she would have been well down the list for potential successors to the presidency. *What was it? Twelfth or thirteenth?* she thought. So little of the cabinet was left that she had been pretty sure she was up to fourth or fifth. After confirming earlier in the day that the downed jet was carrying the VP, she may even be the third surviving person in line for the office. Not that it mattered, she knew now what the future held for her.

Madelyn began picking at the sheer, white nail polish on her slender fingers. It was a nervous habit, years in the making. She prided herself on being perfect. In forty-five minutes, the tiny bubble in the finish on one nail had caused her to scrape polish completely off several fingers. "Shit," she said to no one. She knew it was a weakness to worry about her nails or her appearance. Hell, the world was coming to an end, but she continued to scrape. Tiny flakes of pearlescent white fluttered down to the rich, dark carpet below. She liked the color, what was it? Moon Shadow or Luna Sea or something like that. *Lunacy*, that was what all of this was, and she was right in the middle of it.

There was no way the Council knew in advance that the solar flare would be this bad, but they had been ready nevertheless. Things had moved like clockwork since that day, at least the parts of the plan she had been read in on. Ms. Levy and the Council had contingency protocols for everything. They were a precision instrument it seemed. Like a metronome, nothing interrupted its rhythm. She brushed more of the flakes of chipped nail enamel from her charcoal black designer dress.

One of the pilots opened the cockpit door to the private jet. "Secretary Chambers?"

Her thoughts disturbed, she stopped fixating on her fingers and slid the envelope back into her bag. "Yes, Donald?"

"We'll be landing in fifteen minutes, just wanted to make sure everything was secure." He took the crystal highball glass from her outstretched hand and offered her the dangling seatbelt with the other.

She watched as he retreated and left her again alone with her thoughts. *This will likely be the last flight on this tiny jet or with these pilots,* she thought. The next "event" would see to that.

30

Steve saw JD scurrying along a narrow path just below the water's surface. The old mill dam seemed to be made of rock or maybe cement. The top had been worn nearly smooth after decades of water spilling over its brow. Now it was a path to the shore for the two of them. He had no idea where Gerald was, or even if he was still alive, but he had to try and find him. *God, the river was so wide here.* Thankfully the current was not strong enough to push them over. An occasional glance down at the riverbed below sent shudders through him.

JD stopped and yelled back, "We can get down on that."

"That" was a fallen pine tree hanging precariously from the lip of the dam to the rocks and water below. The blackened tree was bare of needles and slick with moisture. The skeleton of wood had obviously hung up there for a long time. "It doesn't look safe," but the boy was already using one of the limbs to transition over. The tree was much closer than the distant shore they had been running toward, but using it as a ladder down . . .

"Hurry up! We have to get to him!" JD yelled up from halfway down. He had never seen the kid so animated or focused. The top of the tree was moving around as JD climbed, so Steve steadied it and decided to wait until JD was off before attempting his own descent. He couldn't believe they had been on the river such a short time before this happened. He was so unprepared for the dangers of this world.

Gingerly, he climbed down the tree and stepped over to the closest outcropping of rocks. He caught sight of JD already approaching the remnants of the raft. Steve dreaded what they might find; may not be best to let JD be the one to discover it, but—it was what it was. He sloshed through the pools of water and over the gray rocks to get to the mangle of drums and pallets.

"He's over here!" JD was pulling on a hand. Nothing else of their friend could be seen underneath the pile of debris. Steve started digging, pulling loose boards, ropes and drums away.

"Can you feel a pulse?"

JD looked up. "I don't know. Just wet and cold."

That didn't sound good to Steve as he doubled down on his efforts to free his friend. Finally, he could see much of Gerald's body. He wasn't on the bottom of the heap so possibly had not been beaten against the rocks. As he touched an exposed leg, he heard a moan. "Hey, old man, you still in there?" There was no response.

JD climbed up and helped remove the last few items. One of the drums of supplies went rollingoff and down into the river. Steve glanced at it as it picked up speed floating downstream, but knew there was nothing he could do about it. As they uncovered Gerald's upper body and head they saw the blood.

GERALD WAS STILL unconscious and shivering. They had made him comfortable, retrieved his bedroll to keep him warm and treated his head wound. The nasty gash ran from his forehead to back above his left ear. It still wept drops of blood, but the flow was lessening. Steve was unsure if that was good news or bad. *If his blood pressure was dropping, it would bleed less, too,* he thought.

"Is he going to be okay?" JD asked. The deep concern evident in the boy's voice. This man—this stranger—was the closest thing to family he had right now.

Steve shook his head. "I don't know. We've done all we can for him out here." The sounds of the falling water and constant mist provided a surreal backdrop for the disaster. Last month they could have waited for river rescue. An ambulance or EMTs would have been waiting onshore to start treating the patient. He thought he had seen a hospital back near the shore of the little town they had just floated past. Gerald could have been in a room receiving medical care within minutes. Now that hospital was abandoned; the signs of the fire visible from each window as they passed. No fire or rescue would be coming. It was up to them.

"That cut looks deep, and he may have a concussion," Steve said.

"Is that bad?"

"It can be . . . I think. I'm not really sure. I mean, I know it's not good, but I guess there are varying degrees of one. All are bad, but some are probably worse."

JD kept the makeshift bandage pressed against the wound. "So, what else can we do?"

Steve tried to think, but most of his medical knowledge revolved around his son's condition, not first aid. "I remember hearing that you shouldn't let someone with a concussion go to sleep." They both looked at Gerald's still unconscious face. He had resisted all attempts at awakening. "Guess we failed on that one. Probably just an old wives' tale anyway." He had checked the man's body for other injuries and saw none. Nothing obvious at least. Numerous other cuts, scrapes and bruises. He had no idea how they might recognize internal injuries.

They sat there trying to revive him, giving up eventually and just trying to make him comfortable. "JD, I think we are doing all we can for him. Keep him as warm as we can, apply pressure to the wound until the bleeding stops and wait." He leaned up, looked again at the broken wreck of the raft. "Hey—if you are ok for a few minutes with him, I'm going to see if I can find any of our missing supplies. A few of the drums floated off; they may still be close enough to find."

"You aren't leaving us, are you?" The boy asked, worry noticeable in his voice.

Steve gave a practiced smile meant to offer reassurance, but JD was not one of his customers wondering if this was indeed a good deal on a new car. The smile disappeared. "I'm not. I am going to take these two drums and use them to swim down to the next bend. If I see our stuff, I'll go after it. If not, then I will be right back. The water looks shallow, and the current isn't very strong here, so it should be easy. You should be able to see me most of the time. JD, we need those supplies, I have to try before they get away."

He tied the two drums together with a small piece of broken pallet between and floated it out into the main body of water. It was only up to his thighs, so he walked it as far as he could. He told JD to yell if he needed him but realized he'd never hear him over the sound of the waterfall. The river ahead seemed to fork into several narrower channels. A large island with a small hill was in the middle. As he got closer, the water began to deepen, so he pushed himself up on the platform and began to kick with his feet. As the depth increased, the meager current slowed even more.

He chose the right side of the island and searched the overgrown banks for any signs of the supply drums. The island was several hundred yards long, and he had made it nearly to the end when he spotted something blue bobbing beneath a grove of overhanging limbs. Maneuvering his makeshift raft was hit or miss, but eventually, he got close enough to see it was indeed one of their drums. He pulled it free only to realize it was one of the empty ones, only useful for flotation. He tied it off to his raft and continued to circumnavigate the island.

Things kept bumping into his submerged body. The dark muddy water was hard to see through, but he didn't really want to know what it was. They had seen hundreds of turtles all at least the size of a football with pointed, beak shaped mouths. Several huge catfish as long as his leg had also been spotted as they floated downriver. Gerald had mentioned that they should try and catch some to eat. Steve was just hoping they didn't eat him.

Paddling back upstream was more difficult than he expected, but not impossible. He could see the dam in the distance and knew the spot in the white mist where his friends were. It got closer each time he looked up, so he concentrated on searching for more supply drums. Something on the island caught his attention. He paddled nearer to that side to get a closer look. What first appeared to be a small bit of clothing morphed into a tarp as he got closer. Hidden on this far side of the tiny island was a campsite with a ramshackle looking fishing cabin. He paddled up parallel with it and saw no sign it was occupied. No smoke from a campfire, no noise, no signs of cleaned fish. He checked his movement down-current by holding onto a limb as he scrutinized the scene intently.

After ten minutes, he was convinced it was unoccupied. Someone had set this up out of sight of anyone. This was probably state-owned land, so no permits would have been issued for its construction. He decided to go and take a look.

31

It took several hours for them to move Gerald to the island and into the cabin. "He looks kinda blue," JD stated.

Indeed, his color wasn't good. He hadn't regained consciousness all day. Other than a few moans when they moved him, he hadn't made a sound. "I think we need a fire. We have to warm him up." A fire was risky, smoke could be seen and smelled, but he felt they were not likely to be easily detected out here. JD gathered dry wood from the abundant deadfall of trees and began piling it near the cabin.

Steve had rewrapped Gerald's head wound with a fresh bandage and now covered the older man with his blanket. The day had been warm, but a slight early autumn chill hung in the evening air. He tossed JD the lighter, and the boy soon had coaxed a nice fire in a shallow pit. "Don't make it too large. We don't need a lot and don't want it to be seen." JD nodded silently.

They had warmed some cans of soup and sat listening to the various sounds of the river. "He saved our lives, didn't he?"

Steve had been so lost in his own thoughts, the boy's words barely registered. "Huh? Oh yeah, he did. I suppose he did . . . again. He's a good man, JD. We are lucky we found him."

"I think he found us," the boy said. "Why would he bother? I mean he could have gone on alone, and he would probably have been home already. Why, why did he do this?"

It was a good question; one Steve thought he understood but had wondered on it as well. "I don't know." He knew Gerald's reasons for sticking with JD, but the man's determination and commitment to him and the boy went beyond even that. "Something in him that is different than most people, I guess. I suppose it could be just what he said, strength in numbers and all, but I believe it's more than that. This isn't even the best route to get to his place—I think he wanted to make sure I could get home first."

"He did," JD agreed. "He told me that when you were out with that headache. That we should try to get you back to your family."

"My family?"

"Yeah, he said you needed us."

"JD, what about your family? Aren't you ready to get back to them?"

In the fading light, Steve could just make out the boy's shoulders shrug. "I'd like to get home I guess, but . . . "

The silence grew. "But you aren't sure what you will find there?"

JD remained silent, images of finding his grandmother still fresh in his mind. He felt the sting of tears as his eyes began watering.

Steve placed a hand on the boy's knee. "I do understand. I have the same fears about mine. Are they ok? Will they still be there? We know how tough it is right now, but at least our families were at home. They are probably doing fine and more worried about us. I'm sure yours is, at least."

JD nodded noncommittally. He poked at the fire. "Steve, do you think your family is? Ok, I mean. So, you think they are ok?"

Steve leaned back and stared out at the silhouettes of treetops swaying in the gentle breeze before answering. "My son, Trey, is autistic. He has . . . he can be quite challenging. Trey won't understand any of this. All he will know is his games don't work, and his shows won't come on. He needs a lot of stimuli, otherwise, he gets very agitated. My wife doesn't deal so well with him when he is like that. She gets impatient and upset herself, which doesn't help keep Trey calm at all." He leaned back against the rough lumber siding the cabin. "I think things may have gone very badly there already, JD."

"Wow . . . sorry, man," JD said in a near whisper.

Steve had no idea why he had been so honest with the kid, sharing fears and shadows of ideas that he refused to even let himself consider until now. He looked at JD and marveled at how composed the young man was. How adaptable he was.

"I get in trouble a lot at school."

The boy's sudden confession surprised him. Then he realized he was probably just attempting to empathize with his son's condition. "Oh? Why is that?"

"I dunno, just get bored and would rather be doing something else."

"Lots of us do that. I get bored in business meetings and let my attention drift every day."

"But, you are the boss. . . . You can get away with it."

It was Steve's turn to shrug. "True, but it's not smart to do it."

JD looked deeper into the glowing embers. "I wish school had taught us more about this stuff, life . . . how to survive. Things that I could use now."

"Very true," Steve agreed. "That would have indeed been helpful. I suppose they were training us to survive in the world we had . . . not in this one. Now we get to learn 'on the job' as they say." He leaned forward. "JD, let me just say this. I have only known you for a few days, but I believe you're very well equipped for this world. Even if things don't get back to normal, you will be fine. You're smart, quick thinking and you pay attention. Maybe school wasn't your thing, but survival . . . well, that seems to be. If I was a betting man, my money would be on you."

JD nodded. The sounds of the night were interrupted by the sound of Gerald retching from inside the cabin.

$\sim$

GERALD WAS in and out of consciousness all night. When he was awake, he was nauseated—vomiting on himself several times before either of the others could get to him. Steve felt helpless as he watched his friend resting fitfully. He recalled again the old wives' tale of not letting someone with a concussion sleep. He still couldn't recall any reason why, and it was not like they had much of a choice. The fall had knocked the man unconscious. Rest was about the only treatment they could provide. He had managed to get Gerald to drink some water when he woke before. Just enough to rinse his mouth, but maybe it would help.

He and JD took turns keeping watch through the night. They banked the fire, and the residual heat kept the small cabin comfortably warm. Steve was unsure what to do next. Who knew how long Gerald would be out of commission. *Will he even recover?* Questions and uncertainty stormed through his head. A whippoorwill began to croon somewhere down the river. *Focus on what you can control, not what you can't.*

They would likely be here a few days. What did that mean? Well, they would need to make it a real camp. They had lost half of their supplies, so they needed to forage and maybe fish. Keep what food they had as a reserve. He had seen lots of the big turtles. Maybe they were edible. Lots of water obviously, but it would need to be boiled and filtered. They needed medical supplies, bandages and probably antibiotics. Gerald was now running a low fever. Perhaps the burned-out hospital he saw would have something useful. He thought on all of this for several more hours, and by the time he woke JD for his shift, he had a plan. First some rest, but come daylight, the rat would need to come alive again.

32

Gerald regained consciousness the next morning but seemed confused. Steve thought the fever was worse, too. The older man remembered none of the accident but was eating a little and drinking some of the sports drink. JD had found an old fishing line in the river. Something Gerald had called a trot line. It had hooks dangling from lead lines every few feet. JD was scouring the island looking for something to use for bait. Steve remembered something a friend had told him once: "The catfish will eat nearly anything, don't be too picky."

JD was also going to keep a check on Gerald while Steve crossed over to the far bank and went ashore looking for supplies. He took only his knife, small pack, one of the pistols and just enough food for a single meal. Gerald tried to talk him out of it but didn't have the energy to really argue. As soon as JD had secured the now baited trot line, Steve grabbed one of his barrel floats, carried it to the tip of the island and jumped into the river.

The river carried him several hundred yards downstream before he reached the shore. He climbed out of the water and up the small bank, then used an attached rope to pull the drum back up near the old mill dam. There was a sandy beach area he hadn't noticed before, and he tied the drum off to some trees on the near side. He started to cross the sand, then noticed the animal tracks. Deer, birds and what he thought might be raccoon tracks crisscrossed the light brown sand. His tracks would stand out as well. Instead, he walked along the river edge until the sand gave way to more grasses and rocks. *Think like a rat. Focus!*

He guessed the old hospital was back upstream about a mile, but the overgrowth on the river's edge was too thick to penetrate, so he veered away from the Chattahoochee hoping he would find a road or other development. The remnants of the mill were beside the river just ahead, the red brick being slowly overtaken by kudzu vines. He had no idea what kind of mill it would have been. *What were the crops and industry around here back then . . . cotton, maybe?*

Ok, it's an old mill. There should be a road coming to it, look for that. The "road" turned out to be more of an overgrown walking trail now, but he could see it open up not far away. There, it intersected with what looked to be a major road with numerous houses and busi-nesses. As he neared, he eased into the shadows of the trees again. While the numbers of people they had seen on the interstate had diminished over the last few days, small towns like this could be a different story.

As he had done when he was on his own, he stuck to backsides of buildings and side streets as he moved toward the hospital. Every move was planned, and he took time to sit, listen and scout before moving across any open space. The area was typically small town: barber shops, auto repair, hardware and pet grooming. The appear-ance was deceiving; he knew that. Everywhere seemed to hold secret dangers these days. What was hiding in this one?

His goals were food and medical supplies, but he also wanted a waterways map. He and his companions' lack of knowledge on the river had almost been fatal . . . still could be, in fact. Here he was, a man who had it made, owned multiple houses and a life most would envy, reduced to sneaking and stealing what he could to survive. The irony was a kick to his ego, but *shit,* screw his ego. He wanted to survive, and he had to get home.

He saw small groups of people out. All were armed. Most were checking abandoned cars and buildings, presumably doing the same thing he was. He hid and waited for them to move on before continuing. It took a couple of hours to get near the medical park. The large, gray monolith in the middle was the hospital. Various smaller buildings surrounded the complex. Medical services and doctors' offices, he assumed. They, too, might have the supplies he wanted.

As he neared, he saw most of them had been broken into already. Doors hung ajar, windows were broken and trash littered the parking areas and sidewalks. Maybe a lot more people were having medical issues than he realized. His assumption had been the food stores and gas stations would have been the first thing to go. Then maybe liquor stores, but he was now looking at a small dentist's office that had been ransacked completely. It made no sense to him. He moved along the edge of the small road noticing a road sign announcing it as Medical Parkway West. Somewhat grandiose for the modest establishments, but he was used to exaggeration—he was a car dealer. *Now . . . I'm a rat.*

He heard voices and then shouting from the direction of the hospital. Melding back into the thick shrubs along the road, he slowly eased forward to see who was out there.

WELL, shit. In front of the old hospital was a lush green lawn, several acres at least. Possibly land for expansion that now, would never happen. The lawn seemed to be crawling with people. Some were obviously high, dancing, shouting, even having sex. Others appeared to be former patients, some still in tattered hospital gowns. He realized that many of the people lying on the grass didn't move. His eyes began to pick out more detail including what had to be stacks of bodies on the far side, the unrecognizable mass covered with vultures and crows. *Oh shit!* . . . the nausea hit him about the time the smell did. He fought to keep it down, then gave up and just tried to be somewhat quiet as he vomited.

"Why are all these people here?" he said quietly to himself.

"Drugs," came a small female voice from even deeper in the overgrowth.

He jumped back involuntarily. So surprised was he at not being alone, that he all but leaped out of his concealment. "Wh . . . who's there?" he asked nervously. He scrambled in his pack for the pistol. He should have kept it in his pants pocket . . . *stupid, stupid.*

"Calm down," the voice came again. "I couldn't hurt you if I wanted to."

His heart was racing, and he couldn't find the gun, so he just gave up. Better to just run away anyway. "I'm not looking for trouble, ma'am."

The tired sounding voice came again: "Good to hear, now will you please give me a hand?"

A slender arm and outstretched hand extended into the dappling of sunlight. He tentatively reached out his own hand and took it. A sudden weight pulled at him, then eased off. He realized the woman had stood up from where she must have been crouched. "Oh damn, thanks. My legs had gone to sleep I had sat there so long. She moved closer, and he could see she was young, probably only in her early twenties and very pregnant. "I'm Janice."

"Steve," he responded, nerves finally beginning to calm. "So, what is going on over there, other than the obvious?"

"Oh, you mean the screwing, shooting and get'n high?"

He nodded.

"They are just celebrating, or mourning . . . not really sure which. Maybe an end of the world party. I heard them yelling the president was dead. Hell, I don't know."

He took a better look at her. She was still in a thin hospital gown. "And why are you here?"

"I was a high-risk pregnancy on mandatory bed rest. When the power went off I came down here to the hospital. They still had lights on, and they admitted me. That only lasted about a week. The generators ran out of fuel. The nurses and staff stopped showing up, probably because they realized they weren't going to get paid and had their own families to worry about. Patients started dying. No one brought any food for a few days. It was getting pretty desperate, then all the meth heads and druggies started showing up. I guess their normal supplies began drying up, and this seemed like the best place to get more. Do you have any food? Anything I can eat?"

"Um, sure, a little." He rummaged in the pack and came up with a few snack bars and the can of soup he had brought. She popped the top off the soup and drank it down cold.

"Oh my God, thank you, thank you. I haven't eaten anything in days, and I am starving."

She pointed back out to the mass of people. "They cleaned out the pharmacy in hours. Most got so high they couldn't handle it. They took whatever meds they found, some of them died immediately, I guess from whatever they took. Others went a little crazy, hallucinating, shouting and stuff. It was scary." She wiped an errant noodle from the corner of her mouth then licked her lips. "They started gathering up patients in wheelchairs and gurneys. Just dumping them out here or throwing them out windows if they were too high up to get 'em downstairs. I hid inside but decided to sneak out here a few nights ago. Not sure what they would do if they found me."

"So, the entire hospital has been looted, no supplies, no medicines anywhere?"

She gave a sober chuckle. "I don't think you would find a dirty aspirin in that place now. They even ripped the meds dispensers out at all the nurses' stations. Those things are like ATMs for pills. Didn't slow those bastards down a bit."

Well, he assumed he didn't have to risk going in and checking it out now. "What about these other offices around? I just need to find first-aid supplies. Maybe some antibiotics."

"Oh," she said brightly. "That's easy. I thought you needed like, cancer drugs or something."

"Do I look like I have cancer?" he said concerned.

She studied him and pushed his face up into a beam of sunlight. "No . . . not really. Just old, I guess."

Wow. He loved young people. "Ok, so where would I look for that stuff?"

"Make you a deal," she said. "Help me get back home, and I'll tell you. It's not that far."

He was sure he was being played, or maybe even set up, but he also couldn't abandon a girl in her condition. "Ok, deal."

33

Steve helped Janice out of her hiding spot, and she leaned on him as they turned away from the hospital. Her feet were clumsy, and she nearly stumbled several times. "I'm sorry, miss, but I don't think you are in any condition to walk home."

"It's Mrs., and you're right, Captain Obvious, but it's better than taking my chances with these fruitcakes."

They wound their way back through a maze of paths in the foliage and out the far side. "So, where is your husband?"

"No idea," she said as she straddled a small hedge that separated the small medical office buildings. "He's a Marine, or was a Marine. Not sure they are even a thing anymore. Not sure what or where he is either. Last contact I had he was on temporary assignment on a Navy ship."

Damn, he thought. That would suck. People in the military might be stuck wherever they were deployed and might not get to check in with family even in an emergency like this. Hell, especially in an emergency like this. He offered a weak, "Sorry," but she just shrugged and kept walking. The girl may be in the late stages of pregnancy and supposed to be on bed rest, but now she was outpacing him. "Don't you need to . . . I dunno, take it easy? I mean, it's not a race. We can move a little slower, can't we?"

She twisted her head to face him. Her sharp angular features and jawline set in a grimace. "Look, asshole . . . I mean, Steven. I am about to pop, I have to pee every goddamn minute and this freaking monster keeps flooding my body with hormones. Oh yeah, and the world went to shit, and my hospital was burned out. I am about to snatch the head off of the next person that speaks to me, so yeah, we are in a hurry. She stepped away from him and began walking unassisted. "I need you to watch our back and be ready to catch me when the flood of adrenaline is gone, which will likely be in the next few minutes."

Nothing he thought of seemed particularly useful to say at that moment, so he simply nodded and fell into lockstep behind her. Her curly brown hair bounced as she basically waddled across the litter-strewn lots. She had spunk. He could only imagine how difficult forced bed rest must have been on her. They cleared the medical park and turned back in the general direction he had come from earlier, but several streets over from the busy main highway.

With the stress of the hospital scene well behind them, he caught up to her and began helping her along when she struggled. Twice she stopped and put her hands on her hips and leaned back. "God, this hurts!"

He briefly feared she was going into labor and had no idea what he would do if that were the case. He knew the basics, way back when he had taken the Lamaze classes with his wife and was prepared to go in. Trey decided to come early, though. Emergency C-section in the middle of the night. He had paced in the waiting room just like new fathers had done for many years. "Are you going to be ok?"

"Dude, relax. I'm not having a baby. It's called pregnancy. It's like an alien has invaded my body. It's not pleasant, and today he doesn't seem to want me to move, so I think he is pressing on my bladder and my spine. Oh fuck, I gotta pee."

She squatted where she stood pulled her panties down and let it flow. The sounds of water on the pavement was matched by a huge sigh. Steve was uncomfortable and tried to look everywhere except at Janice. She looked up and laughed. "Man, what did you do before all this?"

"Me? Oh...I um. . . ran a car dealership."

"Seriously? You ran a car dealership, and you don't know where to look for first aid supplies?" She scanned the scattering of cars and walked up to a newer model luxury SUV that was blocking most of an intersection. It was unlocked. She opened the door reached down and found the manual release for the trunk lid. He followed her back as she ripped a black first aid kit that was held in place by Velcro to the sides of the cargo compartment. She tossed it to him. "Soccer moms have to be able to treat lil' Johnny's boo-boos. I guess you didn't sell a luxury brand, huh?"

"Thanks, and no, I mainly sell . . . or sold Fords."

"There you go, see, I love the domestic stuff, but you gotta admit these import guys know how to set themselves apart. They get the little things right, man. Shit like this. Useful, ya know?" She lowered the hatch and started walking again.

This girl was not stupid; she was resourceful and tenacious. If this pregnancy didn't kill her, she would make it. He felt sure of that. "Excuse me, did I hear you say the president is dead?"

"Yep."

He waited, but she didn't elaborate. "Just yep? You can't just give a one-word answer for that."

"Sure I can, just did. Besides, not like that is even the most important news anymore."

Frustrated, he caught up beside her again. "Ok, well do you know any of the details?"

"Not really. Some of the dopeheads had a radio. I could hear parts of it from my hiding spot. Said there had been some kind of incident. The president and several members of his cabinet were killed. They were invoking a succession pact or act or whatever. Now some secretary person was being sworn in. The junkies thought it was hilarious, yelling some anarchist bullshit and firing guns in the air and crap. That was when one of the dipshits set the hospital on fire."

∼

THEY WALKED in silence for several minutes before Steve asked, "Janice, what did you do before all this?"

"Mostly followed my husband around the country. I was staying here with my mom for the pregnancy. When he gets a permanent assignment, I'll move there." She went silent for several steps. "I guess that probably won't be happening now." She stopped and bent over, catching her breath again. "Ok, I need you please." She reached out and wrapped an arm around his waist. He supported her as best he could as they resumed walking. "Before that, I worked at several vet clinics."

"Like veteran hospitals?" Steve said.

"No, not that kind of vet, vet-er-i-na-rian." She drew the word out like she was talking to a child.

"Oh."

"Yeah, I like animals. Wanted to be a vet, and there is almost always a couple of veterinary clinics no matter where I was living. You know it is harder to get in vet school than medical school now? Anyways, that is where we are going to get your antibiotics."

"What? Animal medicine?"

"Sure, Humans are mammals. Not that it really matters, we give fish the same antibiotics. Lots of it works just fine on people. Same stuff, really." She pointed to a small, neat house on an upcoming corner. "That's one there. I used to work there when I was in school."

Steve was surprised the office hadn't been looted. In fact, nothing seemed to have been touched. Getting in the old office was painless as the spare key was still in the same hiding spot they used when she had worked there. Fifteen minutes later they were on their way again. He now carried antibiotics as well as several other medicines and some stretch bandages. He was again upset with himself for not thinking of this, not that he would have known about the antibiotics. "Thank you. This really means a lot. My friend's life might depend on it."

She gave him a brief head nod. "Only a few more blocks to my house. I wasn't going to ask, but I'm pretty sure you aren't from around here. Where are you and your friend at, and where ya going?"

He was uncomfortable telling her much, but increasingly he thought he could trust her, and she seemed to have better survival skills than himself. "Heading close to Albany, my friend is back at our camp. We have been on the road heading south since the . . . the thing happened."

"So, you were farther north? What, like Atlanta?"

"Yeah, basically. My friend was, at least. I was a bit farther than that." He had not mentioned JD to this point and decided to still keep that to himself.

She turned down a side street. It looked idyllic with a thick canopy of shade trees overlooking rows of identical small, older homes. "But your friend is hurt? How did that happen, were you attacked?"

"You ask a lot of questions."

"Sorry, just curious," she said with a smile. "No internet or social media anymore. Kinda starved for new information."

He got that. "We have been attacked yes, but his injury came from an accident on the river. We decided to use the Chattahoochee to go south but didn't even make it an hour before running into trouble. We went over an old waterfall."

She stopped and looked at him. "You got on a river without knowing the dangers? Are you stupid?"

He was embarrassed but nodded. "Obviously."

"Damn, I mean dam. You only went over one? You were lucky. I think there are six or seven dams and two large lakes in the next forty miles of river. You went over the first one—the old mill dam. There will be another one just downstream, called Crowhop, nearly as dangerous, possibly another one about five miles farther, although I believe you can stay left and bypass it. Y'all are really taking some chances out there though. This is what they call the fall line, the river drops hundreds of feet before reaching Columbus. Several other dams downstream."

"Wow, had no idea there were more ahead of us, thanks for that.

We knew it was dangerous, but the roads and towns are worse." He told her more about some of what they had seen. She had no idea what the Army, or whoever they were, was doing at the big camp a day's walk back up the interstate.

"Got no idea on that, nothing really important around here. The closest military is Fort Benning down south. Doesn't sound good, though. Maybe we are being invaded. I mean if our president is dead, and the rest of our government is probably non-existent, maybe Russia or China decided to take us over?"

To Steve, it was not an unreasonable assumption. It was one he had considered as well. "If what happened was only to the US, I would accept that possibility, but I think the blackout may have been worldwide, or most of it. Not based on many facts, just a feeling."

"Hmm, great, that would mean we probably aren't being conquered but also means it's going to be even longer before we get beyond this." She slowed and pointed at a house with a neat yard and said, "We're here."

A voice called out from behind a screen door, "That's far enough, mister." The thick barrel of a shotgun slid through a slit in the screen. "Don't move a muscle."

34

"Whoa," Steve raised his hands, full attention focused on the black barrel aimed at his chest. He slowly eased himself behind a white SUV that was parked by the house.

"Mom, put the gun down. He was just helping me get home."

The mean looking gun dropped slightly but was still pointing in his general direction. Janice waved him forward. "She's harmless . . . mostly."

He walked up the few steps to where Janice held the door open. He could now see the woman with the gun was in a wheelchair. Greetings were quickly exchanged, and Janice brought her mom up to date on the situation at the hospital.

"I told you, honey, I told you. After the police all went AWOL, the hospital would be overrun. Didn't I tell ya that?"

"Yes, Mom, you said it." Janice gave Steve a wink as she rolled her mom back deeper into one of the small dimly lit rooms. "What is all this stuff out for?" She pointed at numerous bags and boxes scattered around the floor. Steve stepped inside the house uncertainly. The door swung shut behind him.

Her mom answered, "Your uncle is coming by tomorrow to take me, uh, take us out to his place."

"His place, you mean out to the farm? How is he going to do that, and how do you know?" Janice responded looking through some of the bags.

"Your cousin Will came by on his bike earlier and said his dad finally had a truck working and could come get us. I wasn't sure how we would get word to you, but I am almost out of water and food here."

"So, you were just going to let me and the new baby come back to an empty house?"

"What baby? You still just as pregnant as when you left, child."

Steve was uncomfortable intruding on this family's internal discussions, but neither woman seemed to care he was there. The discussion seemed to escalate into full-blown bickering within minutes. Janice was going through cabinets looking for something to eat, her voice raising with every cabinet door she slammed. "Did you eat everything in the pantry? We had enough food here for weeks." She stormed back out. "How much did you give to him? How much, Mom?"

Her mom tried to look defiant but meekly said, "Only a little. He said the church needed it."

"Mom, the church was burned over a week ago, nothing down there anymore. He's . . . ugh! I bought that food for us. For you, for me, to eat after the baby . . . "

Steve made a slight sound. "Maybe it's better if I am on my way. Very nice meeting y'all, and thanks, Janice."

Both women turned to him and smiled, then began to laugh. "Oh, hush up and have a seat. We'll be done with this in a minute." The mom pointed at a faded gold loveseat for him to sit. Over the next hour, Steve came to realize the banter back and forth was just how the two communicated. Nothing mean-spirited about it, just blunt, raw and apparently, very normal.

Janice had heated up several cans of chili and brought him a bowl. "Thanks again for helping me get home." He nodded. "I know you need to get back to your friend, but I have a few things for you first."

He stopped eating. "Janice, I can't take anything from you. You have been extremely kind already."

'Hush, it's not like that anyway. Hell, you can tell we don't have much to offer." She gave a lopsided grin. "No, I have a river map that might help you, and I think I have an idea on something else you might want."

He had told her about losing the raft and supplies on the journey from the hospital. She again asked if he was stupid trying to make that run on a makeshift raft. She left the room and he heard shuffling and rattling papers. Minutes later she returned holding a faded map with "Chattahoochee River System" printed on the front flap. She then proceeded to give him some ideas on where he might find a boat or two.

"Janice, thank you for everything. You have saved my life several times already, I'm sure."

She leaned in and gave him a hug and a peck on his bearded cheek. "Just stop being stupid. You seem mostly like a good guy. . . . I mean, for a sleazy car salesman. Try and stay alive, not many good ones left." He thought he felt a brief kick from her swollen belly before she smiled and pulled back.

He paused while walking back up the street to look back at the small house with the neat yard. A pregnant woman and her disabled mother had just helped him. It should have been the other way around. His karma bank had to be running low. He had been lucky too often already. He was right to be worried.

JD WAS CLEANING two large fish when Steve returned. "How is our patient doing, doc?" The boy just shook his head.

"I don't know. In and out, but he's hot and he stopped drinking anything."

The infection Steve had feared was real. He would have to get him to drink water and keep it down for the antibiotics to work. He was out of his league here, but all he could do was try. "Those fish look great, how you want to cook 'em?"

"Sticks over the fire, I guess. Unless you have a different idea."

He briefly thought about maybe having him make a type of soup, something they could get Gerald to eat; then he realized they still had canned soup. "That sounds good, may want to make a rack of green sticks as catfish won't hold together well when it cooks; it will flake apart."

"Oh, these are catfish? I wasn't sure. I love catfish, especially fried with hushpuppies."

"Damn, JD. Yeah, I do too," Steve said. "I am sure these will be delicious, though." They were, too. The two of them ate all they could and still had fish leftover. Steve finally got Gerald awake and forced a bit of water down him. He had ground up one of the tablets into the water, and he prayed it would stay down. The man was burning up, but the head wound finally looked better. The swelling was nearly gone. Five minutes later he was vomiting again. Gerald had too many things going wrong; Steve didn't know what to do for him, so he decided to just treat him with what he had. Each time Gerald woke, Steve tried again with the antibiotic-laced water. Finally, late that night, Gerald went back to sleep without throwing up.

"Is Mr. Gerald going to make it?"

"I don't know, JD. He's tough, and the medicine should help. You like him, don't you?

"I trust him. He helped me when I was about to make a big mistake, I think. He knows a lot of stuff."

"You're afraid if it is just me and you, I won't be as good as him at keeping us safe or getting you back to your folks?"

"Kinda, but not really. I mean, Y'all are different."

Steve loved the honesty of kids. "It's ok. I am worried about that, too. I'm not good at this stuff."

The fire was down to just glowing coals now. JD was looking out over the rolling waters. Hearing more than seeing their passage south. "Mr. Steve, I did a bad thing."

"Just call me Steve, and when was this?" JD's shoulder shrugged. Steve heard a sniff and realized the boy was crying. All they had been through, this was the first time he had seen JD seem anything like a child. He moved over near the boy, uncertain as to what to do, but then the dad in him took over. He pulled the boy close and patted his hair. He knew the words would come when they were ready. Through sobs and sniffles, JD eventually got himself under control.

"I don't want to go home. . . My mom—she isn't there."

This was not something Steve had expected. Gerald seemed determined to get JD back to Jacksonville no matter how dangerous it was. "How do you know? Where is she? What about your dad, will he be there?"

JD was leaning up straight now, trying to dry his eyes. "Mom was on a trip overseas, a European vacation with her boyfriend. Dad," he took a long pause, "he's been gone a long time. I have no one to go home to."

Shit, the boy was right. If she were out of the country, she might never make it back. The boy had been carrying this around with him for weeks. So many lost souls, broken families. He thought again to the people walking the roads. American refugees. They were all that now. "I'm sorry, JD. We will figure something out."

"I'm sorry I lied. Mr. Gerald's going to be mad, isn't he?"

"No, son, not at all."

"I wanted to tell him. I was just afraid he would leave me behind. I didn't want the soldiers to put me in the prison camp."

"He wouldn't leave you. He cares for you, as do I. We are family now, ok? We can be your family if you want."

JD looked at him without speaking for a long time. Then he slowly got to his feet and hugged Steve tightly around the neck before quickly heading to bed. *So many lost souls in this new world, lost parents, lost children; will any of us ever be whole again?*

35

MOUNT WEATHER ANNEX – BLUEMONT, VA

The look from the younger woman was withering. "Yes, Mrs. Levy, I . . . " Whatever she was about to say died on her lips.

"Madelyn dear, please don't mistake my faith in you for anything other than what it is. We are all here to serve the republic and our cause." She stepped out of the way while two security guards removed the body of the former director of Homeland Security. "David had a simple mission to do; bring the Navy back under control. He failed to do so. We have no time for failure, dear. As the appointed first secretary you are now the acting president. Now. . . you read the directive, dear, yet you did not take action once being sworn in. Can you please explain why?" She drew out the words for emphasis, the anger evident with each syllable.

Cold sweat ran down Madelyn's spine. The atmosphere here at Bluemont was palpable. The swearing-in had been done in the Council Meeting Room shortly after she arrived. Her newly assigned security detail, who had been her constant shadow since then, waited just outside not daring to enter without permission. She was now president, the first female president of the United States, and she thought, *the one most likely to rule over its demise.* "The initial instructions were challenging to carry out. Communication channels with much of the military leadership are still cut off. We deployed the TSA agents backed up by Homeland's people in the urban resettlement camps. The military has been less cooperative, many of them are questioning—"

The other woman cut her off. "I am not concerned with those— we are dealing with them. Why did you not order the Joint Chiefs to proceed into phase two?" She went on, not waiting for an answer, "You did understand that this was going to be necessary, didn't you? Perhaps, Madelyn, you don't have the stomach for this fight, hmmm?"

While the acting president did not have the stomach for it, she was not about to show weakness. To do so would be suicide. "Mrs. Levy, there has been initial resistance to my authority. My ascent to power was not recognized by some in command. They have been removed, and P5 commanders are now assisting in the establishments of the refugee and resettlement camps. Even you and the Council anticipated some resistance; the First Secretary Protocols were not widely known. Most of the country assumed the Twenty-Fifth Amendment was the only way one could become a non-elected president."

"That amendment was intentionally flimsy and vague, and everyone knew it. If we had allowed it to play out, the leadership would have been in legal limbo for months, while the courts and Congress fought it out. Hmmm . . . I should more accurately say, what's left of those branches. The First Secretary Protocol was approved in secret just after 9/11. The same week as the Patriot Act, in fact. It was designed for just such a situation as now. In the case of incapacitation of the presidency, we could have continuity of government."

Madelyn was quite familiar with the what and how of the law that moved her into office. She was the lone cabinet member who was never allowed to be in the same location as the president. Her former cabinet office in DC was almost never used. The First Secretary Protocol was a safety valve for a potentially catastrophic collapse of the U.S. government. A permanently designated survivor of the executive branch. Strangely, the CME was not the catastrophe that had necessitated the activation. The cause was, instead, something entirely man-made. "Ma'am, it has taken longer than expected, but we will be on schedule by next week."

Mrs. Levy sat on the edge of the polished mahogany desk. "Everyone of any importance is already in the bunkers or protected zones. Our operations overseas are well underway. I don't care what happens anywhere else. Is that clear? What is important is that our supplies are not wasted. The cities are going to fall—they must in fact, fall, and the quicker the better. Use the TSA force, FEMA, Praetor and the military. Make sure they all understand the mission."

The mission . . . that was what she was struggling with. "Yes, ma'am." How to convince them—*order* them—to abandon US citizens to an almost certain death. Not just that, but to hunt down those that might band together and be a threat. Everyone in the military and most in government felt a duty to defend the constitution and, as an extension, the citizens of this country. Now they were being ordered to do just the opposite.

"Madelyn, you will have to purge the ranks. Get rid of those who find phase two distasteful. This is survival. No assistance to major population centers and no resistance that possibly could become organized can be allowed to survive." Mrs. Levy waved a hand dismissively. "Go . . . and make it happen, my dear."

The unspoken threat hung in the air like a sword. Madelyn excused herself and hurried down the concrete corridor, her security detail close on her heels.

36

Gerald was awake the following day but still running a fever. Reluctantly, he agreed to rest and take some of the animal medicine to fight the infection. JD sat with his back against the log door frame holding the soup can and a spoon. "Mr. Steve says you need to eat more."

Gerald gave a crooked smile. "Mr. Steve is a horrible cook and a worse doctor." He took another bite. "And didn't he say just call him Steve or Porter?" The boy nodded. Steve had filled him in on the conversation about JD's family. Something he had already begun to suspect. The twelve-year-old had never seemed all that eager to get back home. Steve also filled him in on his foolish trip into the town. While it was dangerous, he did appreciate the effort, and undoubtedly the drugs would help.

"How's the old man doing?" The voice came from just down the red-clay embankment toward the river.

The boy shrugged. Gerald winked at him. "I'm fine, you mothering old fool, except for being poisoned by . . . what is this stuff anyway?"

Steve edged up to the cabin and sat down the body of a large turtle he had captured. "You aren't fine, you have a fever and quite possibly, a broken rib. That divine elixir you are consuming is a bouillabaisse. We are running low on food so trying to stretch it out."

Gerald took another reluctant bite. "Bouillabaisse, huh? You mean fish soup? Looks more like oily water with bits of . . . of . . . something." He pulled a remnant from his tongue and stared at it with a look of puzzlement. "So, when are we leaving this luxury establishment?"

Steve glanced at JD. "Well, here is the thing. I was ready to leave yesterday, but the boy here, well, he wanted to wait and see if you pulled through." They all laughed somberly. Gerald grasped at his side and shook his head.

"Don't. It hurts to laugh."

"That . . . is why we are staying put. You need to heal, and you won't be any use to us on this river in the shape you are in. We are somewhat safe here, have water, and food is not that hard to get. Also, I have a tip I need to follow-up that might make the rest of our cruise a little less . . . eventful. That is if you can manage to stay alive without us for a while."

JD HELPED DRAG the final kayak up into the bushes. He and Steve had found the location Janice had mentioned the previous day. It had taken a full day to get through the security gate of the old auto body shop to the storage shed. Once there, they had to pry loose a locked iron security bar to open the door. He still had no idea why they would have kept kayaks and canoes locked up behind the business, but he was glad they had.

He and the boy had struggled to carry, and at times, pull the faded plastic boats the half-mile down to the river. Trying to be quiet was hard. If the owners showed up, they would simply look like the thieves they were. Steve was slowly coming to terms with that aspect of himself. On the third trip to the shed, they had gotten the double seat kayak and paddles that were stored on the rafters overhead. Just as they crossed the road and into the woods, they began to hear voices. The two of them had crouched down and hidden for an hour waiting for the sounds to fade.

Gerald looked the boats over. "They ain't pretty, but damn, that was a good find, Steve."

Steve nodded, Gerald was doing better, but after five days they were all ready to leave this muddy fish camp. "Thanks, should help. We still need more supplies, though. Should we head back up to the interstate and scout some more trucks? We still have the bolt cutters." They had found the heavy tool at the bottom of the dam near the wrecked raft.

"No, I don't think we should backtrack. Not really looking forward to going over that waterfall again."

They all agreed. Steve had already gone downstream and checked out the next one. It was an old dam that was even harder to see, but hearing the water pouring over it was obvious. He found a well-used path on the bank for bypassing it. Gerald had studied the map and suggested an afternoon start. He wanted to get into a large lake downstream before making camp. "I do not want to take any more chances out here. Bright afternoon light, we can better see what is coming up."

The meager supplies loaded, Steve took JD out to make sure he could maneuver the boat. "I've kayaked before, Mr., uh, I mean, Steve." The kid did know, too. He stopped dead in the river and rotated the boat in a smooth 360 before continuing. "I grew up near water."

Steve laughed at the remark "grew up" when he was still just a boy, but growing up was exactly what was happening. The boy had matured just in the days he had known him. His childhood was receding from him like a leaf drifting away on the river. The thought saddened him more than he wanted to let on. Every kid should have a childhood. He thought of Trey and the unborn child of the girl, Janice. Did they have a chance? Not to even just be kids, maybe not even at surviving this mess.

They paddled back to the island where Gerald was finishing tying down the last bundle on his canoe. The man still moved wobbly and favored one side but was not complaining. "Load up, man. We are shipping out." The older man grinned as he pushed his larger boat off the bank and into the muddy water.

37

They struggled over the next ancient dam—the one tagged as "Crowhop" on the map. Steve thought there had to be a story with that name but forgot about it as they beached the boats and portaged around the falls. He and JD helped carry Gerald's canoe down as the older man was on light duty. Steve thought Gerald was still a bit wobbly and weak, but, *Damn, the man wouldn't slow down.*

Soon the river began branching into smaller and smaller tributaries. It became difficult to know if they chose the right path or to keep up with exactly where they were in relation to the map. The buildings had disappeared behind them, and for miles, they saw nothing but forest and marshland. The current was gentle, and the three found themselves relaxing for the first time in weeks. JD was uncharacteristically chatty. Getting the nagging secret out about his parents being gone seemed to unleash the boy's social side.

"Mr. Steve?"

"JD, you don't have to call me that. Just Steve or Porter or chief or 'hey you', I don't care, but the mister isn't needed. That's for old folks . . . like him." He motioned with his thumb toward Gerald who answered with an amused huff.

"Sorry, I was just wondering, do you think I'll have to go back to school this fall? I mean, will they be open?"

Steve thought about it. He wasn't even sure what day it was. Must be early September by now, and most schools around here would have already had classes. Stores would hold the back-to-school sales, Friday night football games. It shouldn't have surprised him that this was on the boy's mind, but it did. The mundane, the ordinary . . . how hard it was to leave it behind. He kept thinking about work and his business. School would have been the big thing in a child's life. "Kid . . . I think you are going to get a break this year—in fact, your summer holiday may last a long time." JD grinned. He didn't seem to mind that at all.

Gerald paddled up beside him, "Hey, Chief."

Steve caught the man grinning. "Yeah?" He was clearly feeling better. Something had changed between them. Perhaps it was mutual respect. Steve wasn't sure, but he found himself hoping that was the case. Gerald was the most important member of this group by far, but maybe he had sort of proven some value to the man—he hadn't let him die, at least.

The older man paddled sporadically as he talked. "Tell me again about what the girl said . . . about a new president."

Steve had relayed it all to him back at the fish camp, but the man apparently thought he had misheard some of it in his diminished condition. Steve sighed and went through it all again, everything he could think of Janice saying. They had tried the little radio a few times, but apparently, the river valley blocked them from hearing any broadcasts.

Gerald mulled it all over in silence for several minutes. Steve knew that mind was working; he wasn't particularly sure he cared that it was on this topic. Politics had never been much more than a casual interest to him before the CME. Now it seemed completely pointless. As Janice had said, *it was not the most important news anymore.* "It just seems odd."

Steve looked over at him, "How do you mean?"

"She said. Your pregnant friend . . . she said a secretary had taken over as president?"

"Yeah."

Gerald continued, "I assume that would mean a cabinet member. The Twenty-Fifth Amendment covers succession. To be honest, it is not all that clear on a lot of things, but cabinet members are pretty far down the list."

Steve navigated his kayak around the roots of a downed tree. "How can the constitutional amendment on who can become president be unclear?"

Gerald just shrugged. "It just is. Hard for them to cover every possibility. After the vice-president, it goes to the House speaker, the Senate president pro tem, and then to the cabinet in a rather obscure order. Also. . . no one is actually sure any of that is actually legal . . . I mean constitutionally legal. Members of the legislature are not actually supposed to be able to serve in the executive branch." He stared off into the cloudless sky for several minutes pondering the point. "I wonder how much of our federal government is still left? You have to assume the president, VP, top members of Congress are all gone. It must be absolute chaos."

"It's chaos everywhere, my friend. Washington has just always had a head start on the rest of us."

"Point taken," Gerald said. "Just when we need strong leadership, they put someone completely untested into the Oval Office. Probably one of the former president's old cronies who doesn't know shit and will have his hands tied for years as the courts try to validate his authority."

Steve heard his stomach rumbling as he watched JD go around a bend ahead. In a low voice he said, "Leighton, I don't think this country will have years. It has gone to hell in less than a month. Whoever is in DC will be ruling over a mass cemetery if something doesn't change."

Just then they heard the boy shouting from up ahead. Both men picked up the pace fearing what they would find.

~

THEY PADDLED into the shoals of the river where JD had beached his kayak. Both men eased up gingerly from the hard seats. The four hours of paddling had made them ache all over. JD's enthusiastic gestures got them moving quickly. Gerald reached him first. "Ok, kid, what's got you—" He stopped in his tracks. "No way!"

Incredibly they all were staring at one of the escaped drums of supplies. With all the twists and turns of the river and the myriad of splitting into smaller streams finding one of the lost drums was inconceivable. "Nice find, JD." Steve patted him on the shoulder as he waded into the undergrowth to retrieve the rusting blue cylinder.

"Please be food, please be food," JD began chanting. While they had managed to make their rations last, the food lately had not been great. They were down to emergency supplies. Gerald had estimated that wouldn't last more than four days, maybe six, but only if they cut their intake down to a bare minimum. As long as they were on the water, they felt confident with getting fish, frogs or turtles, but the plan was to get off the river in the next few days and head east.

The drum's lid clamp was clogged with mud and rust, but all of them took turns loosening it, and finally, Steve managed to get it off. All three looked into the barrel expectantly, each of them let out a groan. The drum held nothing but spare clothes, empty knapsacks, some tools and a few plastic tarps still in their wrappers. JD let out an exasperated yell and kicked a rock into the water. Gerald was smiling and began removing the clothes. He divided them up, so each person could carry a bundle.

"Jackpot!" Reaching deep into the bottom he pulled out a stack of canned meat tins. "Tuna fish, of course." Then some sealed desert cakes. "I thought I remembered putting these in this one." JD's eyes lit up seeing the familiar packaging with the little girl on the box.

"Oatmeal cookies. Yes!" he pulled his arm down in a sign of triumph. It wasn't much, but it brightened their spirits. They split one of the tins of tuna, and each took a cookie before continuing on. They all doubted they would spot any of the other drums. At least they had a change of clothes and some shelter for the night.

By late afternoon, the river began splitting and narrowing again, and they could see the trees opening up. "Coming up on the first of the lakes," Gerald said.

"Good, I'm beat. How far do you want to go before stopping?" Steve asked.

Gerald looked uncertain, "Not sure, depends on how developed the shoreline is. Probably best we avoid people for now, if what you saw back at the hospital is any indication of how the rest of the world is. Well . . . think I'm fine being anti-social. According to the map, both sides are only sparsely developed, but the Georgia side is a little more direct to the dam. Let's go to the left and scout the eastern shore for a good campsite.

It took until nearly dark to find an area that was remote enough to feel safe. A copse of trees near the shore with a large fenced pasture behind it gave them some sense of security. "We should be able to see anyone approaching at least," JD said. They were all exhausted and had a cold camp before going to sleep.

Several hours later a booming retort tore through the dark night. "What the fuck?" Gerald was up in an instant looking around. The others groggily came awake just as another flash and boom sounded. Then the rain started to fall. *A thunderstorm, how lovely*, Steve thought. Then he realized—they were no longer alone.

38

The three of them stared into the darkness feeling more than seeing the shapes. "Wh . . . what is that?" JD whispered.

"It's a herd of cows. They must be looking for shelter," Gerald said calmly. "Just don't make any sudden moves. They aren't dangerous unless they get excited. You don't want one running over you." The storm began with the pattering of raindrops building up to a crescendo as the deluge reached its full force. Lightning streaked and forked across the sky, frightening both man and beast.

Steve and JD had taken shelter under one of the blue tarps, and slowly they handed another to Gerald. "Where should we go, back to the lake?"

The older man shook his head, then realized they couldn't see that. "No, lightning and water are much worse than cows. Standing here under these trees isn't smart either." The sounds of the storm made it nearly impossible to hear, but he motioned for the other two to follow. Steve began grabbing up the few supplies they had brought up from the boats. "Leave it," Gerald yelled.

They followed Gerald's billowing blue tarp out into the field until he dropped down in a low spot. They were well away from the cows and the trees. They huddled together trying to keep the rain out of the makeshift shelter. "Are we hiding from the cows or the lightning?" JD asked. Steve thought he knew the answer, but was glad the kid asked anyway.

Gerald had been watching the scene outside through a small opening. "The lightning. Cows are not all that bright. They don't get hit by lightning often, but when they do, it's often like this. They will huddle to get shelter from the rain under trees, and when lightning hits the trees, it may kill a bunch of 'em."

As if on cue a powerful arc hit one of the pines like incoming artillery. Several of the cows ran in the other direction, but the others just stayed where they were. The scene repeated over and over as the storm raged on. "Our camp is toast by now," Steve muttered.

The others nodded. "Just hope the boats are still there in the morning." They had pulled them pretty far up on shore, but Gerald was right. If they lost those, their journey south would be a lot slower. The lightning eased off after a half hour or so, but the storm kept up for much of the night. Rivers of water and mud washed through the depression they were lying in. Sleep was impossible, and trying to keep up a conversation was pointless with the staccato of rain pelting the plastic tarps. It was one of the most miserable nights Steve had ever endured. He imagined it was for his fellow travelers as well.

No matter how much he willed himself not to, his mind kept going to the familiar, he had always loved rainy nights. Sitting in his den with a good book or maybe even a drink. In colder weather, a fire in the big stone fireplace would be crackling. No television or music playing, nothing to break the spell. He would just sit and listen to the rain coming down outside, knowing he was going to sleep soundly that night. Now he lay shivering in the mud with two strangers, praying they didn't get trampled by a stampede of cows or struck by lightning. *Yep, the old life was definitely gone*, he just had to find a way to erase the memories of it.

~

THE LAKE they were on was remarkably undeveloped. It was narrow enough to see both sides most of the time, so they could hug the opposite side whenever they saw houses or the occasional marina. Steve and JD now shared the double kayak, and Gerald was in the other. A tree limb had come down in the storm and punctured the kayak the boy had been using. The cows had also destroyed everything left at the campsite. Luckily, there was not much in the way of supplies there. They had lost the river map, which was disappointing. They knew they had a series of dams coming up, and somewhere ahead was Columbus, one of the largest cities in Georgia.

They were planning to be off the river before reaching the city, but without the map, it was more of a guess now. The next day they portaged the boats around an older hydroelectric dam. The river on the far side seemed wide for just a river, and calm. Steve thought that it, too, must have a dam, but neither of them could remember for sure; nor where it might be. They camped again in deep forest on the river's edge.

"I've been thinking . . . " Steve resisted the urge to make a smart-ass comment, so Gerald continued: "Without power to operate the floodgates on the dams, these reservoir lakes are just going to keep filling until they overflow."

"Wouldn't they have spillways open to prevent that?"

"I dunno . . . maybe. Not sure they will help. If one dam upstream fails, then all of 'em could. You saw how high the water was on that last one. I don't think it was always that way. The storm dumped a lot more water into that reservoir. Even spillways will get clogged with fallen trees and debris if they aren't maintained. How long can that go on before something bad happens?"

"Wow, thanks, Leighton, for cheering us up with all your optimism. You are just a beacon of dark, aren't you?"

Gerald patted Steve as he pulled the plastic bag with the small radio out of his pack. "Just doing my part, Porter. Need my fellow travelers to be ready for anything."

They all gave a nervous chuckle as he powered the little radio on and began spinning the dial. On the first pass, all they heard was varying levels of static. Gerald then checked a series of specific frequencies he seemed to have memorized. On one of these, they could faintly hear a woman's monotone voice repeating a random series of numbers. Gerald got a puzzled look on his face, and Steve was about to ask what the numbers were, but the broadcast faded, and he went to another channel.

Gerald didn't want to run the batteries down so was limiting himself to how long to keep the little unit on. This had been the first night in weeks they had heard anyone transmitting. Just as he was about to call it quits, he stumbled across another very faint broadcast. The white noise nearly drowned out the man's voice, but he could just hear it if he used small earbuds that were packed with the radio.

Steve watched as his friend listened intently to whatever the conversation was. He would have never guessed that his desire for information could be nearly as strong as the need for food. Living in this vacuum, purposefully out of contact with people, felt unbelievably isolating. His life and his business had all been about people. He enjoyed the social interaction, even the casual banter, between acquaintances. Now he lived in a world that was mostly silent. The noise of daily life he'd always taken for granted was now nothing more than a muted breeze blowing over a lazy river.

Gerald suddenly grabbed a pencil stub and the notebook from his pack and began writing. Finishing, he removed the white earbuds and turned off the radio. "Whoa . . . man, we gotta talk." His voice left no doubt that something serious was up.

39

"In short, the world has gone to shit."

"No, duh!" said JD.

"Ditto," echoed Steve.

"No, worse . . . much worse," Gerald sighed.

Steve leaned up against a tree. "Who were you listening to?"

"Just a guy, says he's a patriot. Wouldn't give a real name, not even his official call sign. Said he was worried about 'them' triangulating his location. Probably just some prepper, but he's got a good radio rig and must scan for radio signals every night. He seems to know a lot that is going on."

"Like what?"

"Well, he said something is going on in Tallahassee, at the college there. He also said our new president has issued several emergency orders limiting travel, hoarding of supplies and temporarily outlawing firearms."

Steve looked shocked. "He can't do that, it's unconstitutional."

"She."

"Huh?" Steve said confused.

"*She* can't do that. Apparently, we now have our first female president." Gerald paused and let that sink in. "People are also being 'encouraged' to vacate the larger cities for the aid camps." He did the air quotes thing while saying encouraged. "The camps are being run by TSA, FEMA and Homeland personnel as well as another para-military group that no one seems to know much of anything about. He thinks they may be a mercenary army. In short, America is turning into a police state."

"So that camp we saw was one of those—an aid camp?"

Gerald shrugged. "I suppose. He said they were set up along major travel routes and near significant population centers. From what he is hearing, the larger cities have fallen into anarchy: food has mostly run out, clean water is scarce, medical care is gone. Those people that relied on handouts to survive have nothing. Judges made the prisons release all the inmates since they couldn't feed 'em. No standing police force remains anywhere, so every gang member, drug dealer, and petty thief is now able to operate without much fear of consequences."

"My God," Steve said in disbelief. He stared over at JD, wondering how much of this the young boy understood. "But still, why would anyone voluntarily go into one of those camps? They look like prison camps—hell, they *are*."

Gerald rubbed a hand through his thinning hair. "Well, that's the really bad news. Apparently, the officials are saying there is also a pandemic sweeping through Europe and Asia. The government is saying that they will close these camps if or when it reaches the US. If you aren't in the camp before that, you won't be getting any protec-tion or ... treatment."

"That sounds like bull. If they had a treatment it wouldn't be a pandemic," Steve said with a tone of disgust.

"Yeah, that is what the guy on the radio said, too. Just scare tactics. He believes this is some mass depopulation scheme. Hey . . . he's probably just some conspiracy nut, but—that doesn't necessarily mean he's wrong."

Steve looked up into a darkening sky, the first few glitters of stars beginning to shine. "God," he sighed, "I have to get home."

"I understand, but that's not going to be easy. If we can't travel the roads freely nor go into any major cities, I'm not sure how we can make it. One other thing, this guy did say he talked with someone over near the Georgia-Florida line. Said smaller cities all through South Georgia had been burned. The man said it looked like Sherman had marched through again." Gerald paused like a doctor about to give bad news to a patient. "Steve, Tifton and Albany were two of the ones he specifically mentioned."

"Well, shit..."

THEY ATE several small fish JD caught before heading downriver again the next day. None of the group spoke much. The news from the previous day was weighing on Steve most of all. He had to get home to Trey and his wife. The questions just kept swirling through his head. *Will there even be a home anymore?* Once he got there, would he even be able to survive? His main thought was that he was leading his new friends into unnecessary dangers. They had decided to stay on the river simply due to the lack of better options. The Chattahoochee ran through the middle of Columbus and its Alabama counterpart Phenix City on the other side. On the southern edge of the city was one of the largest Army bases in the world, Fort Benning.

Both cities had a bit of a rough and tumble history. The one on the Alabama side, in particular, had a rather sordid past. These were the closest big cities to his home, and Steve knew them well. He recalled a story his father had told of when General George Patton had been stationed at Benning. He had once threatened to roll his tanks across the river into Phenix City and destroy it. Since then, the towns had grown, matured and now possessed beautiful downtowns, colleges, museums and the typical urban sprawl. Steve was hoping that the military presence might still have a calming effect on the area. Deep down, he knew that was just wishful thinking.

At midday, they had to cross another of the dams. This one was another tall hydroelectric which they had to navigate to one side, then portage the kayaks and supplies up and over to the other side.

The descent to the river below was steep and the footing treacherous. "Whoa, let's stop for a second," Gerald said. "We are making too much noise, and one of us is going to turn an ankle or worse if we aren't careful."

Steve sighed, released his grip and sagged to the ground. "I could use a break anyway, how 'bout you, JD?" The boy nodded and set the end he was carrying down as well.

"Steve, you come up with any better options, or do we stay on the water?" Gerald asked the question while fishing in his packs for something to eat.

"Options? Hmmm, no, not really. I wish I knew what we were heading into. I have to say again, guys . . . y'all can choose your own path. I don't want to be making these decisions for everyone."

"We know," Gerald said as he chewed on something. "I think the boy and I will head east once we are below Columbus. JD and I have been talking, and I think he is good staying at my place until things get better. You should only be a few days from home then, an easy walk to Albany."

Steve asked, and JD confirmed, that was indeed the plan. "Sounds good, guess we just got to get through the next ten or so miles, then get off this river for good."

"Using the river was smart, Steve. I know it didn't start out so good, but it was a good plan. We've not been threatened. Hell, barely saw any other people. Had food and fresh water. Yep, things could have really been a lot worse."

The men nodded in agreement. Gerald spoke again, "What do you think you will find?"

Steve knew what he meant. The same thought kept going through his mind over and over. "What I think I will find is . . . " he stopped trying to bury the fear, "what I hope is I will find my family safe. Right now, I just pray they are alive. Beyond that, I have no idea."

Gerald gave a somber nod. "Porter, if you need, you can always come stay with me and the kid."

"Wow, thank you. I really couldn't, though. I know I must find my own way. I have relied on others my whole life. This time it's really up to me."

The other man just shrugged.

"Besides, I have no idea where your place even is. You've kept those details to yourself, friend."

"Not totally," Gerald said glancing at the youngest member of the group. "Seriously, my place is pretty well stocked and could sustain us all for a while. Next spring, we would have to plant some crops, but it could work. Consider it a standing invite for you and your family. I'll leave the radio with you when we part ways. I have one at the cabin. I'll show you how to contact me. Just in case . . . you know." He winked and stood. "Guess we might as well see what's down there."

40

They watched the procession from the trees overlooking the four-lane road. Mile after mile of weary stragglers, most with packs or bags, some pulling luggage. Steve thought again how much the scene reminded him of the images from 2016 of Syrian refugees as they fled their war-torn country in a desperate trek toward Europe in some vague hope for safety. These people had that same defeated look. Many were dragging luggage, small children; a few pushed shopping carts.

JD leaned in close. "There are thousands of them. Are they all going to the camps?"

Gerald sighed. "I suppose so. Most are probably trying as much to get away from something as get to something. No food, no water, no money or anything to trade. Hell, nothing really out there to trade anything for. The camps may be the only real option most of them have."

"Why are they dragging all that stuff? The Army isn't going to let 'em bring any of it into the camp."

"They probably don't know that yet, JD. They haven't seen or heard any of the things we have," Steve answered. They had left their kayaks hidden in the undergrowth far below. As they approached the bridge, they heard the sounds coming from the mass of people up above. They had decided to climb the steep hill to get a look.

"Look there," Gerald whispered as he pointed.

Steve focused in and saw it, too. "Armed roadblocks at the exits. They aren't letting anyone head back south toward town."

"They aren't letting anyone back on any of the roads." He scanned the area with the compact binoculars. "Those don't look like Army uniforms. They are all black, even a few with gray camo. These must be the FEMA and DHS people your guy on the radio mentioned. Those agencies don't have troops, do they?"

Gerald made a sound like a snort. "Essentially, yes. The DHS alone has almost a quarter-of-a-million employees, many of whom are in some form of enforcement."

"Holy shit!" Steve muttered. "We've lost our country, haven't we?"

Gerald eyed JD before answering in a hushed tone. "Afraid so. This is looking more like North Korea than Columbus, Georgia."

The three of them sat there for hours watching, but the line of people never seemed to diminish. As the afternoon sun began to dip, they saw small campfires appearing along the road. Soon after, the gunfire started. It was unclear if it was the troops that started it, but they engaged quickly. The shots seemed to be going in all directions. Screams and moans were interspersed with orders being issued over loudspeakers. Several rounds ricocheted off nearby trees.

"Back to the river," Gerald ordered.

The shooting began to lessen as they descended the hill. Once they reached the river's edge, all they heard was someone on a loud-speaker.

"This is your only warning! Stay on the highway, keep heading toward the camps. All other travel is prohibited. All firearms are prohibited. Failure to comply will bring immediate consequences. Approaching official vehicles and personnel will be dealt with the same way. These are emergency executive orders."

The sound of the broadcast faded, presumably as the speakers' vehicle traveled farther down the road.

"What now?" Steve asked.

"Should we toss the pistols?" JD said looking through his bag.

"No!" Gerald said. Then in a slightly calmer tone. "If it looks like anyone official is about to stop us, then, yes, toss it. Keep it out of sight but close, we may need it. Steve, we need to keep moving. You know this area better than me—is it safe to be on the river in the dark?"

Steve shook his head. "No, definitely not. There are numerous rocks and eddies as well as another old dam with a fairly good drop coming up. Below that, they actually have a whitewater course running beside the city's Riverwalk. We don't have life vests, and I assume it is too dangerous to use our lights."

"Damn . . . we have to do something." Gerald moved over to the kayak he had been using and slid it back toward the water. I have an idea, but the rat in you is not going to like it."

Steve regretted ever telling him about the advice he had gotten back in Charlotte. But indeed, he did not like Gerald's idea at all.

"OH MY GOD, this is so gross." JD's voice was muffled, but the complaints were shared by all.

"Quiet, kid, your slime will get messed up."

Gerald's bright idea was to submerge the kayaks partially, so they didn't so much ride on top of the water as in it. In the dark water, they looked more like logs floating downstream. Logs without any humans on top as the three of them were hanging onto the sides also mostly submerged. The parts that were exposed were covered in green slime and mud scooped from the bottom of the river. The goal was to present as small a profile as possible. He also figured it would be safer to be able to feel the water hazards coming up in the dark.

To some degree, Gerald had been right. Steve felt everything in the river, and it all scared him. Fish, limbs, squishy things. It was disgusting, and he was cold on top of it all. The water wasn't that chilly, but his fear was amplifying the effect of the water. "Hey, Gerald," he whispered. "I hate you."

"Me, too," came JD's voice from the darkness in front of Steve.

"Me, three," Gerald muttered to himself.

A few minutes later Steve's panicky voice came again from the darkness. "Oh man . . . there is the city, looks like it is . . . on fire, too." They could see silhouettes of taller dark buildings backlit by a red and orange glow. The scene began filling the eastern sky. They watched entranced as previously burned-out buildings and homes passed by. The closer they got, the more fires they saw. Finally breaking the trance, "We should see a bridge coming up, and I think the old dam is right under it, or maybe just before. I only did the whitewater course once . . . sorry."

They saw the bridge a few minutes later and began to swim toward the eastern shore. Steve had thought that side was more manageable for bypassing the dangerous drop-off. The water slowed and began eddying back on itself. Debris was circling in small whirlpools. "Yeah, the dam must be a few yards ah . . . fuck, what is that?"

"What is . . . holy shit."

Steve was trying to figure out what was bumping into him just below the surface. Gerald was looking up at the underside of the bridge. JD was simply clutching his end of the kayak and staring straight ahead.

"It's a body."

"Its lots of bodies."

"Huh?" Steve glanced around, panicked. They could hear the sound of the flowing water. He had stopped swimming to the side. "No, it's . . . " he pulled on the thing bumping him and realized. It *was* a body. Stiff and decayed; the skin and meat sloughed off the arm he was holding. "Oh shit," he vomited as the reality of what he was seeing set in.

Gerald pointed. "More up there." Hanging from the bridge were at least two dozen bodies, the flickering firelight casting the bodies into evil apparitions.

"Some are hung up on the dam, too," JD said now viciously

paddling to keep from colliding with the first of the dark humps ahead.

"Keep your mouth closed, don't let any of this water in," Gerald said as he too began pushing his boat to the side. "No telling what kind of diseases are in here with us."

Steve stretched his feet trying to find the river bottom, but it was too deep. He swam with one arm and strong kicks to get to the shore, the other hand holding firmly to the kayak. He could see the darker shadow of the embankment leading up to the bridge above. It seemed to get closer with frustrating slowness. Thankfully, the current pushing them was not strong, but neither wanted to repeat the lessons that first dam had given. And, this one was already encrusted with dead people; how much more fun would that be?

"Oh, Geeze, they are here, too," JD said as the front of the boat finally nudged into the bank. "At least parts of them are."

Steve could see more of the misshapen lumps on the bank above him and a creepy movement on the shadowed corpses. "What's that on them?

"Turtles, rats . . . probably catfish as well on the parts that are still in the water," Gerald said. "Come on, just get through this, guys. It sucks, but we only get to live by doing this."

"That's a terrible speech, Coach," JD said as he helped pull the larger boat up on shore.

"Screw you, kid," he said with a grunt. "I'm up to my ass in dead bodies, ok?"

41

The three of them struggled to pull the water-ladened kayaks up onto the shore. The putrid smell was so strong it seemed to be a physical presence. JD was rubbing his eyes and spitting. "I think it's in my mouth," he cried. Steve fought to keep his stomach under control. Even Gerald seemed shaken, but he was the first to recover.

"Can't stay here—we've made too much noise. Grab your boat and get your shit downstream below the dam."

Steve stopped his coughing and grabbed for the handle strap on the kayak. JD did the same. "I'm not getting back in that."

He was glad the boy had said it because he felt the same way. The idea of all that death, all those bodies, and having to be in there with them made his skin crawl. *He couldn't do it.*

"Just move for now. We can discuss it when we get there," Gerald's voice was labored as he dumped the water from, then hoisted his own kayak from the carnage-riddled ground.

"Do you think they did this? I . . . I mean did it to themselves?"

"I dunno, Porter . . . maybe. If so, that's sick. Probably a few did, but I think most went involuntarily. Somebody probably hung them there as a warning."

Steve cocked his head. "A warning?"

"Yeah. This is our city—stay the fuck out."

And we just ignored that completely, Steve thought as he tipped his own kayak and heard the water draining out over the gruesome landscape.

~

THE SOUND of powerful water rushing against rock was just one more reason to stay on land. Steve knew by the sound that this was the beginning of the whitewater course. They were all cold, wet and scared. The journey had just come to an abrupt stop, and neither Gerald nor Steve seemed sure what to do next.

"Guys, I'm sorry. Coming down this river was my stupid idea. We should have taken a safer route."

"Cool it, Steve, the river was fast, we made good time . . . or would have if I hadn't gotten hurt. Besides, traveling any other way would likely have gotten us stopped and herded into one of those damn camps. None of us want that. At least here, we have a fighting chance."

Steve appreciated what Gerald was doing but wasn't buying it. He felt like an idiot, and he had failed his friends. "So, what do we do?"

JD's body shivered violently enough for the other two to notice. Gerald was concerned but knew sitting here accomplished nothing. "We only have two options, leave the boats and try to get through the city on foot or back on the river, but we have to do it now."

"There are bodies out there . . . m, more bodies."

"I know son," Gerald offered, "but the people that killed them are on land. The bodies can't really hurt us, besides, most will have washed way downstream, away from the dam here."

They all knew they really had no choice, but the debate still went on. Too late, they realized they had been discovered. They heard sounds of running on the bridge above at the same time flashlight beams stabbed out from the top of the bank behind them.

"In the water now!" Gerald yelled, already pushing his boat into the river.

A single gunshot pinged off a rock behind them. Steve grabbed JD and pushed the stunned boy to the front of the kayak. "Hurry, JD!"

Shots began hitting all around them. Thankfully, the flashlight beams had not centered on them yet, but it was only a matter of time. They managed to get in the kayak only to get immediately picked up by the current and slammed into a boulder. Steve struggled to find his paddle; he briefly glimpsed Gerald's red kayak as it slipped into the darkness thirty yards ahead. Glancing back, he saw almost a dozen people up on the bridge. The firelight giving just enough illumination to see they each carried weapons, and they all were pointed toward them. More of them were scurrying down the eastern bank and lining the rail of the once pristine Riverwalk. Some carried lights, but all seemed to be shooting. "You motherfuckers better stop or we gonna kill yo ass."

The laughter and threats came at them over the rushing water. Steve was disoriented and unable to see any of the obstacles in the river. The only good thing was the boats being dashed back and forth kept the bullets from finding their mark. "Paddle, JD . . . paddle!"

His world and his focus narrowed down to a ten-foot boat on a dark stretch of water. Steve dug the paddle hard to carve a path around things he felt more than saw. He had come down this river in an inflatable raft just after the whitewater course opened. He briefly remembered how much fun it had been. Even Trey seemed to enjoy it. What else could he recall from that day? Would anything help? Everything seemed to be moving in slow motion. Another attacker had started firing an automatic rifle. He watched each round's impact as they entered his tunneled field of view. The bullets stitched a line across the water and right across his kayak. JD screamed out in pain. Even in the dim light, he could see a dark patch spreading across the boys back. "Shit!" *We should have gotten back in the water, sitting on top was stupid*, he thought.

He had no time to think about the child's injury. *Just get away.* More shots came, this time from another position downriver. He caught sight of the red kayak again as it darted in front of him at an extreme angle. The incoming fire was coming from another bridge just ahead. Gerald was attempting to distract the shooter. The slight glow of the burning city provided little illumination here. The banks were higher, and the river current slowed. The barrage of shots was relentless. Steve could feel the kayak becoming sluggish to maneuver and knew it must be taking on water. More shots came, and then the shadow of the bridge passed overhead. It was a four-lane with a gap in the middle, so the shooters on top couldn't cross and had no line of sight to the river on the far side. The two kayaks slipped through and into calmer water.

"JD? Hey, JD. Talk to me, man." Steve whispered between paddle strokes. He couldn't stop paddling but wanted to know if the boy was ok. JD let out a moan as he reached a hand toward his bloody back. Steve's focus zoomed back out, and he now recognized the sounds of battle receding as well as the shouts and jeers from the attackers. The edge of the kayak was just inches above the water and handling like a fat cow. "Hang in there, buddy. We're nearly out of this." His voice was shaky and unsure, not at all reassuring. "Leighton, you out there?" He called again in as loud a voice as he dared. JD moaned again from the front. "Gerald, our boat got hit. JD is hurt. We are sinking."

He tried to remember what the river was like on the other side of that bridge but couldn't recall. He wasn't sure they had even come this far on that whitewater rafting trip. The only thing he remembered was afterward he had gone to a really cool place in the old downtown for a beer and some barbecue. *Well shit, that's helpful.*

The dark silhouette of a large building passed by, and he recalled it was an indoor arena. Beyond that seemed to be a parking lot, and if he recalled correctly, mostly undeveloped land. He saw JD's hand motioning at something, then caught sight of Gerald's kayak just up ahead.

"Oh damn!" The older man was slumped over the kayak which was now drifting in lazy circles.

42

"JD, listen to me. Where are you hit?"

The boy was still sitting upright but unresponsive. Steve was paddling hard toward the circling red kayak ahead. He scanned the bank on both sides seeing nowhere to land. All he could really see was shadows, but it seemed the overgrowth on each side was thick with plenty of concealment for more attackers. He also couldn't move forward in the small boat without tipping JD out. "Shit, the boat is sinking anyway." The water was running freely in and out of the flimsy plastic shell, but it didn't seem to be getting any lower in the water. *Must be some trapped air somewhere.*

Steve knew how totally screwed they were. "JD, find where you are hit and put pressure on it. Hold it tight with your hand or arm." He saw some movement from the boy, but it was achingly slow. Gerald's kayak was coming into reach. "Leighton, how bad are you hit?" Gerald was slumped forward in his boat. His head was resting on the plastic hull. Steve hooked the kayak with his paddle and brought it alongside.

Putting a hand on the man's shoulder caused no reaction. He felt cold, but that could just be the wet clothes. "Gerald, hey man, stay with me." The two kayaks picked up a current and began moving faster into the darkness. Steve struggled to keep the other boat beside his own. *God, don't let us run into any boulders*, he thought. If either of his friends went in the water, he knew he wouldn't be able to find them in the dark. He checked Gerald over the best that he could with one hand. He thought he felt a slight pulse when he touched the side of his neck but couldn't be sure. His own heart was racing so hard he might just be feeling that.

Find a place to land. The river banks were closing in, narrowing the channel and increasing the current. He scanned the dark shore, but saw nothing but trees and brush crowding the approach to the bank. As he neared one side, limbs began whipping by—some crashing into JD up front. He used the paddle as a rudder to guide them back toward the middle.

He had so many conflicting ideas: get away, pull over, check on his friends, paddle faster. He should have stayed a rat. The move to go through the city had been rushed, and it had been a fatal mistake. His seat was half full of water, and he felt his kayak scrub against the riverbed a few times. The river level had been incredibly erratic the entire trip. It might be six inches one second and twenty feet the next. They seemed to be in an area of shallows, so he decided to stab the paddle down in the mud and see if he could slow their momentum. If he could get the kayaks stopped, he could at least see how JD was doing. He dug the nose of the paddle in, and the boat spun around on its axis. JD leaned heavily to one side and let out a painful groan. The other kayak was torn from his grip and kept floating downstream. "Crap, crap, crap!"

He pulled the paddle up and counter-leaned to right the boat. JD shifted back toward the center. *Ok, that didn't work as planned.* It took him several minutes to chase down the other kayak. When he neared, he realized that Gerald was close to falling out; his upper body had slid off the blood-slicked plastic and was now in the water. The red boat was riding at a precarious angle. Steve shifted his approach to the other side and came up alongside him. Lifting the man's head and shoulder from the water he could now see the bullet wound. Gerald's right side was a mass of blood. The darkest spots were just below his ribcage. "Come on, buddy. You can make it."

He heard a sound from up ahead and looked up. The darkness faded in an instant, as powerful spotlights lit up the entire river. A booming voice rang out, "That's far enough. Stop your craft. You have just entered the controlled space of a U.S. military base. Stop and raise your hands, or you will be fired upon. Do it now!"

Steve cautiously raised his one hand while holding his friend up with the other. JD still sat motionless. "We're unarmed and injured." Technically incorrect, but good enough for now. His panicked voice sounded weak and scared. The light blinded him from seeing much of anything. He was vaguely aware of something approaching, although the light stayed motionless. "You in the back, show me both hands!" Steve released his grip on Gerald and raised his other hand. The red kayak began drifting away. He went to grab for it.

"Let it go. We have him. Keep those hands up, no sudden moves. He saw another craft now and men lifting his injured friend from the red boat.

STEVE KNEW they were all fucked. The Chattahoochee River ran beside Fort Benning, and why they assumed the river wouldn't be monitored, he had no clue. At least it wasn't the gang up on the bridges. He was quickly examined before having his wrists zip-tied and being roughly thrown into a larger black boat. To his surprise, they were much gentler with JD. He now saw the boy's eyes were open, but his face was etched with pain. He heard calls for a medic somewhere else and hoped that was for Gerald. He would accept being thrown into a camp or even killed as long as they treated both of his friends' injuries. A muffled engine started, and as the water-craft he and JD were in made a sweeping turn, he saw the battered kayaks drifting lazily past, all their gear and meager supplies still onboard. The little kayaks had done their job and gotten him within a hundred miles of home. Sadly, it seemed this was where they parted ways.

He had a sense of speed as the boat skipped quickly over the water. He and JD were accompanied by at least six uniformed soldiers. None of them spoke except one who seemed to be checking JD's injuries. Steve couldn't hear any of what the man was saying and made a move to get closer. A hand restrained him. Looking up into the face, the man shook his head. His dark camo greasepaint making the gesture even more non-negotiable. Steve slipped back down to rest his back against the side walls. The tension, the drumming of the engine and the bouncing of the boat were too much. He felt the twinge of an old familiar enemy. "No, no, no," he whispered. "Not now."

An oncoming migraine hit with the fury of a prizefighter. Within minutes he felt himself curling into a ball and the nausea building. Steve hated himself for it. His friends had both been shot. Gerald may have been killed, and now he was going to be unable to do anything because of a goddamn headache. After all they had been through this night—this was more than he could handle.

HE FELT the soldier poking him. Steve knew he must be speaking to him as well, but didn't hear anything. He wasn't even sure he was still in the boat. He felt arms around him tugging, and something solid underneath, then he was out again.

43

"Madam Sec . . . so sorry, I mean, Madam President," her longtime aide said before handing her the file.

Irritation clouded her face as she took the envelope without responding. The envelope was coded for "Special Access Only." It contained a sensitive "Mission Action Report" and was at the highest level of secrecy. She dumped the contents out on the table. Photos, papers and a flash drive spilled in all directions. The aerial photos showed scene after scene of utter devastation. The world had not seen a CME this large since the 1800s. Back then, it had a negligible effect as electricity was only sparsely used. Now though, it was a vital part of daily life in most parts of the world. She knew some of what she was looking at was a direct result of the CME; some was the result of the Council's direct actions.

She inserted the flash drive into the laptop and looked at the data. Just as Ms. Levy's letter had indicated, the death rate worldwide was soaring. Estimates here on mainland US were over twenty million casualties. In Europe and Asia, mortality was estimated at over 50 percent already. She couldn't look at the photos of what that damn virus was doing over there. Levy had already indicated one of her elite Praetor Battlegroups had been wiped out in Pakistan. That, on top of the main Praetor 5 base getting slammed in Florida. *Damn that woman, served her right. Where was Levy at now?* She was glad the evil bitch was no longer here in Bluemont, but she didn't trust that her vile machinations had slowed.

What bothered Madelyn was it could have all been prevented. She knew before even reading the reports. Systems could have been hardened to protect the power grid. Redundancies could have been put in place to make quick repairs, and FEMA could have been given an actual humanitarian mandate instead of what it really had.

No . . . this had not only been expected; it had been wanted. She understood how many great civilizations had crumbled under weak leaders and a constant bleeding away of wealth into a doomed welfare state. Even the mighty empire of Rome had fallen into this trap. *The Council members must hate that reminder*, she thought. Now they saw all this as its mission. It was simply . . . a course adjustment. Something to keep the republic on track.

Before the end of this, the projection was that 90 percent of the American population would be dead. The Council had identified the 10 percent they wanted to survive, many of whom had been remanded to protectorate camps already. She had been instructed to clear roads, railways and airports to allow for this to take place. Then she was to empty the urban areas to both speed up their demise and develop a new agricultural basis, the farming communes that would spring up all over the country. They were literally taking food out of the mouths of Americans and giving it to the chosen survivors. The thought of it all made her sick, but she had a duty. Something else— she realized the Council was right. Maybe not in their methods, or who they chose to live or die, but doing nothing would have meant losing it all.

This virus, though, that was another matter entirely. She knew there was another level to the story. Something major that Ms. Levy had neglected to tell her. She wasn't even sure the other Council members knew. The clues were starting to add up, but she couldn't see the bigger picture yet. She shut down the computer and placed the horrid pictures back in the envelope with the papers. The U.S. was doomed—the entire world for that matter. While the Council might envision this as a—what did they call it?— the catalyst for a brilliant new age, she saw it for what it was—*the end.*

44

Steve came to, tasting bile in his mouth. Rolling to one side, he threw up, unable to care who or what was in that direction. His head was spinning, and the intense pressure behind his eyes made every movement laborious. He heard voices, then a light so bright even his closed eyes couldn't block it all. A deep voice asked him questions. Something about the river. He couldn't answer, couldn't even remember. Another voice: "No sign of a concussion. Must be something else." He wanted to tell them it was simply a migraine, but this one was unlike any he had before. All the tension, stress, anger he had endured the past month had twisted his mind into an elastic knot. Like a rubber band wound too tight, it had snapped. Nerve synapses fired at pain receptors like machine guns. He felt his body giving up, succumbing to whatever was in store. The sounds became muffled, he felt himself sliding down into the darkness yet again.

∼

LIKE A FEVER DREAM, the images in his unconscious mind made no sense, yet still had an effect on him. He was convinced he was being tortured, then paralyzed and finally drowning. He panicked for air as he tried to make unresponsive limbs swim—push—to the surface. Some of this he had experienced before, but never to this magnitude. How many times did he come to, only to be pulled back down? Finally, more of his senses began to come back online.

Eyes still closed, he dared not move as nausea and a pounding head were still there, like a cat waiting to pounce. *How much time had passed?* Each time he surfaced back into consciousness he took in a bit more of his surroundings. His head still swirled, and unanswered questions drifted by like flotsam on the ocean. *Why am I here, who are these people, had I been alone?*

Slowly, his mind began separating the dream world from reality. Most of the tortured images faded back into the fog of his battered brain. The light was back, hands on his back and shoulders.

"Sir, you are going to feel a pinch."

They were injecting something in his back. The surprise hit him almost as fast as the spreading cold. He knew this feeling; it was a treatment for the headaches. Wherever he was, maybe they were trying to help. More thoughts returned as the pain ebbed slightly.

"My friends . . . Ger . . . " the voice croaked and didn't sound like his own.

The deep baritone was back asking him more questions. "Sir, what were you and your friends doing on the river? Who are you with?"

The interrogation would have to wait; he simply couldn't focus. He tried to answer the man, but apparently, the words would not travel from his brain to his mouth. Surprisingly, the man didn't seem to get upset. Steve thought the man's voice was vaguely British, or maybe something . . . the thought was lost as the curtains of his mind closed again.

"He's in no shape for this, Major. Mr. Porter, just get some sleep," the voice he now recognized as female said. He heard soft footsteps walking away, and the muffled voices resumed, discussing someone, possibly him. He now realized those voices had been part of his dreams, they had been talking while he slipped in and out of consciousness. As he lay there, he struggled to try and separate what he remembered from what was simply a delusion. In his migraine-driven fugue-state, nothing made much sense. They were U.S. Army; he knew that. *Think, Porter, think! It's important.* He slipped back down beneath the waves of consciousness.

War is coming! Where the hell did that thought come from? He knew he had been asleep. The spinal blocker had done its job. The massive headache was now lessening its grip. The monster was still there, but on a leash for the moment. *War.* The conversations he had been concentrating on before had coalesced into this while he slept. The U.S. Army, or at least this base, was preparing to go to war, but the enemy they were fighting was the most jarring part.

"Oh good, Mr. Porter, you're back with us," came the voice a short while later.

The light was subdued but still painful as he cracked open crusty eyelids for the first time. He rolled toward the voice and coughed. "How long?"

"Two days," the woman said. "I am Sergeant Lackey. I'm the one who has been treating you. Are you able to sit up? We need to ask you some questions."

He nodded, then regretted the movement. "Yes," he said as he maneuvered up on what he realized was a real bed. Not a cot or even a hospital bed. "Where am I?"

"That can wait," she said dismissively. "Do you have a history of migraines? Were you under treatment for them?"

"Yes, most of my adult life." He told her the medications he had been prescribed. "Of course, that was before . . . "

She nodded as she made notes. "So, you know what I gave you then? It is a pretty final option, but it was what I had. Sorry, this is not a clinic, but the epidural kit was part of our standard medical supplies. Our CO wants to know what you were doing on the river."

He briefly thought of trying to lie but didn't have the energy. "Just trying to get home, trying to get out of that city."

"You and your friends breached the perimeter of a U.S. military base. You were lucky our river patrol didn't shoot you. They had standing orders to do just that."

"Why didn't they?"

She ignored the question.

"You are from Albany, Georgia?"

"Yes, I was on a business trip when the lights went out." He wondered how long ago that had been now. "I've been trying to get home ever since." He then asked the question he and she seemed to be avoiding. "How are my friends? Are they . . . "

"What did you do . . . in Albany?"

He realized now a compact but solidly-built black man had stepped into the room and was leaning against the room's door. "I . . . I owned a car dealership, Ford's . . . Porter Auto Group."

The man stepped forward, the deep singsong voice was familiar. "Are you related to the other man or the boy you were captured with?"

"No, we were strangers until a few weeks ago. Just happened to be traveling in the same direction and became allies and friends. How are they doing? Did . . . did they survive?"

"Why the river? Surely you knew it was dangerous?" the sergeant asked.

Steve hesitated, he didn't want to seem dishonest, but the truth might reveal too much. "We were avoiding . . . other dangers. It was a quick decision by him to be vague, but obviously not the right one."

The man pressed. "Meesta Porter, what other danger?"

"I'd rather not say."

"I apologize to you, sir, but I am not giving you that option. What other dangers made you risk all of your lives?"

Steve shrugged, defeated by the man's words. "We saw your friends herding people into those camps. Shooting broke out, people were killed, and . . . we fled downriver."

The man got noticeably agitated. "Not our people; not our camps. Is that who shot at you? Our river patrol heard a lot of shooting."

"No, just some hoodlums or gang . . . we never knew." He took a cold rag from the sergeant's outstretched hand. "Wait, what do you mean not your people?"

The man, who Steve assumed was the major, shook his head and turned to leave. "We will talk later." He nodded at the sergeant before walking off.

The sergeant put a hand on Steve's back in a reassuring move. "Please try and stand, you need to come with me."

HE HAD BEEN SURPRISED when he woke that he was not restrained or handcuffed. His assumptions were that they would be prisoners, but here, treatment had been cordial and professional. The major had used the term "captured" though. *When will they send us to the detention camps?* Maybe when they were all recovered, but that made no sense either. He had seen the troops shooting at people that were already heading toward the camp. They were not concerned with their health; anyone could see that.

Sergeant Lackey had not been lying, this was certainly not a medical facility. She led him through a maze of hallways to the door of a large room with several beds. This area looked to have been hastily converted to a surgical wing. Plastic drapes separated several beds. Most were unoccupied. She paused and drew in a long breath. "Your friends are in here. Mr. Leighton has been asking for you." Hearing Gerald was alive was such a relief that he found himself grinning, and inside he was exuberant.

Her eyes did not mirror the same emotions; in fact, she was stoic to the point of morose. "Listen, I'm sorry, I did all I could for him. He . . . he needs more extensive surgery but, well, he wouldn't . . . he isn't going to make it. The damage is too extensive. His organs have started shutting down. I just wanted you to have a chance to say good-bye. The boy had asked me to bring you when you woke."

45

Gerald's pale skin was cold as Steve laid a hand on his friend's arm. Steve was surprised to see him open his eyes and even more shocked to see JD curled up asleep on a nearby cot. "Hey, man," he said with tear-filled eyes.

"Wow, look who is back with the living," the older man wheezed, "Just don't ask how I am doing, I'm sure that is pretty obvious." His head nodded slightly to the side. "No idea why they let the kid stay in here. He doesn't need to see this." The man's words were weak and slurred. "They gave me morphine . . . said that was 'bout all they could do for me." He gave a feeble lopsided grin. "Hey, that's some good shit, you should try it. Might help you kick those headaches."

How these two strangers could have become so close in just a few weeks was a mystery. Steve knew few details about him. Where was he born? What was his faith? The minutiae that is the fabric of most friendships was completely absent here. What he did know was the man's character. He had saved JD and then saved him. He had put himself between danger and them time after time. "I'm sorry, Gerald."

"Not your fault, Steve. They had us in a shooting box. It was a trap. I should've seen it coming."

Steve couldn't find his voice. The man was dying, but here he was trying to absolve him of the guilt he was carrying. Gerald closed his eyes, and Steve thought he was asleep. He wiped his eyes clear and looked at the sleeping form of JD. The boy had a small bandage on his neck, and Steve could just see the edge of a larger wound dressing on his back. Unlike Gerald, he had no tubes or monitors attached. Hopefully, that meant the boy's wounds were not life-threatening.

Gerald's drowsy voice pulled his attention back. "He's doing fine." He waved a hand lazily in the direction of the sleeping child. "Going to have a nasty scar, but neither shot punctured through to anything vital."

"That's good. I hate that he was injured, though."

"Me, too. Kid's a trooper. Barely a complaint. Look, Steve, I don't know how much time I have, but try and bear with me. Listen, I'm not sure what is going on here, but it's more than we imagined."

"Yeah, I gathered. Surprised they haven't locked us up by now."

"Some of them want to, things seem to be . . . uncertain here. I think that is why we are being kept here instead of up at the main base hospital. The commander of this unit seems to want to keep our capture under the radar, which might be a good thing. My feeling, Steve, is that you will get home, not sure what you will find, but . . . stay alive." He closed his eyes briefly before continuing. "Look . . . to have a life, you must live. The secret to getting old is simply just not dying. I am going to meet my sweet bride, and I'm ok with that." He took a labored breath before continuing.

"What I am asking you is not fair, but I have to, Steve. . . I want you to please take care of that boy—you are all he has. He looks up to you; said you don't treat him like a child, he likes that. Get out of here with him, find your family, then get to my place on the lake. Trust me. It has all you guys will need. Can you do that for me?"

Steve nodded numbly, the cold reality that this man was telling him goodbye and giving him a mission. "Of course I will, and thank you."

Gerald reached a trembling hand beneath the bed covers, then handed Steve a small, battered notebook. "I've tried to keep this updated, it's an old habit of mine. It's my notes and a few more survival tips. It might help you guys. One more thing, Porter. Get in touch with that man on the radio. His frequency and times are written near the back." His voice started to fade, and Steve thought he might be going back to sleep. Then he spoke again in the familiar, confident tone: "Listen to me, Steve. This . . . *this* is important. It will be up to people like you and him to take this country back. To give these kids a chance at all. Some hope for a better tomorrow. Can you do that . . . will you do that?"

Steve fought the urge to offer an easy answer. He knew his friend didn't want to be placated. He wanted a commitment. He also knew what this request meant. "I'm not a fighter, Gerald. I've never been. But . . . I would never have thought I was a survivor either, not until now. I will do my best. I'll do what you ask."

The older man nodded, his strength obviously ebbing. "Hope is a hunger, Brother. It is something those in charge cannot allow to feed. All you have to do is help light the flame. Like hope, fire exists only to feed, and the fire of a patriot is all that can stand against the darkness of tyranny. Help light that fire of rebellion. Others will be ready to take up the call. Please take my place to help them."

They sat there together in the large, empty room. Gerald growing weaker and weaker. Steve felt a small hand on his back and realized JD was standing there with him. Gerald motioned the boy to come sit beside him on the bed. They all seemed to realize the end was coming. The man's eyes were beginning to dim. The thought of being without Gerald frightened him. Steve didn't know if he could let go, but he knew that was simply being selfish and weak. Gerald was not family, yet in many ways, he was closer. Gerald reached out and took hold of JD's hand and told him one final story.

His eyes focused somewhere above them as he began to speak. "Nancy was the most beautiful girl I ever saw. We were both standing in line to buy movie tickets. We noticed each other, and she smiled at me. That was all it took; one smile and I was forever and hopelessly in love. It took me years to convince her to marry me, but eventually, I wore her down and she agreed. They say love makes you weak; don't believe it. Love makes you whole. We were unbelievably happy—more than we had a right to be. When I held her, I could hear the music and feel the magic. In all our years, we only had one regret, we couldn't have children.

JD, I'm sorry your family didn't have that kind of love, sorry you aren't going to have the perfect childhood. I don't know what's in store for you now, but I know you will be fine. You are an amazing kid; you and Porter make a good team. I just wish I could stick around to see what an awesome young man you will become."

JD leaned down and put his arms around Gerald's neck.

Gerald whispered something into the boy's ear, and Steve watched as the dam of tears began to flow from the boy's eyes, then he, too, began to weep. Gerald inhaled deeply, sighed and then he was gone. His fight was finished.

46

Major Kitma sat across from him at an ancient gray metal desk. The thin, light veneer on the top worn through to a dull brown on most of its surface. The man's deep, black skin seemed to burst out of the tight-fitting uniform. Steve was still processing the passing of his friend as well as the residual effects of the migraine. The commander seemed in a rush to get the words out as soon as he could. "Did you not know your freend was former meleltary?"

Steve focused on Major Kitma's pronunciation of the words. "No, he never mentioned it. Just said he was an analyst with the government."

The large man smiled. "He was that, too, but that was after he served your country. You never noticed the tattoo on his shoulder, no? He was an Army Ranger. From what I gather, back in the day, he was an exceptionally good one. You probably couldn't have found a better ally to travel wit."

"Is that why you have treated us so well?"

Kitma shrugged. "It's part of it. We take care of our own."

"But you are not even an American, are you?"

"These are strange times, my freend. South African. I was here on an officer exchange program when the event occurred. No way to get back home now. Things on the base have been challenging. Many of the officers of the camp left or . . .simply disappeared. I volunteered to help wherever. Now, I serve as a commander of this unit."

"I guess I understand," Steve responded unconvincingly.

"You don't, but that's ok. Much here that you are unaware of. Da meletary is having some issues with its commander-in-chief. In particular, her response to this crisis." The major picked up a cup of tea. The delicate mug lost in his huge hands. "She ordered us to help with the 'humanitarian mission,' as she called it. Da Army, *your* Army, is prevented from carrying out operations on American soil, it's illegal, in fact. Not without executive order at least. So, she ordered dem, and at first, some of our commanders agreed. She wanted dem to clear da roads and help build aid camps. Then we saw what they were really doing: clearing out the cities. Afterward, meeny of your meletary leaders had some big disagreement on conducting further operations."

"That sounds like the beginning of a military coup or something," Steve said

"No, no . . . " Kitma stared off into space for a moment. "Well...it's probably not off the table, but I doubt anything so drastic. Right now, we are isolating ourselves. Dey leave us alone; we don't bodder dem. Just the circumstances of Mrs. Chambers' ascension to the presidency is, well . . . questionable, as is the fate of your former president and VP."

"I do find it strange. I mean how does a secretary of transportation become president? Wouldn't she be way down the list?"

"Yes, Mr. Porter, as I understand it, that is correct. According to the FEMA official who gave us the certification validating her as the new president, she was a designated survivor."

Steve nodded. "I've heard of that. A lower ranking member of the executive office that is held away from the president in case of an attack or something. A continuity of government contingency."

"Partially true, dat is one scenario. Dis one is what they called a 'First Secretary Protocol.' It was apparently instituted in secret, after your nation's 9/11 tragedy. The first secretary survivor is chosen at the outset of a presidency and doesn't change without an official order. Madam Secretary was that person. Your military was unaware of that protocol's exeestsance or the role of FEMA in validating its process. Since dis bypassed most of da known steps of a non-elected succession to the highest office, most of the Joint Chiefs rejected her legitimacy to hold it. So you see, as of now, we are neutral."

Steve's emotions took over. "How can you stay neutral? You are the fucking Army. My country is falling apart."

Kitma raised his hands in a calming gesture. "Belief me, it pisses us off, too, we have seen what is going on out dar. We don't like it."

"If it isn't Army out there rounding up Americans, who is it?"

"Dem guys, hell, I dunno. National Security Force, your National Guard probably. We even heard a bunch of TSA agents were armed and helping. Imagine that, the pat-down guys at airports now rounding up civilians and putting them in detention camps. Our base commander was away when it all went down. The colonel who is in charge now . . . well, Colonel Willett, he's now something of a renegade warlord in the government's eyes. He is refusing their orders, and he isn't alone. Other bases, other branches are refusing the executive order to depopulate the urban centers. Not all of the soldiers agreed. Defending your country and all. Like I said, many, many of da troops and officers went AWOL, probably tried to get home to their own families. Others were purged due to divided loyalties. That is why I serve now as a commander. I have a family, too, back home, but no idea if I will ever see them again."

Steve rubbed between his eyes as he tried to process it. "Why are you helping us?"

"Officially, we aren't. Right now, dar is no record of you and the boi, but your friend in there is one of us. He say you saved his life many times. As I said, we're honoring his service to his country and, by extension, your service to him. We will take care of his remains, but unfortunately, no service for him. Meester Leighton only had one request. Get you and da boi to safety. We will do dis tang for him,

oke? He says you are a good man, a patriot. We need more of those. If
so, we may talk again."

~

THE DEPARTURE from the small outpost hidden away on the edge of
Fort Benning was not a quick event. Sergeant Lackey wouldn't release
JD until his wounds had knitted together well enough to travel. Steve
used the time to learn what he could about what was going on. The
Army had working equipment and communications with much of
the world. The major had said they could not give them transport
beyond the base, but that the route into Southern Georgia was not
being blocked by troops. For whatever reason, those were only
around larger towns and major roads.

So much of this was still so confusing. Why would they want to
depopulate the cities? Hell, seemed like that would happen on its
own. On the third day of waiting, he was watching the sergeant check
JD over. She smiled and said one more day and he should be fine, no
signs of infection. The words triggered a recent memory: "Sergeant,
we heard a broadcast indicating some outbreak overseas and that the
president was using that as justification to move people into the
camps. Was that just a ruse to panic people into doing what
she wants?"

The worry lines above the woman's eyes told him he had hit a
nerve. She pulled off the latex gloves and expertly hit the refuse
container. She glanced at JD who was putting his shirt back on.
"That, unfortunately, is not a lie. What she is using it for is manipula-
tion, but from what we are hearing, the pandemic itself is sweeping
across the entire continent."

"Geeze, but maybe the president is right, isolating healthy people
so they aren't exposed might be smart, and if it does hit, much easier
to treat. Right?"

"No, Mr. Porter, not right. These camps are already breeding
grounds for disease. Thousands have already died from simple stuff
we already are familiar with. We hear the radio reports of what is

going on. Our drones overfly the compounds and see the cremation pits. You cannot gather masses of people who are weak, undernourished and without hope and not expect to lose many of them to illness. From what I know, there is no treatment for the disease overseas. I'm not sure anyone has a clue as to what it even is or how it is transmitted. All we've heard so far is mostly rumor and speculation, but it sounds horrific."

"Just what we need," Steve said idly. "Is there anything out there that isn't trying to kill us?"

She looked defeated. "It's a dark time, I agree. Perhaps we can make things right again, but the coming dawn seems distant. Look, my job is to follow orders, but lately, even that has been uncertain. Soldiers don't like unclear directives, so who knows what happens next? You two got lucky. I'm sorry about your friend, but . . . you both just need to take care of yourselves out there, ok?"

47

It was still three more days before they were allowed to leave the base. No handshakes or good wishes, just instructions to follow a corporal to a waiting Humvee. They were dropped off on the far side of the massive Army base an hour later. The corporal handed them each a rucksack from the rear compartment. "What's this?" Steve asked confused. He knew they had lost everything in the river.

The corporal just shrugged. "The major told me to kit you guys out with one of our three-day packs. It's not a lot, but it'll get you started." He then gave them each several liter bottles of water, then got back in the driver's seat and, with a brief nod, drove back the way they had come.

The two of them stood there on the overgrown dirt road on the edge of an ocean of pine trees. "Well, JD, I guess we are heading to Albany; you good with that?" The boy had been somber since Gerald's death, but he gave a nod. "If that pack pulls on your wounds too much let me know. Sergeant Lackey had given him precise instructions on changing out the dressings and what to look for in the way of infection. She had also slipped him a small container of antibiotics and some pain meds, including some that might help with his migraines.

They left the dirt road and safety of the base, turning south onto the two-lane blacktop. While Major Kitma had assured them the federal militia wasn't patrolling below the base, they still had to worry about local threats. Gerald had drilled them on what he called "situational awareness" over their weeks together. Now they found themselves doing it automatically. Looking for anything that seems out of place, unusual. Glance to your rear and sides regularly. Stop and listen, stay in shadow or deep woods if you think others are around. Essentially, make sure you see them before they see you. This approach slows your progress but can keep you alive. While they first thought it was a stupid routine, neither felt that way now. "Head on a swivel, right?" he asked JD. The boy nodded.

"MR. ST . . . I mean, Steve, why did those people want to hurt us?"

They had been walking for hours, the last two in silence. JD's words shook him out of a memory. He knew that JD meant the people that shot him and killed Gerald. "I don't know. Maybe they are angry at someone, scared, not sure what comes next or . . . maybe they were just always bad. Now they don't have to fear the police or being caught and punished. It's a different kind of world, JD. For now, we have to share it with those types."

"I hope we don't see any more like 'em."

Steve nodded his agreement. "We probably should have avoided that town, we were doing pretty good up until that point. I just wasn't expecting them to be forcing people out of the cities and into the aid camps at gunpoint."

They walked on in silence for several more minutes before JD asked, "Are you really going to go to Mr. Gerald's cabin?"

"Yes. I wasn't sure at first, but even if my home is still there, it isn't safe. I have no supplies there." How odd it was for him to be thinking in terms of tactics and strategy; how defensible the location was, how far to fresh water. "JD, I was totally unprepared for this disaster, hell, any disaster. It never even crossed my mind. I relied on others, assumed I would never be in a situation that I couldn't buy what I needed. I wasn't like Gerald; he was prepared. He..." His voice broke. "He should have been the one to survive—not me." He walked on several more steps before continuing. "I think his place will be the best option for us all to get through this. We'll go to my house and get my wife and son, maybe Elvis if he is still there, and head to the old man's lake house."

The boy looked puzzled. "Elvis?"

"My rescue dog, just a furry ball of fun." Damn, he missed that mutt almost as much as he did his son. JD had told him where the cabin was. Steve figured it was a good eighty miles from Albany. That kind of distance would have seemed impossible until the last few weeks. Now it simply meant a couple more days on the road.

They bypassed several small towns by a wide margin but had passed no one on the road. Steve wasn't sure the travel restrictions scared everyone so much they didn't venture out, or maybe no one was left down here. As the sun began to dip, they found a concealed spot to rest for the night. As he dropped the pack, he decided to see what was included in the Army rucksack.

It was surprisingly well equipped with a first-aid kit, spare clothes, light-duty sleeping bag and rain gear, as well as knife, matches, chemlites, signal mirror, binoculars, paracord, and several food pouches, energy bars and six MREs.

"I have to admit, I think this is the best equipped we've been since getting on the road. Thank you, U.S. Army."

JD was inventorying his supplies as well. "Can we eat one of these tonight?" He held up one of the MREs.

"Why don't we share one and split an energy bar? We probably want to make them last." They had been fed well at the base, but non-stop walking all day had burned a lot of calories. "We also need to find water each day and any other food that we can."

"I know. I thought about that today, but I was . . . "

"You were what?" Steve asked.

He shrugged. "I dunno."

Steve had an idea of what it was—the boy was scared. He was, too, and it was not going to go away. Fear is a tool, not a weakness when the threats are real. "We can stick together when we go scavenging, ok? Also, I think we need to make some weapons, even just a sharp stick. Right now, we have nothing."

JD jumped on that idea and went around the immediate area looking for suitable sticks. Steve had figured out the boy did better if he had a project, something to focus on. He made up his mind to come up with something new each day for him.

They shared the cold meal, and Steve got ready for sleep while JD sharpened the end of a long staff. Tomorrow would be another grueling hike, and his feet were throbbing from today's march. "Get some rest, JD. Another long day tomorrow."

"We probably need to keep a watch tonight," the boy said without looking up.

"Leighton taught you well, son. I think we are well concealed back here, but you are probably right. You want me to take the first shift?"

"Nah, Steve, I got it. I'll wake you when I get tired."

Steve smiled—the boy was maturing with every passing day. He would be a survivor. He owed it to Gerald, and he owed it to JD to make sure that happened.

THEY WERE TRAPPED. Neither had expected the threat, but they had been discovered and outmaneuvered. The second and third day back on the road had seemed ordinary, almost boring. That changed on that third night. They had walked until well after dark just to put some additional distance between them and a light industrial and residential area. The entire area had a dangerous feel to it and a lingering smell of decay. Both had gotten the bad vibes and wanted to keep going. As the cover of trees was nearly non-existent, they had moved into open pasture land away from the roads. JD spotted the first one, a dark shape moving fast through the weeds.

Steve heard movement to his rear and side. Their path ahead was blocked by a shadow and then a growl. They now stood nearly surrounded by the beasts. Steve wasn't sure if they were coyotes or just wild dogs, but the danger was the same. He pulled the hunting knife from its side sheath. In the other hand, he clutched the sharpened staff. JD was doing the same. "Back to back, JD. No sudden moves." He felt the boy's backpack as he backed up close. The animals were all snarling, and he could see their bared teeth. *Find the alpha*, came some memory from deep in his past. Hell, I can't tell which is the leader in the dark. They all look terrifying. His mind raced for a solution as he felt the boy's trembling turning into outright shaking.

One of the animals moved in close enough for him to see it was a dog. In fact, it looked like a golden retriever. These were pets, their owners probably weren't alive or could no longer feed them, so they were reverting back to become pack hunters. Another of the snarling dogs moved in close and snapped. It was a mixed breed, some terrier, and . . . something. It was compact and aggressive. Steve kicked out at it, and it went sailing. He heard JD yell and felt him lunge at something behind him. He caught sight of a large muscular brute charging in from the side. The dog was totally silent but had the face of a Rottweiler.

He could be the lead dog. Steve lowered the long spear just as the dog came into range. The point pierced the animal's chest with a violent thud. The animal's retraction tore the shaft from his hands. Howls of pain erupted from the downed animal. The others fled in fear.

Steve nervously walked over to the writhing animal. It was biting at the wooden spear sticking from its body. JD came up behind him excitedly. "You got him, Mr. Steve."

"Just Steve, ok? Keep an eye out for the others." The dog was losing a lot of blood. The fight was all but gone. Steve saw a collar around its neck, *Someone's pet*. As he reached to see if there was a tag, the dog turned toward his hand, not to bite, but to lick it. God, he hated this world. He laid a hand on the deep fur and felt the breathing begin to slow. He felt all the anger, pity, sorrow, everything encapsulated in this one poor suffering animal.

He petted the animal and scratched behind its ears. The dog gave out a whimper like a puppy. "I have to end its suffering, JD. You may not want to watch."

"I know . . . but I probably need to."

Steve fought back rage and tears as he slid the knife across the dog's throat in as quick a motion as possible. The dog spasmed once, then lay still.

JD looked over his shoulder at the scene. "We going to eat it?"

"Do you want to eat it?" Steve was taken aback, but deep down, knew it was the right question. He wouldn't be able to do it, not yet anyway.

JD looked away. "No, not really. I just know Gerald would have been mad at us for wasting supplies."

"It won't go to waste; his friends will be back. He will be their meal."

48

"The spears worked well against the dogs, but that's not going to help us with anything more dangerous."

"I know, JD," Steve whispered to try and let the boy know this was not the time. *It wasn't working.*

"I'm just saying, we need guns, dude."

Steve looked through the compact binoculars that they found in one of their backpacks. "We had guns if you recall. We never shot them, and in the end, they didn't help us. Also, they are completely illegal right now."

"Who cares? There is no law, and the only reason our guns didn't help is the bad guys had bigger ones."

He had to admit the kid had a point. His traveling companion had been somewhat obsessed with getting weapons since the attack several days earlier. JD didn't like being scared; it seemed to push him to toughen up. Steve was more interested in avoiding trouble. The old farmhouse ahead was part of that plan. "Still no signs that anyone is there. I think it is abandoned."

JD was bored with the surveillance. "We have been watching it all afternoon. Of course, it is empty."

"We thought that last time too, remember?" They were within two days of reaching Albany, but they were out of the water and running low on food. Steve was somewhat familiar with the surrounding area and thought the owners of this farm had moved off and listed it for sale. "Ok, I am going to approach the house. You stay here, and if anything happens to me, stay hidden and get away when you can. Do you understand?"

"Duh, I'm not a retard."

"Don't use that term, please."

This was the second house they had surveilled hoping for food or water. The first house had looked abandoned except it wasn't. Steve had gotten an uneasy feeling someone was inside. After watching it for several hours, they were about to approach when a man walked out with a bat, went into a side yard and swung at a small dog that had been tied to a tree. The wet smack of the bat and the dog's head had lolled to one side, obviously dead. The man had picked it up by the hind legs and took it back into the house. He was glad JD has not asked what the man was going to do with it. It brought up fresh memories of the Rottweiler. He had had to kill that poor guy; it was survival. But this? *Pets for lunch* . . . what was next?

Thankfully, he wasn't getting that same vibe from this place. Standing up, he dropped his pack beside the boy and walked toward the white, two-story clapboard house. His hands were raised about halfway. *Very non-threatening, Steve. We are all just friends here.* Twenty feet from the front door he stopped and called out, "Hello, is anyone there? Not looking for trouble, just want some water."

Nothing . . . he tried again and got the same, no-response. He stepped up on the front step, a screen door separated him from a small covered porch and a solid wooden door on the opposite side. He knocked on the screen door and asked again if anyone was home. Finally satisfied, he opened the screened door, crossed and knocked loudly on the entry door.

No sounds came from the other side. Nothing about the house gave any signs of life. Most homes they passed now that had people in them had several obvious signs they were occupied. Clothes drying on a line or tree limbs, refuse, piles of garbage you could smell from a distance and some sort of cooking fires of which the smoke gave away the location during the day, and the fire often did at night. Usually, there were other sounds or sights which revealed the presence of others as well. Not the case here. Steve agreed with JD that it was abandoned, but the rat side of him wanted to make damn sure.

The door was locked but had a decorative side glass panel on each side of the door. Steve took out his tactical knife and flipped it around, so he was holding the blade. He used the metal knob behind the handgrip to break the pane nearest the doorknob. He knelt, still hidden behind the solid door and listened. Satisfied, he took a glance through the glass—open and very empty rooms were all he saw. He reached through the opening and unlocked the door.

He opened the door and motioned back for JD to join him. He saw no sign of the boy, but he had told him to hide. Walking into the house, he called out again. "Hello, is anyone there?"

"Just me," came a voice from an open room ahead.

"Shit, JD, don't do that."

"Sorry man, couldn't help myself. You never checked the back door. It wasn't even locked."

Crap, the boy was right again. "You know, kid, I liked it better before you started talking."

JD smiled. "No water, I tried the sink. House looks empty."

"Let's check it out, top to bottom. Make sure it's safe. If nothing else, we can at least sleep inside tonight."

"I CAN'T BELIEVE you are going to do that."

Steve filled the water bottle, lifted it to his parched lips and downed most of it. "Aghhhh."

"That's gross," JD said.

Steve thought of all the money he had wasted over the years buying bottled water. He had even ordered hundreds of cases with his company's name on it just to give out to customers looking at cars. Now he was drinking from a toilet. "It's not from the bowl where the poop goes. This is from the tank. It's all fresh water, a bit stale, and I probably should boil it, but it's clean."

"This was in Gerald's notebook?"

"Yep, one of several ways to find water in unexpected ways. Another would be the hot-water heater. I checked that too. It seems full of water, but I couldn't get the water valve on the bottom to turn. We need a few tools for stuff like that." Slowly, the boy's thirst overcame his disgust, and he began filling his bottles from the back of the toilet as well.

Dinner that night consisted of the last of the MREs. One was chicken with noodles, and the other was beef brisket. Neither was particularly good or bad. Actually, neither tasted like what they were either, but knowing this was the last of the food made them savor every bite.

"You have any food at your house?" JD asked.

"I did. Doubt there is any now. I would assume my wife and son have eaten most everything in our pantry."

"You don't talk about them much." JD's statement was neither accusing or questioning. He simply stated it as a fact.

"I know. I'm just not sure what I will find. I have been trying to brace myself for the worst."

"You think they're dead?"

This kid has no filter. "No . . . maybe, I don't know. I told you about my son's condition." He stared down at his filthy hands, thought briefly of what he was having to do now just to survive. " . . . I'm just not sure he can make it in this new world. He had a hard enough time in the old one."

"My mom is dead."

"Huh? That's terrible. Why would you say that?"

His shoulders shrugged. "It's true, I just know. Not sure how to explain it. She ain't the surviving type. Always had to have a man. One boyfriend after another. They all treated her bad, but she seemed ok with it as long as they didn't leave. Someone like that, well . . . no way they can make it now."

Steve watched as the boy spread some oily peanut butter on a stale cracker and shoved the whole thing in his mouth. Again, he felt the boy was right. It hurt to let go of the niceties of the past, but what mattered now was facts. The truth was most people probably wouldn't survive. He wasn't even sure if they themselves would. The lack of electricity was bad, but the possible pandemic was worse, and on top of it all was what the government was doing. Their chances of getting through all this seemed to be diminishing by the day.

The somber mood was lightened somewhat by having a roof overhead. JD was right on a lot of things. Staying smart was what Gerald called it once. Survival means outthinking death more than anything else. He wanted to survive, and he wanted to get to that cabin as quickly as possible. First, they had to go get his family. "Get some sleep, JD. I may have an idea on how we can speed this trip up some tomorrow."

49

"According to Gerald's notes, there are three basic options for surviving conflicts with others, JD. Stay hidden, fight, or flee. If you choose to flee, you have to be faster than the other guy . . . and his weapons."

"What's wrong with hiding?"

"Nothing wrong with it; that's what has kept us alive until now," Steve answered.

"Yeah, yeah, *Be the rat.*"

"I know," Steve laughed. "It doesn't make for a cool story, but it has kept us alive." The statement hung in the air just a moment too long. "Mostly," he amended.

Continuing, he said, "We know it won't always work, so I want us to try speed. We haven't seen a working car since we left Fort Benning. That would be my first choice, but I have a feeling that even the ones that might still function are probably out of gas. My second thought was horses, but the ones we've seen seem wary of us. I can ride, but don't know about doing it bareback, nor do I know much about taking care of one."

"So, that is why you chose this?" JD said as he pointed to the building.

"Yes, bicycles are a nearly perfect means of transportation. I remembered seeing this shop every time I passed through this area." The bike shop was on the corner of a small, nondescript shopping center. Steve knew this was a good mile from the rest of the small town. The other shops were a mixed bag of insurance agencies, a clothing boutique, a title pawn and one he guessed from the name as maybe a tattoo shop. The entire place had a "rough around the edges" feel to it, but just like the farmhouse, they had staked it out for most of a day already.

Several of the stores, including the bike shop, had front windows broken and litter streaming from the interior, obviously already ransacked. The two of them had moved to within twenty yards of the store. "I'm going to go check it out, just like before," Steve told the boy.

"Let me go," JD whispered. "I'm fast, I can peek in the window and take off if anything seems sketchy."

"No, too risky."

"Steve, you know I got this. You know I'm right."

He shook his head, marveling at how quickly the boy was learning. He wanted to argue, but he did know the kid was right, and he had to learn how to do this stuff. "Ok sport, go do it. Be safe."

He watched as JD sprinted to the edge of the building, ducking low before peeking around the front. Seeing nothing, he crawled up under the broken window and eased his head up briefly to see inside. Steve's insides were in knots watching as the kid took a longer look, then motioned for Steve to join him.

Inside the shop was a wreck, bike parts, and ruined frames were scattered everywhere. It appeared that all the adult bikes were gone or destroyed. A few kid-sized bikes were still intact, but they would do no good. "Was this part of your plan?" JD asked.

"It was about what I expected. Come on." They headed to the rear of the shop. A small repair area was set up behind the smashed sales counter. He opened a door to a darkened storage area. Here too, the place had been ransacked. He flipped on the small tactical flashlight from the Army pack. The light swept around the room, old tires, bent bike wheels. Boxes of helmets. Then he shone the light up toward the ceiling. A loft area extended back toward the front, over the retail space. He could just see the edge of large cardboard boxes. "Bingo! Look for a ladder or stairs."

They walked around the small space, shining the lights around the unfinished chipboard lined area. No stairs, but JD found the metal ladder hidden away between a far wall and the outer edge of the building. Removing the ladder from its hiding spot and leaning it against the overhead mezzanine was a noisy maneuver. They took a ten-minute break to go back out front and make sure no one had heard and was coming to investigate. "So, what do you think is up there?" JD asked as they looked out at the empty parking lot.

"Inventory. Extra bikes that haven't been put out for sale yet, I hope," Steve answered, finally satisfied no one had heard them. "Let's go see."

THE CLICKING SOUND of the racing bike made Steve nervous. As long as he was pedaling it didn't make that sound, so he tried to keep pedaling. He had been an avid bike rider in his teens and twenties, but that was many years in the past. Even then he had never been on a bike this nice. They had found a row of boxed bikes upstairs. Most were mountain bikes, but several were adult racing bikes in various sizes. He thought the racing bikes would be faster, although the more rugged durability of the off-road bikes was tempting. They had selected two lightweight racers and spent most of the next day putting the wheels and brakes on. Even with the instructions and tools handy, it had taken time to get them to spin and shift correctly. Out on the road, the bikes felt like a dream, so much quicker than walking. They were much faster than he recalled from his youth as well. JD kept pulling away from him and was grinning ear-to-ear each time he caught back up to the boy.

They had found some other items of use in the shop's storeroom and added what they could carry to the packs. Spare tubes and patches, toolkit, a small pump, an overlooked box of energy bars and a few packets of sports drink mix. JD had fussed about leaving the sharpened spears behind, but there was no easy way of carrying them on the bikes. In the end, speed and maneuverability had won out.

"Dude, we should have done this from the very start," JD yelled as he went by him again.

It was a valid point, but the roads were packed back then both with people walking and the militia's random roadblocks. Steve didn't think they would have gotten far before being attacked or stopped. Here in the rural part of the state, he felt more comfortable staying on the roads. Generally, they could see for miles, and they got in the habit of slowing or stopping regularly to listen for any dangers that might exist.

They saw a black column of smoke on the horizon about mid-afternoon. JD had been reading the road signs during the ride just like Steve had. He knew what was ahead. "That's Albany, isn't it? Your hometown."

Steve nodded, Albany was a little less than twenty miles ahead. Just an hour or two by bike, yet he was no longer nearly as anxious to get there. The man on the radio must have been right; Albany had been torched. His anxiety grew as they continued heading toward the billowing black cloud of smoke.

An hour later on the edges of the town, they began passing burned-out cars and homes. Steve pulled to a stop and looked at the charred shell of a large building ahead. What remained of the distinctive blue trim was scorched, only part of the name remained intact.

"Porter Ford. That was your place?"

Steve nodded. Probably a million dollars in inventory lay in ruins around the massive parking lot. New cars burned and smashed. Part of the collapsed building lay atop a group of high-end Mustangs he had special ordered. Each would have been a collectible one day. Now they were junk, like everything else here.

"Not going to go look around?" JD asked as Steve put a foot back on the pedal.

"Nope, nothing here." He started pedaling toward an intersection ahead. That was his yesterday. In the end, it meant nothing. What mattered lay ahead.

50

The route home was so familiar to Steve and yet so alien. The area looked like a war zone with burned buildings, graffiti and a general smell of rot. The streets were littered with debris, clothes, toys. It looked to him like a great migration must have occurred. If so, where had the people gone? Nervousness had him on edge. He couldn't feel the bike's handlebars in his grip; his chest was growing tighter by the mile.

They passed the church where he was a deacon. The pastor was a kindly man in his mid-sixties. A body lay in front of the broken entrance doors. The white hair looked . . . Steve turned away as he rode by.

"Steve, this doesn't look safe."

The boy was right; this wasn't home. Not anymore. They hadn't seen anyone alive since getting to Albany, and now . . . he wasn't sure he wanted to. Other than his family, of course. *Did he actually want to?* See them alive, that is. That was the buried question he couldn't allow to surface in his mind. Deep down he knew his wife, Barbara, was just as weak as Trey. Neither was equipped to survive in this world any more than he had been. He had adapted though, and so did JD. *Could they?*

Dodging a burned-out car brought him back to reality. "You're right, JD. It isn't, we turn back west at the bottom of this hill and head farther out of town. Should be better there." The level of destruction here was overwhelming. They had bypassed most of the other towns the last few weeks. *Were they all like this?* he wondered.

"How are you going to get your family up to Gerald's place? Are we gonna walk again?"

Steve had no idea. It was just one of many things he had refused to think about. Coming home had been a duty, an obligation. He should feel overjoyed being within six miles of his objective. Instead, he only felt dread. Somehow, he already knew what he was going to find. The panic had become a wholly palpable thing. He'd known for weeks. *Please God, let me be wrong. Let that just be the fear in me.*

AS THEY BEGAN to get into the nicer neighborhoods, an area called Arlington, their progress was slowed by numerous makeshift road-blocks. Stalled cars, barrels filled with rocks, wire strung across the road. This was the area of the "haves." Apparently, they had been determined to keep the "have-nots" out. Steve knew the area well, had numerous friends who lived in these houses.

Several miles before reaching his subdivision, the way forward was blocked by a scene of bloody carnage. Dark birds circled the area as a warning to others. Decaying lumps of flesh and body parts littered the road ahead. A massive roadblock made up of two bright yellow school buses and a dump truck blocked the road. A line of barrels plugged the openings under the vehicles. No one seemed to be moving on either side of the blockade. "Slow to a stop, JD," Steve whispered. "Raise your hands."

They both did that, and after several minutes lowered one hand to slowly guide the bicycles toward the carnage. "Hello?" Steve yelled. He didn't want to surprise anyone.

"We don't want any trouble," JD offered in a well-practiced

cadence. "Nothing to see here, we are no threat to anyone." He chanted softly as they gingerly approached the blockade.

Steve spotted a lone rifle barrel sticking from one of the bus windows. It moved slightly and seemed to be indicating they move to the left. "Hello, in the bus." *No answer.* The gun stayed on them. "Far enough. JD, let's ease over to one side." Nothing about this was smart or safe. No one in this neighborhood would recognize him anymore. In tattered clothes and sporting a full beard, he doubted his own family would even know him.

As they moved gingerly to the end of the bus, JD whispered, "The rifle isn't on us anymore."

Steve looked back, the boy was right. The gun was still pointing in the general direction they had been. "It's still moving, though. Someone is guarding the approach. They may have other shooters concealed. "Hello, my name is Steven Porter. I live back in the Fox Run subdivision—just trying to get through with my boy." JD gave him a curious look.

The gap between the bus and the dump truck was nonexistent, but underneath, one of the barrels had been rolled aside slightly. *This is not smart.* Steve told himself as he leaned his bike and began to crawl through. "Stay here and let me explain myself to them. If they start shooting, or I yell . . . get the hell out of here." For once, the boy nodded in agreement.

The scene on the far side of the roadblock was a mirror image of the other. Dead bodies lay everywhere. These people had been his neighbors; now they were unrecognizable. From the state of decay, this battle had been a few weeks earlier. "Hello?" He walked into the area with both hands up. He noticed guns and spent shell casings littered the roadway. The smell of death hung in the air like a morbid fog. He turned to the bus, to the one person he was sure was alive here. The one holding the gun on them earlier. His heart was pounding as he pushed the middle of the folding bus door and planted his worn sneaker on the lowest step. "Hello, the bus, coming in. Don't shoot."

A twinge in the back of his skull let him know the tension was too high. He could ill afford another headache now. He forced himself to focus on each step. The interior of the bus was dark. It looked like they had spray-painted over many of the windows. His fate and JD's depended on being smart; approaching an armed guard in this hellish scene was anything but that. He stepped to the top and grasped the vertical metal pole. The gun was still pointing out the window a few seats back. That was good. *At least he hasn't turned it toward me*, Steve thought.

"We're just passing through, ok?" He thought he heard movement from the seat. The guard may be injured, he thought briefly. He could see the shirt sleeve holding the rifle shaking now. Was he scared? Maybe the gun wasn't even loaded. He was out here just for show. With all the empty rounds outside he could certainly believe they had run out of ammo. He took one more step down the aisle and went to speak again when a flurry of black rose up from the seat.

Steve flailed with his hands as whoever. . .whatever it was attacked him. He felt sharp cuts on his hands and arms. He turned to flee back toward the entrance as the entire bus erupted into a cacophony of squalls and the wingbeats of large birds drove him from their lair. As he jumped back out of the bus, a half-dozen crows flew out over his head. JD was leaning against the hood of the bus having also crawled through. "That was funny."

"Don't be an ass, kid."

The carrion birds flew briefly, then settled back down to continue feeding.

"We have guns now," JD said as he picked up one after another.

"Not sure there is going to be any ammo for them, though. Looks like this was their last stand."

They spent a half hour matching guns to the few rounds of unfired ammo they could find. Most of it was hunting rifles or small caliber handguns. Gerald's notes had suggested several calibers of weapons they should look for. The ones where ammo would be more common. They chose several 9mm, 5.56 and .45 caliber handguns, a compact shotgun and a rifle. They strapped everything to their packs except one handgun each which they wore in holsters they had also recovered. JD seemed relieved to have a weapon again.

Steve didn't want to think about it, but to him, it was pretty obvious the "have-nots" had gotten through the roadblock. No one was left alive to defend it. Who was he kidding? Everyone was a "have-not" now. As they remounted their bikes and began pedaling, the sense of dread returned like a dark passenger. None of the elegant houses they passed showed any signs of life. Many had been burned, and all looked to have been ransacked. Remnants of expensive drapes hung out through broken windows like withered ghosts.

"How far is it to your house? I'm starving."

Steve was looking at a thin body lying on the edge of a driveway as they rode by. A dingy and stained dress still fluttered in the slight breeze. She was so thin—everyone had been starving . . . except the dead. "Two miles."

51

Steve pedaled against the sense of foreboding just as much as the small hill leading up to Fox Run. This was his home, these were his neighbors, yet nothing seemed familiar. His community was gone. Now, what would he find of his family? The anger at what was going on overwhelmed him. Gerald had been right—they were losing the country.

They slowed to a stop before the entrance to his neighborhood. The gated community was the gem of Albany's elite. Steve saw one of the gates lying on the road; the other side was hanging precariously by one hinge. The ornate stone entrance monument with the stylized fox sign was a scattered mess. This was his worst fear coming true.

"Come on, Steve." JD's hand rested lightly on his shoulder. Glancing over, he saw his own concern reflected on the boy's face. He gave a small nod and pedaled through the debris of the entrance.

The Porter home was one of the oldest in Fox Run, located on one of the rear streets. Each cross street showed more destruction. The once-manicured lawns were now a chaos of junk. From broken furniture, clothes and even massive flat screen TVs, to simple things like a baby swing with two of its legs twisted up behind it.

"Looks like a tornado hit a community yard sale. Doesn't it?"

Steve just nodded, he was growing numb again. His legs felt like they were moving through mud. He couldn't seem to catch a breath. This was not another migraine coming on. It was simply blind fear. They rounded a curve and his street. The top of his house came into view. The familiar red brick and steep dark roof of the second floor. His heart hammered in his chest.

"There it is," he said softly. Hundreds of miles he had traveled, and now he wasn't sure he could make it just a few more yards.

"Dude . . . sweet. That's the biggest home in the hood."

JD was right, and now it had become the biggest target. As more of the structure came into view his heart sank. His home had not escaped the plague of chaos. They saw the same evidence of looting and destruction as all the others. *Oh God, Trey.*

They dropped the bicycles in the front yard. Steve saw a framed picture of his son and himself resting against part of a broken Transformers toy. The yard was a surreal snapshot of his life. An old yearbook from his high school junior year. Remnants of a formal jacket he had worn when he and Barbara married. A broken plaque presented by Ford several years earlier at a dealer awards dinner. His gaze fell on one object after another, each transporting him to another place and time for the briefest of seconds. The wrongness of it all was overwhelming.

As they neared the door, Steve noticed JD had dropped his pack and was holding a pistol. *Smart.* Why had he not thought to do that? *Because this is your house, dummy. Why would you need a weapon to enter it?* He pulled the shotgun out as he sat his pack beside the steps. Stepping across to the door he tried the handle and was surprised to find it locked. Should he knock? He hadn't had his keys in weeks. JD was scanning the yard for dangers. "I'm going to try another door."

He moved around to the side of the house. The garage door was a dented mess with one panel missing entirely. Glancing to the back of the yard he saw Elvis's paddock shrouded in late afternoon shadows. A dark mass lay inside. His heart sank even further; his hand began to tremble. He handed JD the shotgun while he contorted himself to get through the hole in the white garage door. It would be too high for JD to get through without help. The gun came pushing through the opening along with a flashlight. "Thanks, JD, I'll let you in the front door," he whispered.

~

How could he feel like such a stranger in his own home? Everything seemed almost familiar, yet also completely alien. It looked like there had not been one part of the house that had not been ransacked. Tools lay scattered in the garage. A pile of what appeared to be shit was in one corner. His wife's car, another new Ford from his lot, was in its normal place. The large Viking, stainless-steel freezer was open; no food remained inside. The door that led into his kitchen was missing, and he could see the kitchen was in even worse shape. *Should I call out?* He heard no sounds, but maybe Barb and Trey were hiding.

Trey could never hide, he couldn't stay quiet that long. His mind wouldn't be able to comprehend the danger until it was too late. No, whoever did this could still be here. Steve needed to stay silent. Hopefully, his family had gotten away to someplace safe. He moved through room after room as silently as possible. Anything of value in the house was gone, in fact, it looked like the worst moving job in the world had happened here. Broken dishes, torn magazines, smaller stuff he had no idea what it had been littered the floor. He made his way to the front door only to see it had not been locked but *instead,* nailed closed. The hammer and a box of nails were sitting on the adjacent floor against the wall.

He could see JD's face in the tiny window inset in the door. He shook his head and shrugged, not wanting to speak. He motioned for him to try the back door. The boy's head nodded, and he disappeared. Steve resumed his hunt. Each of their bedrooms had been on the first floor. Upstairs were guest bedrooms, an office and a crafting room Barb had insisted upon *but never* used. He moved first into Trey's room whispering his son's name. "Trey. Son, are you here? Trey, it's Dad." Nothing. He tried several more times as he looked behind the upturned bed and in the empty closet. "S-P-3 ... where are you?"

With nowhere else to look, he moved to his and Barbara's room. Food wrappers and empty soup cans littered the floor. A scattering of his wife's clothes spilled out of the closet like they were trying to escape it. Expensive containers of makeup and lipstick were smashed along with pictures and mirrors. "Barb," he called as he went through the massive room toward the darkened bathroom. What little remained of his seemed to be broken, shredded, or . . . well, used as toilet paper from what he could see. Shining the light around he realized the toilet was overturned and spilling out a vile mass. The glass shower doors were broken as well.

A thought occurred to him, and back in the bedroom, he shone the light into his wife's closet. Her main travel bag was gone as was one of the wheeled suitcases. He heard a sound from another room, then JD's voice.

"Steve, you should probably see this."

He eased out of his room and went toward the sound of the boy. He saw him standing near the rear door looking at the wall of his dining room.

"Backdoor was missing altogether. Hey, man, I believe you are on someone's shitlist."

He was shocked at the boy's language, but looking at the wall he understood. "Fuck you, Stevie" was smeared onto the wall, and it did look like it had been written in actual shit. She was the only person that ever called him Stevie. She had given up on him and fled. His fears about her had been correct. When he was no longer there to provide the life she needed, she'd left.

"Any sign of your son?"

Tears were welling in Steve's eyes as he shook his head. "Nothing downstairs, about to head up." They searched the upper floor with the same result. The house was empty, although it looked like people had stayed here. What appeared to be remnants of a small campfire had been made on the tile floor of his office. The ceiling was stained with smoke. The guest toilet was full to overflowing. In fact, the entire house smelled noxious.

Steven Porter had never felt so isolated, so completely out of his element. Where would his family have gone? Well . . . fuck that—he didn't give a damn about her. She had abandoned them both. Where was Trey? He rested his head against the window in his office. The view of the backyard was just as bad as the scene out front. Nothing had escaped the intruder's attention. What they couldn't take or use, they had destroyed. Eyeing the dog pen again, he decided to go take care of one thing at least.

Steve grabbed a shovel that was lying near some uprooted shrubs, and JD followed dragging a dirty comforter that Steve motioned for him to grab. As they neared the fenced pen, Steve saw the dark head of the dog rise briefly and look his way. He gasped. Dropping the shovel, he broke into a run. At the gate, he was stopped by a chain and padlock. It was one of his, but they never locked Elvis's gate. A simple latch was all that was needed to keep the sweet dog inside. He could see Elvis clearly now about halfway down the concrete pad. The dog was in bad shape, but *how?* How could he still even be alive?

"I don't have the key. We never locked this."

JD looked at him confused. The pitiful looking dog needed help. "Just tear the fencing loose."

"I would, but it's...very well made, bolted to the top, and both the post and the wire is embedded at the bottom in the cement." A thought occurred to him: *I saw some cutting pliers on the floor of the garage.* "Be right back, keep talking to him." He took off running back to the house.

JD moved down closer to the whimpering dog. "Hey boy, good puppy. Going to get you . . . " His words stopped as he could now see into the doghouse down on the far end of the pen. "Oh God."

52

JD threw the comforter over the top bar of the pen and began climbing the chain link fence. He dropped into the pen and pulled the dirty blanket over. He patted the dog, feeling bony ribs beneath the dark fur. "Good boy, Elvis, good boy. Back in a few." He raced down the twenty feet dreading what he had to do. Curled inside the doghouse was the unmistakable shape of a human body. As he got closer he could smell the rot and make out more of the form. It was a young man or an older boy. He knew who it had to be. "Oh Jesus. . ." he couldn't let his friend find him like this. Over the last few weeks, he had grown accustomed to seeing the dead and the decaying bodies, but rarely this close.

As he reached in, he closed his eyes and pulled the boy's body toward him and into the blanket. His fingers slipping into the rotted flesh and he felt bone. *How did the dog not eat his body?* he morbidly wondered. Sounds from the yard let him know Steve was returning. He worked fast to move the stiff body as gently as he could from the dog house. "Steve—stay back!" he yelled.

Distantly he heard the panicked, "Why, what . . . ?"

The sound of wire being snipped and Steve making pained sounds were becoming too much. Finally, he wrestled the frail body fully into the comforter and wrapped the withered remains completely in the death shroud.

Steve leaned through the half-cut slit in the fence and looked at JD and the bundle he held. He couldn't ask the question that he knew he had to. He knew his son was indeed dead. JD was holding Trey's body. He dropped to his knees beside the dog and wept. His body was wracked with the sobbing pain that only a grieving parent would ever know. All of his effort to get home had been in vain. He had been too late. He hadn't prepared for a disaster. He had married badly, again. He had failed his son. The guilt and the shame mixed with the pain to complete the triad of misery. Glancing at the bundle JD was still holding became too much for him to bear, and he closed his eyes to the pain. Elvis's wet tongue weakly licked at the arm of his owner's shaking body.

JD KNELT with the dog and watched as Steve carried his son's body into the shallow hole. It had taken an hour for the man to make it the few yards to verify it was indeed Trey. JD had spent that time digging a hole on the backside of the property near a playset and a large oak tree. He hoped it would have been a spot Trey would have liked. He liked it, so . . . *maybe,* he thought. Truthfully, he was out of his league here. He knew nothing of loss like this, not really. The man had just lost his child and been betrayed by his wife. Heck, he felt like she was probably the one who locked the kid in with the dog, but who really knew? What he did know was that this wasn't a time to talk. Let his friend find some peace if that was possible.

Elvis had drunk so much water he had thrown up. JD had found several sources inside the house including the back tank of the nasty toilet. The dog seemed to be much better. He had also found the remnants of a bag of dog food in the back of the garage. He had brought several handfuls out to where the dog now lay in the yard. Elvis nudged some of the food toward JD in a gesture he couldn't fully grasp. "It's yours, boy. You eat it." The dog's watery brown eyes seemed to thank him, and he lowered his head and hungrily devoured the pile of dry nuggets.

JD walked over and joined Steve at the grave. Looking down at the wrapped bundle, it seemed too small to be human. The tears still flowed down Steve's face, and JD hurt for the man. He had never known his father but wondered if he would have cared for him like that. He placed his hand on his friend's back like he had seen Gerald do a few times. He could feel Steve shaking and wondered if he should leave him to his grief. His hand stayed, and in time Steve turned and embraced him in a fierce hug. JD, too, began to cry.

THEY SAT on the floor with their backs against the wall and ate energy bars and warm sports drinks. Steve kept staring at the words on the wall. JD hadn't asked, but had come to the conclusion that it had been written by his wife. Steve had been unable to fill in the grave, so JD had done that while Steve walked back to the house carrying the dog. He had found Steve there afterward clutching the broken frame with the photo from the front yard. The cracked glass making his son's face unrecognizable. He looked up where his friend was staring.

"You going to look for her?"

JD's words seemed to break the spell that hung in the foul air. Neither had spoken much all afternoon. "No." Steve thought he was angry with her, should be furious in fact, but the word held no emotion. He was now completely numb. In his mind, she had abandoned his son, her stepson, to die. She may have killed him herself, for all he knew, her actions certainly contributed to his end. Now he was shutting down that part of himself. No revenge, no hate, no love and as far as she was concerned, *no loss.*

"I'm sorry, Steve."

He nodded. "Sorry, I drug you all the way down here."

"Steve, I have a question. Where is everybody?"

It was a good question, but unfortunately, he had no idea. "Don't know, some are probably hiding, many probably traveled to one of the camps or somewhere else they thought might be safer. Obviously, many . . . just didn't make it." *My own son hadn't made it.* He looked again at the broken photo. The rush of pain and tears each time that thought screamed up at him was making him sick. So much of his life had been spent caring for his child's extraordinary needs. While losing him was awful, the fact that on some level he felt a kind of . . . relief, made him hate himself even more. He wasn't sure he could survive the grief, nor was he sure he wanted to. Trey wouldn't have survived in this new world, he knew that, but the reality still consumed him.

"So, what's next?" JD asked as he stroked the dog's matted fur.

"We leave." Steve had nothing left holding him here. He knew this life was gone. He could physically move on and hopefully, in time, he would be able to emotionally. "We go to Gerald's house on the cove and try and wait the mess out. Just you and I."

"And Elvis," the boy said with a grin.

"Of course, Elvis."

53

"President Chambers?"

Madelyn still could not get accustomed to the title. *Perhaps if I were at the White House looking out at the Rose Garden instead of the concrete walls of the bunker*, she mused. "Yes, come in." Her newly christened chief of staff walked in with the daily security brief. She loathed the damn thing—what an absolutely dreadful way to start every day. She had borrowed a page from another president's playbook to deal with it. Taking it from him before laying it down on the conference table behind her: "I'll read it later, give me the highlights, Ed."

His eyes showed disapproval, but the former Wall Street banker dutifully began recounting the newsworthy items listing each succinctly and in some predetermined order of priority. "The outbreak of the SA1297 has now spread to sixty-two percent of Europe. The impact on the Middle East is estimated at eighty-six percent. Cases have also been confirmed in Asia, Africa and several Eastern European countries. No news out of Russia or China at this time.

"Mexico has signaled that they are closing their borders. Canada may be about to do the same, but as you know, there is no functioning national government there, so any effective decisions will be on a provincial basis."

"Ed, the highlights, please. I can read the mundane later for myself." He looked thoroughly chastened, in her opinion, for a man who was used to being the one giving the orders, not taking them.

"Sorry, Madam President." He flipped several sheets in a file folder and began again. "The joint forces are still questioning your legitimacy to hold the executive office. FEMA officials have delivered the certification, but as instructed, we had to remove the two most vocal members. General Ayers and Admiral Mitchell have been replaced.

We still have no contact with several of the carrier strike groups and have to assume they have gone rogue. The Seventh Fleet Command is still intact, but we have monitored much of the Atlantic Fleet relocating toward the Gulf along with several amphibious ready groups."

"I get it, Ed. We have lost control of half of our military. What sort of threat do those assets pose?"

"Madam President, they all have first strike nuclear capabilities."

"But I have the codes. They can't launch without me, right?"

The man began shaking his head, not liking where this was heading. "Ma'am, the 'Gold Codes' you have are not the launch codes, they are the codes to authorize a launch. Any actual launch would come from one of the designated command sites such as the Cheyenne Mountain facility. Even your codes would require a secondary confirmation under the two-man rule."

"So, I couldn't just order the missiles to . . . I don't know, self-destruct in the ships?"

"No, ma'am."

"Well, what fucking good are they? Can we change that? Let's do that at once. I need full authority to launch."

He knew the woman was more rational than this—she was becoming unhinged. Whatever was driving her might take her right over the edge. While he already knew the answer was no, he agreed simply to buy more time. He also decided not to mention the final bullet point on the briefing that NORAD and the entire facility at Cheyenne Mountain had gone silent, severing all communication with the new commander- in- chief.

"Ed, war is coming. You need to make sure we will win."

He closed his book, tucked it back under his arm and stared at her briefly before hurrying from the room.

Madelyn looked at the closed door, then at the morning's playbook on the desk. Gently, she read again the sealed memo her security agent had given her before the morning meeting. "Ms. Levy was dealing with a personal matter and would be unavailable. Deal with the issues per her prior instructions." What the fuck did that mean? She got a distinct feeling that something was going terribly wrong. The Council's plan had a flaw, and she thought she might know what it was . . . or more precisely, "who" it was.

54

JD ran on ahead, Elvis nipping at the boy's heels. A rare smile briefly crossed Steve's face. The pastures and fields running down to the isolated lake were exactly as Gerald described in his notes. They had followed the directions Gerald had made the boy memorize. Getting out of Albany four days earlier had proven to be even more challenging than getting in. The first people they saw after leaving his old neighborhood had been a dozen men, several wearing prisoner uniforms. A few of whom were obviously armed.

Something substantial had changed in Steve back in his old house in Fox Run, he knew that. The car dealer part of him was dead. He'd crossed a line there was no coming back from. The gang had stepped out into the road blocking their path. They seemed focused on the boy. Before leaving his old house that last morning, he had placed an Indian headband on Trey's grave. *Goodbye, my good boy, my little Cherokee.* The folded picture of the two of them being the only item he took from the wrecked house. His life now was what was in front of him. As he had leveled the shotgun on the leader, the *alpha dog*, it was without remorse.

∼

THE STRAPS of his Army pack dug into Steve's shoulders. It now included most of JD's supplies as well as his own. JD had carried Elvis in his for most of the trip from Albany. The dog was recovering from his long nightmare. How he'd survived so long in that pen was nothing short of a miracle. Steve had promised the mutt that he would never be caged again. Watching him chasing JD down the small hill was a tiny victory for all of them.

He wondered what Gerald had whispered in the boy's ear just before he died. JD never mentioned it, and he would never ask. While his relationship with the boy was not the same as Gerald had, it was a tight bond, nonetheless. He wanted to love the boy as his own, but that hole in his heart was filled with something dark right now... *Maybe in time.* For now, he would simply treat him as an equal, a partner. In time, that could grow.

While JD had the general directions, Steve had been given the other half of Gerald's secret. How to locate and get into the cabin. The man had been right, getting there had not been easy. They had left the last paved road at least twenty miles back. The bikes had been left midday the day before when the path they were following disappeared. From what he could see, the property was about as isolated as you could get in the state of Georgia. National Forest parkland bordered much of the land. Beyond that, fifty miles to the northeast was a large Air Force base just below Macon. Virtually no private land between them. Wildlife in the area should be plentiful. No towns or development anywhere around that they could see. Amazing that a place like this even existed.

Dropping the pack, he sat down in the meadow and rested his back against it. Trey would have loved it out here; he should have spent more time with his son. It had just seemed like everything the boy had needed was so expensive. He'd just felt the need to work harder and harder to pay for it all. He now fully understood; he had been trying to fix his son instead of just loving him fully for who he was.

He'd been the best dad he knew how to be, but in the end, it wasn't enough. The world has gone to shit. Millions are dead. America is on the verge of collapse or *maybe* even civil war, yet all he could think about were the deaths of his son and Gerald. The loss seemed so trivial in the scale of misery out in the world. To him, it was everything, though. On some level, he knew it was probably for the best in his son's case, but it still made him feel awful to think that way. People weren't disposable, everyone had value. Even in his son's limited capacity, he had understood. He had taken care of Elvis, followed his dad's instruction even after his own food was probably gone. Ultimately, he might have even sacrificed his life to protect the dog.

He thought back to the people, the children along the fences in the detention camps. The president had no right to abandon so many of her fellow citizens. We all have as much right to survive. We have to be able to choose our own fate. Even if Gerald was right, and there was no way the government could help everyone, they didn't have to add to the misery.

Looking at the penned notes, he brought the binoculars to his eyes one more time and scanned the slight ridge on the western edge of the lake. He was beginning to think this had all been some elaborate ruse by the old man. It would be just like him to keep screwing with them even after he was gone. The notebook had a crude drawing of the location. The shape of the lake matched, *it had to be here.*

EPILOGUE

They nearly walked into the structure before finding it. The cabin had been completely shrouded by old military camo netting. The shape blended into the surrounding trees perfectly. *How had he built this way out here?*

Elvis ran and barked as they got close enough to see the house. "Hold him," Steve warned. "There are a few things I need to take care of before it is safe to enter."

He took long minutes examining the ground, then gingerly stepped over a set of hidden trip wires. The notebook indicated that activating any of the wires would arm other defensive traps in the area. One of the wooden steps was also rigged. After a half hour of lifting netting and disarming traps, he stood and looked at their new home. It was far larger than he expected, and turning around, he realized it had a gorgeous *and* tactically smart view of the lake and valley beyond. Parts of the cabin looked old, ancient even, but most of it seemed relatively new.

Inside was even more surprising. The cabin had a bank of solar panels supplying electricity, and once they turned the inlet valve on to the tank, *hot water*. Gerald had even equipped the cabin with blackout curtains that closed automatically when darkness fell. The house lights would remain invisible to anyone outside. The kitchen and pantry were fully stocked, and as Gerald had said, it would last them for months. They sat down and ate one of the MREs from the stack on the counter. The food hitting their empty stomachs was a shock. "We probably ought to take it easy on the food. Our systems aren't used to regular calories."

Afterward, they began exploring the rest of the cabin. JD found a small weapons room which was stocked with a variety of defense and hunting guns. Cases of ammo lined one entire wall. The boy sat and began stripping down and cleaning the weapons they had been carrying.

Elvis followed Steve around the bottom floor inspecting every corner. His nose began sniffing along a particular set of boards in one of the bedrooms. "What is it, boy?" Steve asked with a knowing grin. Somewhere along an inner closet was a small handle that would release an access hatch to a hidden cellar. He watched the dog trying to figure it out as his hand found the latch. A small click and the ends of those boards popped up slightly. Steve marveled at the craftsmanship. The hinged door disappeared into the floor completely when closed. If Gerald did all this work himself, he missed his true calling.

"Going into the cellar," he called out as he descended the wooden ladder. As he got to the bottom rung, a set of LED lights came on automatically. The "cellar" was larger than the entire first floor. It had obviously been extended underground back into the hill. Steve's mouth dropped as he took it all in.

He was looking at a large open space with numerous side rooms which were essentially cut-out cubicles. The open space was dominated by a set of oversized leather sofa and chairs, and a massive gun safe. Beyond that, row upon row of cases and containers of freeze-dried and canned foods. A small kitchenette area was along one side. That was followed by a well-equipped combination exercise and first-aid room. Nearby, a radio room surrounded by a strange copper mesh lining the walls, with several of the ham radios Gerald said were there. He also saw a well-used MacBook Pro and a rack holding at least a dozen of the small, fast, solid-state drives. Besides the equipment was a spiral notebook with instructions on how to use everything. Looking around the room, he guessed the mesh was supposed to protect the electronics from an EMP or hopefully, in this case, the CME which had devastated the United States and possibly the whole world. The man had been a serious prepper, but beyond that, he was just smart in his planning. There was nothing in this place that didn't have a purpose.

A mechanical room held the battery bank for the solar array hidden somewhere far above, as well as spare batteries on shelves. Tools for almost any task and surprisingly, a large Polaris four-wheeler and trailer. He had seen no other way to enter the basement, but apparently, there was. No way to get that thing up the wooden ladder. He spent an hour down in the basement before JD came down and joined him. The two of them had walked every inch of the space amazed at the contents, but still, neither saw any other exit. Steve heard Elvis whining up at the opening, wanting to join them. He climbed the few rungs to reach the dog and brought him down as well.

Elvis began his inspection of this space just like the floor above. Even though the dog had never spent much time indoors, he seemed right at home. Ultimately, it was the canine member of the group that discovered the biggest surprise. He started pawing at a section of the wall toward the back of the basement. Steve looked at it for quite some time before he noticed it. The section looked the same as the surrounding walls except . . . *right there*. Steve focused up at the top where it met the floor trusses of the floor above. Running inside a gap in the metal trusses was a flat iron bar. The bar was not unusual as it extended around on both opposing walls, but here it had two black wheels covertly mounted about fifteen feet apart.

Gerald's notebook hadn't said anything about this, but Elvis, and now Steve, felt like something lay beyond the wall. In hindsight, it took way longer to figure it out than it should have. The wall was essentially a large sliding barn door hanging from the iron rail above and riding on casters in a hidden groove below the wall. The system was ingenious and almost impossible to detect. Once JD found the catch, the entire wall slid out of sight behind another section.

"Holy shit, what the hell is that?" Steve said in amazement. What he was looking at was a very large corrugated metal pipe. Something you might see on a construction site or . . . he wasn't sure— maybe a drainage pipe going under something big like an interstate or something. A series of bright LED tubes flickered to life running down the entire length. The shiny metal tube was at least fifty yards long. Hanging at the far end was a set of firing range targets. The floor of the tube had wooden planking to make a flat walkway even with the basement floor.

"It's a hidden firing range," JD said in awe. "I bet you couldn't hear anyone shooting down here if you were outside."

"Smart," Steve said. "You would need a way to sight in guns and scopes that didn't give away the location." Looking just above the targets, he smiled. A hand-lettered sign read "EXIT." They would have to investigate that tomorrow, but at least he now knew how to get the four-wheeler out if needed.

"THIS PLACE IS AMAZING."

Steve nodded at the boy in agreement. Gerald had never talked much about the place, but it was far more than either had expected. Their friend had taken care of them even after he was gone. He knew the house had many more surprises in store. He could see several sets of bookcases along one wall. "I think we will be ok here."

"For how long?" JD asked.

That was a very good question. Yes, they could hunker down to weather what was happening beyond this valley. Deep down, he knew that would not be enough. He felt the rough edge of paper in his pocket and pulled out the crumpled picture. Gerald had offered him this place, but at a cost. He also gave him a mission in exchange for the safe harbor. "Time we start earning our keep, kid."

Steve carefully took the radios and laptop out of their protective sleeves and powered them on. To his relief, they all worked just like the manual indicated. The scanner on the radio began picking up random broadcast almost at once. He and JD studied the guide until they knew the basics of the system. Amazingly to Steve, the laptop had a connector that fit into the second radio. Gerald's notes indicated that radio could be used in something called "packet mode" to receive data transmissions via certain radio frequencies. The laptop could decode these transmissions. It would, in fact, work as a crude form of internet.

He took out the crumpled paper from the back of his friend's notebook. The radio guide had warned him about transmitting too often. They knew some of the story; others must know more. *We all have to know what's coming.* The radio was mainly to be used in a passive, listen/receive-only mode. Apparently, transmissions could be isolated and the sending radio source located if someone was looking. *Someone like the government thugs,* he thought. In this case, though, Gerald had been clear—make contact. . .*light the fire.*

He pushed the button and changed to the frequency listed on Gerald's note. This was the channel of the man his friend had simply called "a Patriot." All he heard on the channel was silence, so he queued the mic, following the exact wording Gerald had listed in the manual. The guide indicated he could choose his own call sign and he almost said, "*The Rat.*" But in honor of his late friend, he kept the call sign Gerald had marked on the sheet as his own; it seemed very appropriate. He was rewarded several minutes later by a male voice with a pronounced Cajun accent: "Acknowledged. We show this as first contact—please prepare system to receive files."

Steve verified the packet radio was in receive mode and the software on the laptop was standing by. He heard sounds that he took to be the encrypted file transmission, although he had no idea what to expect. On the MacBook screen, he saw a filename appear and a checksum data number followed by estimated time to download. The incoming filename was called CATALYST-CME.zip. The time to receive was estimated at more than twenty-three hours. *The system wasn't built for speed apparently.*

The voice came back again, "Hello, Sentinel. This is Pitstop. You can call me Gopher, what's your status?"

ABOUT THE AUTHOR

Fiction author JK Franks' world is shaped by his love of history, science and all things sci-fi. His work is most often filled with vivid characters set in dire situations only a step or so away from our normal world. His focus on gritty realism and attention to meticulous detail help transport his readers into his stories.

The first novel of his apocalyptic Catalyst series, Downward Cycle, was published in 2016. The follow-up to that, Kingdoms of Sorrow, continued the tale of a near-future apocalyptic event and a group of survivors' efforts to hang on to the remnants of a collapsing civilization. The novella, American Exodus, published late in 2017 takes a look at the disaster from a fresh and more personal perspective. Look for at least one more book in the series.

Always writing, JK Franks now lives in West Point, Georgia, with his wife and family. No matter where he is or what's going on, he tries his best to set aside time every day to answer emails and messages from readers. You can also visit him on the web at www.jkfranks.com. Please subscribe to his newsletter for updates, sneak peeks, promotions and giveaways. You can also find the author on Facebook and Twitter or email him directly at media@jkfranks.com.

For more information

www.jkfranks.com
media@jkfranks.com

OTHER BOOKS BY JK FRANKS:

THE CATALYST SERIES

Book 1: Downward Cycle

Life in a remote oceanfront town spirals downward after a massive solar flare causes a global blackout. But the loss of electrical power is just the first of the problems facing the survivors in the chaos that follows. Is this how the world ends?

Book 2: Kingdoms of Sorrow

With civilization in ruins, individuals band together to survive and build a new society. The threats are both grave and numerous—surely too many for a small group to weather. This is a harrowing story of survival following the collapse of the planet's electric grids.

Book 2.5: American Exodus Novella

This companion story to the Catalyst series follows one man's struggle to get back home after the collapse. No supplies, no idea of the hardships to come; how can he possibly survive the journey? Even if he survives, can he adapt to this new reality?

Connect with the Author Online:

** For a sneak peek at new novels, free stories and more, join the email list at: www.jkfranks.com/Email

Facebook: facebook.com/JKFranksAuthor

Amazon Author Page: amazon.com/-/e/B01HIZIYH0

Smashwords: smashwords.com/profile/view/kfranks22

Goodreads: goodreads.com/author/show/15395251.J_K_Franks

Website: JKFranks.com

Twitter: @jkfranks

Instagram: @jkfranks1

CPSIA information can be obtained
at www.ICGtesting.com
Printed in the USA
LVOW03*1020130418
573143LV00001B/1/P